Golden Myths and Legends
of the World

Geraldine McCaughrean was born in North London. Her degree was in Education and she has been writing full time for many years, both adult and children's books. She has won the Whitbread Award, the Guardian Children's Fiction Award, the Carnegie Medal and the Beefeater Children's Book award and has written several books for Orion, including *Myths and Legends of the World: The Golden Hoard, The Silver Treasure, The Bronze Cauldron* and *The Crystal Pool, Britannia, Cowboy Jess* and *Cowboy Jess Saddles Up*. She lives in Berkshire with her husband John and daughter Ailsa.

Other books by the same author

Myths and Legends of the World: The Golden Hoard
Myths and Legends of the World: The Silver Treasure
Myths and Legends of the World: The Bronze Cauldron
Myths and Legends of the World: The Crystal Pool
Cowboy Jess
Cowboy Jess Saddles Up
Britannia
Britannia on Stage
God's People
God's Kingdom

Golden Myths and Legends of the World

Geraldine McCaughrean

A Dolphin
Paperback

First published in Great Britain in 1999
by Orion Children's Books
a division of the Orion Publishing Group Ltd
Orion House
5 Upper St Martin's Lane
London WC2H 9EA

Reprinted in 2000

A catalogue record for this book is available
from the British Library

Typeset by Deltatype Ltd, Birkenhead, Merseyside
Printed in Great Britain by Clays Ltd, St Ives plc

ISBN 1 85881 675 0

Contents

The Golden Wish   1
A GREEK MYTH

Shooting the Sun   6
A CHINESE MYTH

George and the Dragon   10
A PERSIAN MYTH

Skinning Out   14
AN ETHIOPIAN MYTH

Robin Hood and the Golden Arrow   16
AN ENGLISH LEGEND

Brave Quest   24
A NATIVE AMERICAN MYTH

Saving Time   31
A POLYNESIAN MYTII

The Lake that Flew Away   35
AN ESTONIAN LEGEND

Admirable Hare   39
A LEGEND FROM CEYLON

All Roads Lead to Wales   41
A WELSH LEGEND

Rainbow Snake   47
AN AUSTRALIAN MYTH

Juno's Roman Geese   52
A ROMAN LEGEND

John Barleycorn   58
AN AMERICAN MYTH

The Singer Above the River   61
A GERMAN LEGEND

How Music was Fetched Out of Heaven 66
A MEXICAN MYTH

Whose Footprints?   70
A MYTH FROM THE GOLD COAST

The Death of El Cid   74
A SPANISH LEGEND

The Man Who Almost Lived for Ever   78
A MESOPOTAMIAN LEGEND

Stealing Heaven's Thunder   81
A NORSE MYTH

Anansi and the Mind of God   86
A WEST INDIAN MYTH

How Men and Women finally Agreed   89
A KIKUYU MYTH

First Snow   94
A NATIVE AMERICAN MYTH

Ragged Emperor   98
A CHINESE LEGEND

The Boy Who Lived for a Million Years 104
A ROMANY LEGEND

Sea Chase   109
A FINNISH MYTH

Dragons to Dine   117
A HITTITE MYTH

Guitar Solo   120
A MYTH FROM MALI

Sadko and the Tsar of the Sea   123
A RUSSIAN LEGEND

The Armchair Traveller   128
AN INDIAN LEGEND

Uphill Struggle   132
A GREEK LEGEND

Bobbi Bobbi!   136
AN AUSTRALIAN MYTH

The Gingerbread Baby   139
A MYTH FROM PALESTINE

The Price of Fire   143
A MYTH FROM GABON

The Hunting of Death   146
A MYTH FROM RWANDA

Young Buddha   148
AN INDIAN LEGEND

The Woman who left no Footprints   152
AN INUIT LEGEND

Sun's Son   156
A MYTH FROM TONGA

Biggest   160
A JAPANESE LEGEND

'I love you, Prime Minister!'   164
A FRENCH LEGEND

And the Rains Came Tumbling Down   169
A MYTH FROM PAPUA NEW GUINEA

Four Worlds and a Broken Stone   171
A NATIVE AMERICAN MYTH

*The Needlework Teacher and the
Secret Baby*   177
A EUROPEAN LEGEND

Culloch and the Big Pig   183
A CELTIC LEGEND

The Call of the Sea   189
A LEGEND FROM THE CHANNEL ISLANDS

The Crystal Pool   193
A MELANESIAN MYTH

Race to the Top   195
A MAORI MYTH

Lamia   199
AN INDIAN LEGEND

Isis and Osiris   204
AN EGYPTIAN MYTH

The Flying Dutchman   210
A SAILOR'S LEGEND

Proud Man   215
A NATIVE AMERICAN MYTH

About the Stories   219

The Golden Wish

A GREEK MYTH

THERE was once a fool. Of course there have been far more fools than one, and fools more often than once. But this particular fool was a king, so his foolishness mattered. He lived in Greece, at the foot of Mount Olympus, and his name was Midas. All he thought about was gold. All day, while the golden sun shone, he shut himself away in dark vaults counting tinny gold. All night long, while the golden firelight glimmered, he shivered over his accounting books reading the words to himself:

> *Twelve bars of gold in my vaults*
> *Twenty plates of gold on my table*
> *Ten rings of gold on my wife*
> *Four hundred gold coins in my tax coffers . . .*

The centaurs, unlike Midas, valued only fun and wine. One day (and on many others, too) a centaur took too many drinks and stumbled into Midas's garden.

'I am lost,' he told the King.

Midas set the centaur on the right road for Olympus.

'Such a friend! Such kindness!' exclaimed the centaur, joyfully kicking up his heels. 'How can I thank you? A wish? I shall grant you one wish.'

Now Midas knew that these centaurs, these horse-men, grazed on the slopes of Olympus and drew magic from the holy mountain. His heart leapt to his mouth. 'A wish? You mean anything? I wish that everything I touch turns to gold!' He said it quickly, before the centaur could withdraw the offer.

'Ah. I should have warned you. People have asked that of the gods before, and . . .'

'Your magic isn't powerful enough! I knew it.'

'Oh, I can grant it,' said the centaur, flicking flies with his long tail. 'But you'll be sorry.'

'*No, I won't!*'

The centaur pronounced no spell. He did not spit or clap or chant. So when he trotted away towards Olympus, Midas felt sure no magic had passed between them. 'Boaster! Braggart!' he yelled after the galloping horse-man, and pounded the garden wall with his fist.

The wall felt smooth under his hand. It gleamed and glittered in the sunlight.

Gold.

Midas ran to his treasury and touched all the brass coins. They instantly shone gold – and not just the coins, but the jars they were in and the door of the treasure-house.

Gold.

Midas ran through the palace stroking and slapping every stool, bench, table and urn. They all turned to gold. His china and statues, his weapons and chariot all shone, more exquisite and precious than anything he had ever dreamed of owning. 'When we charge into battle,' he told his horse, patting its fat rump, 'we shall dazzle our enemies, you and I!'

The horse did not respond. It stood quite silent and quite still between the traces of the chariot: a perfect gold statue of a horse. Midas was a little startled, but after a moment he shrugged his shoulders. It made a fine statue for his new golden palace. And fresh horses can be bought by the dozen if a man has the gold to buy them.

'A feast! A festival! Where's my Chancellor? Where's my cook? Invite everyone! Spare no expense! Let the world know that Midas has gold! Midas has gold enough to buy up every sword, every horse, every acre of land in the world! I shall be unconquerable! I shall be worshipped! I shall be the envy of every man from the poorest beggar to the richest millionaire! I shall *be* the richest millionaire! A millionaire a million times over! Cook, where are you?'

His cook rushed in, carrying the King's lunch. He could not help but stare round him at all the changes to the room – the gold ornaments, the golden furniture. Midas snatched the bread impatiently off the tray and bit it. 'Huh? What are you feeding me these days? Rocks?' When he threw down the bread in disgust, it skidded across the golden floor. A golden loaf.

Food too, then? Midas took a drink to steady his nerves.

At least, he tried to take a drink. But the wine, as it touched his lip, turned to gold, to solid, metallic, unyielding gold. Midas stared. The cook stared. 'Don't just stand there! Fetch me something I can eat!' And he gave the man a push.

Ah well, there are more cooks in the world, for a man with limitless gold.

Midas sat down on the ground beside the golden statue of his cook. His clothes, one by one, in touching his skin, had been turning to gold around him, and he found that he was suddenly very, very weary from wearing them.

He had not meant it to be like this when he asked the centaur to . . . He had not meant food and clothes and people and horses . . .

Midas began to wonder. How long does it take for a man to starve to death?

Just then, his queen came in and, ahead of her, their little daughter. Midas tried to warn her. He tried to stop the girl running to him with outstretched arms. But the child was too young to understand. Her little fingers closed round Midas's hand – and stiffened, and grew cold, and could not be prised open again. Her face and features, too, hardened and set, and the eyes were plain gold orbs in their golden sockets, the golden mouth frozen, for ever half-open to speak.

'Oh Zeus! Oh you gods! No! Not my daughter! Not my little girl!' He ran past the Queen, past the guards, his arms burdened with the monstrous weight of a small clinging golden child. He ran out of his golden palace and its golden gardens: the flowerheads jangled as he brushed by them. He ran across golden grass to a forest and blighted it with a golden canker. He ran through orchards till the sight of the fruit maddened him with hunger. He started up the rocky slopes of Olympus, staggering under the weight of his lifeless daughter.

How long does it take for a man to die of loneliness? Or a broken heart?

'Take back this curse! What did I ever do to you that you punish me like this?' When he kicked off his heavy golden shoes, the golden grass spiked his soles like needles.

'Curse? I thought I granted you a wish,' said a familiar voice. The centaur trotted out of a nearby cave.

'I was a fool! I see that now! I was a fool! But does a man deserve to lose his daughter – to die – just because he's a fool?'

The centaur picked a few stalks of grass and nibbled them thoughtfully. 'I did try to warn you. Perhaps I've done you a favour, after all, if it has taught you something about yourself ...'

'Wonderful! I shall die wise, then!' said Midas.

The centaur blew through his lips. 'If you take my advice, you'll go to the river and jump in,' he said.

'*Kill* myself, you mean?' gasped Midas.

'No, you fool. *Wash* yourself.'

At the banks of the river Midas did not hesitate. If the water did not turn to gold and crush him, then the weight of the metal child clasping his hand might pull him under and drown him. But he did not care. He flung himself into the river, and its water closed over his head. As he surfaced, his daughter surfaced beside him, spluttering and terrified, not knowing why or how she came to be swimming. 'Father? Where are all your clothes?'

Together they carried buckets of water back to the palace, and flung it over cook and horse, over stool and table and coins. The colour of gold was loathsome to Midas, and he was not content until he had undone all the alchemy of his magic golden touch.

Never again did he dream of gold – except in nightmares. Never again did he yearn to own gilded ornaments and mounds of yellow riches. No, no! For Midas had learned his lesson, hadn't he?

Now he thought about jewels, instead.

Shooting the Sun

IMAGINE a tree with a spread of branches and twigs as intricate as the blood vessels of an eye. Imagine its trunk twelve thousand spans high, roots plunging as far as the earth's hot core. Imagine a rookery of nests in the topmost branches, each the size of a galleon, each the cradle of a boy-child. And imagine the parents of those children, Di Jun, god of the eastern sky, and his wife Xi He.

In the ancient days of China, Di Jun and Xi He had ten sons, strong and handsome, each with a yellow suit, a scarf of orange and a cloak of flame. Each morning their proud mother whistled up the dragon which lay coiled around the great tree where she lived, and harnessed it to her chariot. Then, with one of her boys beside her, she drove to the edge of the eastern sky. There she set him down – Lung or Wu, Yanxi, Ming or Xang – and with a last comb of his hair or damp finger to clean a smut off his nose, she left him there to walk the path across the sky. Each boy, you see, was a sun.

Many footprints tamped flat that blue, celestial path. For many thousands of mornings this same routine took place. But after a thousand years more, the boy-suns grew into boisterous, roistering louts too vain and wilful to do as their parents told them.

They liked to do everything together, and had no patience to wait ten days for their turn to light the world. Thus it came about, in the reign of Emperor Yao, that the Chinese Empire was blighted by a terrible vandalism. The leaves of the trees blackened and curled. The feathers of the cranes singed and moulted. Fishponds boiled and the rhododendrons burned like a million campfires on the hills of China. For there were ten suns burning all at once in the sky.

Corners which were gardens in the morning were deserts by the evening. Even nightfall did not bring a respite from the dreadful heat, the fearful drought, for the ten suns stayed in the sky all the time, playing sports and horsing wildly about. The earth below never knew the healing balm of cool darkness. The people clamoured at the Emperor's gate, begging him to do something. And each one of them had ten shadows at his feet, because of the ten glaring suns in the sky.

Emperor Yao travelled across the ocean to the valley where the great tree grew, and he stood at the bottom and hailed Di Jun with all the respect that one king can offer another. 'O marvellous ruler of the eastern sky, will you not ask your royal children to do as they once did, and walk the sky's path one at a time? The world is burning, the sea is steaming, and soon the only water left will be the tears of my people!'

The great tree shook in every limb. 'O Emperor, no words are harder for a father to speak, but my sons are my shame! They have lost all respect for the word of their parents. Neither their mother nor I can shame them into obedience. Not threats or bribes, not shouts or politeness humble these roaring boys! But tell your people I will not abandon them to fire and scorching. I have sent Yi the great archer of the sky, with his red bow and ten white arrows, to shoot down my delinquent sons!' On an outer branch of the tree, Xi He could be seen sobbing, while her dragon lay panting far below her, half-buried in crisp leaves fallen from the drought-stricken tree.

Emperor Yao bowed low and returned to his people with the good news. Though no one saw Yi in person, nor the red curve of his bow, many claimed to have seen his white arrows streaking skywards.

BANG! One sun exploded in a ball of fire and spun in the sky like a Catherine wheel. As it fell, it changed colour – from white-hot to blood-red, from red to umber, umber to brown. Then each flame turned to a black feather in the body of a black crow, and the dead crow landed, feet up, with an arrow in its breast.

BANG! BANG! The suns fell like oranges from a shaken tree. Four, five, six. 'Blessings on you, Di Jun!' cried the people. 'You have valued our lives and our world above the lives of your ten sons!'

'Ten?' said the Emperor to himself with a start. He shielded his eyes and glanced up at the sky. Four suns were left, blazing down on the earth, roasting the bears in their caves, the turtles in their shells. 'Will he shoot down all ten?' Suddenly it dawned upon Yao that Di Jun meant every last son to die. Yi the archer had ten arrows in his quiver, and when he fired the last one, the world would be plunged into total darkness. Instead of too great a heat, there would be none, and the birds would shiver in the trees and the fish be frozen in ponds of solid ice.

'Quick!' he said to the courtier standing beside him. 'Run to where Yi is shooting, and steal the last white arrow in his quiver!'

Without question, the courtier set off to run – over parched meadow and dry stream, over charred bushes and burned forests. As he ran, the shadows which streamed out behind him decreased in number from four to three, and a black crow fell at his feet. As he ran, the temperature dropped, and another black crow fell.

Just as the courtier glimpsed Yi, his red bow as bent as any dogwood tree, the bowstring twanged and a ninth sun exploded in a whirligig of flame. A ninth crow plummeted to the ground.

Yi reached behind him and felt for the last arrow. He fumbled, looked in his quiver, then looked around. He saw nothing but the dust flying up behind a running man who did not stop when called.

He did not stop, in fact, till he reached the court of Emperor Yao, and presented his emperor with a single white arrow. Meanwhile, the last of Di Jun's suns was running towards the eastern horizon, too afraid to look behind him. He disappeared over the rim of the world, and night fell on the Day of Di Jun's Anger.

That one son was so frightened by what had happened that he might never have shown his face again in heaven. 'The Celestial Bowman will shoot me down, Mama!' he wailed piteously.

But his mother simply bundled him into her dragon chariot next morning, and ordered him out again at the edge of the eastern sky. 'So he will, if you don't behave yourself better in future, my lad!' and she pointed an imperious finger out along the sky-blue pathway.

As soon as his back was turned, she watched him begin his journey with her head on one side and a fond smile on her face. She was so grateful to Emperor Yao for saving the life of her youngest son that she allowed him sometimes to ride in her dragon chariot, and they would tour the boundaries of China together discussing such things as tea and chess.

George and the Dragon

A PERSIAN MYTH

A s THE sun rose, the town opened its gates, as if it were yawning. As if it were yawning, it shut them again. Left outside were a goose and a nanny goat – the last animals in the whole town. The goose honked balefully, the goat pressed itself against the gate, sensing danger. Then a large shadow swamped them in darkness, a flash of flame burned up the shadow, and goat and goose were gone. When the people of the town peeped over their high palisades, nothing remained but a scattering of charred bones and a sprinkling of white feathers. The dragon had been fed for one more day.

No one any longer left the town to tend their crops or travel to market. They simply waited, prisoners within their own walls, while the besieging dragon circled them, scratching its hide against the wood walls, sharpening its claws on the gates. It had slithered out of the lake – a beast longer than night and hungrier than quicksand. Its scales ran with slimy sweat, and its jaws dripped acid saliva. Wherever it trod, the grass withered and died. The stench wilted the cherry blossom and cankered apples on the bough.

Princess Sabra had seen the beast from the top window of her tall room, high in the royal palace, where she watched for help to come. But no help came, for no one knew of the town's plight, or if they did, they dared not come near. Having seen the dragon once, Sabra hung her cloak over the window so that she might never see it again. But she could not shut out the sound of crying in the streets, of screams and shouting, of fights and quarrelling.

All the animals in the city had been fed to the dragon. Now the King had given orders for a lottery.

The name of every man, woman and child was entered in the lottery, and whosoever's name was drawn would be turned out to feed the dragon. The King closed his doors against the angry protesters. 'It is necessary,' was all he would say, shouting through the thickness of the door. 'Do you want the dragon to tear down the city walls looking for its food?'

And the dragon found the taste of human flesh to its liking, and came earlier each morning to be fed.

Then, one day, the knocking at the palace door did not stop. 'Open, Lord King! Princess Sabra's name has been drawn in the lottery!'

'No! No! Her name should never have been entered! My daughter? Never!' But his subjects (though they loved their princess dearly) had no pity left in their hearts. Terror had wrung them dry of it. 'We have lost our loved ones – our husbands, our wives, our sons and daughters. Give up the Princess Sabra, for she must feed the dragon in the morning!'

A flagpost stood outside the gate. To this, each day, the victim was tied with strong rope, blessed with kisses and tears, and left alone to await the dragon's hunger. On the summer morning when Sabra took her place beneath the flag, the sky overhead was full of mare's-tail clouds, and the fields full of poppies. Birds sang in the scorched orchards, and the sun glinted on the poisoned lake. Above her, the blood-red banner flicked its lolling tongue, and the city bell began to toll dully – *chank chank chank*.

Suddenly, a horseman appeared on the skyline: she might not have seen him but for the sunlight gleaming on his metal helmet and the dazzling white of the shield across his back. He stopped to look around him, wondering, no doubt, at the blackness of the countryside, charred, burned, dead. Sabra wondered, in turn, whether to shout a warning. There was still time for him to escape, whereas everyone in her city was surely doomed, one by one, to die in the dragon's jaws.

All at once, the birds stopped singing. Through the soles of her feet, Sabra felt the ground tremble. Through the walls of her soul, she could feel fear crushing her heart. Out of the pool, out of its subterranean lair, the dragon raised its head to see what morsel waited by the city gate. Out it heaved itself, lidless eyes rolling, nostrils dilating. Its tongue unfurled suddenly from behind its teeth, forked and flickering. There was a smell of sulphur and filth.

Sabra opened her mouth to scream, but fear was strangling her. Instead, she heard a voice, loud and calm and demanding of attention. 'So. I have found you at last,' said the knight. 'Evil made flesh.'

The dragon cast a look over its shoulder, and the lobeless earholes sucked in the words. It looked the knight over and then turned back towards Sabra. No meal so delectable had yet been placed before it, and nothing could disrupt its lust to feed.

But as it scuttled towards her, on bowed legs and splayed feet, the knight rode at full tilt and crashed his horse, flank against flank, sidelong into the beast.

It turned in irritation and snapped, but the knight was too quick, and galloped out under its tail. 'Know this, beast, that I am George of Lydda and the shape of your undoing. I am here to make an end of you!'

The baggy jaw gaped in a grimace like a laugh. A ball of fire burst at the horse's feet as the dragon spat its contempt. The mare reared up, her mane singed short by the heat, but George stayed in the saddle, spurring her forwards once more, driving his spear deep into the dragon's haunch.

The beast seemed to feel no more pain than from a bee-sting, and rubbed himself against the town wall, breaking off the shaft of the spear and opening a gap in the long palisade. Its tail brushed Sabra as it turned, and the razor-sharp scales snagged her dress to ribbons. With a single blow of a webbed claw, it knocked over the knight's white mare.

George rolled clear, drawing from the side of his saddle a broadsword, as bright and as long as day. And there, where he had risen, he took his stand, white shield raised over his head. A torrent of fire splashed over the snowy heraldry and turned it to silver ash, but from beneath the burning buckler the knight struck out – a slash to the snout, a lunge to the breast, a charge into the green coils of snaking, dragony neck. Sabra shut her eyes. She could not remember how to breathe, how to make her heart beat. A carpet of fire unrolled at her feet and set her dress alight.

But a hand extinguished the flames, and another brushed her long hair back off her face. 'The beast is down, lady. If I might borrow your sash, you may see foulness conquered by purity.'

Sabra opened her eyes and saw George loop her sash around the dying dragon's throat. Its thrashing tail lay still, its laboured breathing ceased with a quiet sigh, and the fire of wickedness burning in its soul went out like a penny candle. 'I fought you in the name of Christ Jesus, who is goodness made flesh,' George whispered into the beast's ear. 'So you see, you stood no chance.'

Then the gates of the town opened like a great cheer, and out poured the people to stare, the children to clamber over the dragon's carcass. The King embraced George, and thanked him a thousand times. 'Stay! Stay and marry the Princess Sabra and rule the kingdom after I am dead ...!'

But George thanked him graciously, exchanged smiles with the Princess, then remounted his horse. 'I am on a journey,' he said, 'which does not end here.' Sabra watched her knight ride away, she noticed that his shield was no longer scorched, but white again, and that a red cross embellished it now; a simple blood-red cross.

Skinning Out

AN ETHIOPIAN MYTH

WHY GO to all the trouble of creating people and then let them wear out? It is like building a cart and not nailing on the wheels: sooner or later they will fall off – and what good is the cart then?

The Maker, who moulded and shaped the Galla people, was neither forgetful nor slipshod. You may see it in the people – as tall and willowy as fishing rods and beautiful as ebony. And his intent never was to let their beauty wane. But of course the blazing sun over Ethiopia dries soft skin and puckers it into wrinkles. Though the babies gleam like stones from the bottom of a stream, the old men and women bend and wrinkle like the tree whose roots can no longer reach water.

'Go to the Galla, Holawaka,' said The Maker to his messenger bird, 'and tell them, when their skins start to wrinkle and to weigh heavy, to slip them off and leave them where they fall. Underneath hides a new beauty, as the butterfly hides within the caterpillar.'

The brightly coloured bird, who sat preening her purple feathers with a beak of scarlet, cocked her head. 'Very well,' she said. 'But how shall I know the Galla from the rhinoceros or the giraffe, from the hyena or the lioness? These creations of yours all look the same to me – no feathers, no beaks, no plumes . . .'

'The Galla are as tall and willowy as fishing rods and beautiful as ebony,' said The Maker. 'How you do *talk*, Holawaka.'

So Holawaka flew down to the earth, still talking, but only to herself. Presently she met Tortoise. 'This is not the

Galla,' she said, 'for it is squat and round and its face is far from lovely.' So she flew on by. Soon, however, she saw Snake.

'Now this fellow *is* as tall and willowy as a fishing rod and as beautiful as ... what was it, again? Ah yes, beautiful as emeralds.' And she asked, 'Would you care to know the secret of staying young and never growing old?'

Snake, not surprisingly, cared a great deal. So Holawaka showed him how to slough his skin and slither out. The skin was left behind, delicate as paper, diamond-patterned and translucent in the sunshine.

'Of course, if I had been The Maker,' said Holawaka, who liked to talk, 'I would have given you people feathers to fly with. Then you could have nested among the treetops and dived for fish in the lakes, and left single feathers like licks of paint on the ground.' On and on Holawaka talked, though Snake had long since gone to tell his children the secret of staying young and never growing old, and she was speaking only to his sloughed skin. When she noticed this, she hopped back into the sky and home to The Maker's orchard where she perched on his fruit trees.

'Did you give the message to the Galla?'

'Yes, yes ... though I'd have called him *long* rather than *tall*.'

By the time the mistake was realized, the world was set in its ways, and the Maker was busy elsewhere. That is why the men and women of the Galla (and the rest of us for that matter) grow wrinkled and old with passing time, and the passage of many suns. Don't trouble to go looking for Snake to learn his secret. You will never find him – only empty snakeskins, crackling and translucent.

Robin Hood and the
Golden Arrow

AN ENGLISH LEGEND

ENGLAND was a country in despair. When the wind blew through its forests, the trees groaned and the leaves sighed. It was a country ruled by foreign invaders, and while the Normans fed richly off the fat of the land, the conquered Saxons made do with the crumbs that were left.

Saxon and Norman knights had ridden away in comradeship behind the glorious banners of King Richard, and gone to do battle in the Holy Lands. But the Normans left behind to rule England kept up the old tyranny. Prince John, Richard's brother, proved as barbaric as Richard was chivalric. He appointed men like the Sheriff of Nottingham and Guy of Gisborne: robber barons who sat in the great grey keeps of their granite castles and plotted to grow rich. They taxed and fined and robbed their Saxon subjects until starvation sat by every Saxon hearth. They dispossessed the poor who could not pay, the proud who would not pay, and anyone whose fortune they wanted for themselves.

Robin of Locksley, for instance, was cheated of his father's land by Gisborne. Where was the law to protect his rights, grant him justice? Gone to the Crusades with the King. Law and Justice no longer existed in the England ruled by Prince John.

Unless they lived on in Robin Hood.

That same cheated Robin of Locksley, to preserve his life, slipped away into the green forest and disappeared.

Soon afterwards, a mysterious figure was glimpsed by travellers, dressed all in green, with green-feathered arrows in his quiver and green mosses streaking his cheeks. No one knew at first whether the 'Man of Sherwood' truly existed or not. But then strange things began to happen.

Fat Norman merchants were robbed of their gold, and next day thin Saxon children found gold beneath their pillows. Cruel tax collectors were 'relieved' of all their takings. Then money would fly in at the windows of widows, and flour fall like snow on starving villages. The mysterious Robin Hood was robbing the rich to feed the poor, and though the Norman soldiers hunted him like the hind, they could never find him. He had made the greenwood his own stronghold.

One by one, men persecuted or pursued by Norman law headed for the forest to join Robin Hood and to wear the 'suit of green'. They were outlaws to the Normans, but heroes to the Saxons. Their very existence burned like a green gleam in the imagination, a flame of hope.

'A tournament? Will there be archery?' asked Robin casually, waxing his bowstring with a stub of candle.

'That's the main event!' said Friar Tuck, tucking into his meal. 'First prize is a golden arrow, presented by Gisborne himself.' The Friar's words emerged speckled with bread-crumbs and flecks of fat. 'Open to any archer in the land. The Prince himself is going to be there, so they say, the swine.' Tuck was the only man in Robin's band not to wear the suit of green. In his brown habit, he could come and go to town unnoticed, unquestioned, and bring them news, messages from wives and sweethearts, gifts from well-wishers. He was able, too, to deliver Robin's little 'presents' to the poor of Nottingham.

Today his news was of a grand archery contest to be held within the castle walls. The outlaws, sitting around their campfire, greeted the news quietly, remembering other such festive holidays spent with their families.

'We know, without going, who's the best archer in England, don't we?' said Alan-a-Dale loyally, and all the outlaws shouted in one voice. '*Robin Hood!*'

'It would be pleasant to prove it, even so,' murmured Robin.

'You *wouldn't*! You never would!' Much the Miller was horrified. 'Tell him, Little John! Tell him it's too dangerous!'

'S'probably a trap,' said Will Scarlett gloomily. 'The Sheriff probably means to lure Robin inside the castle – thinks he won't be able to resist competing for a stupid golden arrow.'

'Let's not disappoint him, then!' declared Robin, jumping to his feet.

There was a streak of recklessness in Robin which scared his Merrie Men. It was hard enough to keep alive in the inhospitable greenwood, without a man wilfully creeping into the stronghold of his worst enemy. And for what? An arrow of shiny gold that would not even fly?

The sun glinted on the golden arrow. The cushion it lay on was of blood-red velvet.

The castle grounds were bright with striped pavilions and painted flag-poles, the sky jagged with pennons. Tourney armour caught the sun and dazzled the eye. Chargers cloaked in cloth-of-gold stamped their hooves and jingled plumed bridles. It was a holiday in Nottingham and, for once, the brown and ragged townspeople were also allowed inside the castle precincts.

Entrants for the archery contest stood in a huddle: the best archers in Prince John's guard, the best archers in the Sheriff's employ, professional marksmen and amateur huntsmen. There were a few Saxons, too – arrowsmiths and bow-makers, for the most part. Impatiently they queued up to shoot at the distant butts.

Suddenly there was a flurry of excitement, as a young man in a green tunic was seized by castle guards and wrestled to the ground. 'We knew you couldn't stay away, Robin Hood! Got you at last!'

But it was not Robin Hood at all, just a boy wearing green. Gisborne ground his teeth. He found archery tedious, and now he was obliged to sit through a whole afternoon of it.

Some arrows went wide, some buried themselves in the grass, ripping off their feather fletches. The butts looked like porcupines by the time all the bowmen had loosed their flights. Last of all, an old man, bent and bearded, shuffled to the firing line, carrying his arrows in a raffia basket. He began, with shaking hands, to fit an arrow to his bowstring.

'Get away, old man. Clear off!' they told him. 'This is a young man's sport. Go home.'

'All comers, it said,' croaked the old man.

'He's holding up the competition! Get rid of him!'

'Oh, let him make a fool of himself. Takes less time than arguing.'

The old man nodded and doddered, peered down the field at the butts as if he could barely see them, then feebly tugged back on his bowstring. The arrow plunged into the golden heart of the target.

'Fluke.'

'Lucky!'

'Not half bad, Grandpa.'

The competition continued, with everyone disqualified who did not hit gold. Round by round it became harder – the butts were moved farther off – and more bowmen were eliminated. But the luck of the old man held. The crowd began to warm to him: he was a ragged Saxon, after all. Every time he fired, they cheered. Every time a Norman missed, they cheered, too.

It came down to just three men: a Norman sergeant-at-arms, hand-picked by Guy of Gisborne, a pretty French knight in chequered velvet . . . and the old man, frail and lame, whose clothes had more holes in them than the canvas target. The butts were moved still farther off – so far now that they were scarcely in sight.

As the French knight took aim, a silly lady in the stands jumped up and waved to him for luck. It spoiled his concentration and the arrow went wide.

But the sergeant-at-arms fired the perfect shot. His arrow hit the gold dead centre. Even the Saxon crowds gasped with admiration and began to turn away. The contest was plainly over.

The old man congratulated the sergeant, who spat in his face and laughed. The nobles in the stand were rising and stretching themselves, stiff after so much sitting. The old man took a green-tipped arrow from his raffia basket and laid it to his bow. 'I'll just see what I can manage,' he quavered.

His arrow flew like a hornet. The thwack, as it hit canvas, sounded like an explosive charge. It pierced the selfsame hole as the sergeant's arrow, and dislodged it, leaving only one arrow thrumming with the force of impact.

'Did you see that?'

'Why? What happened?'

'He did it! Old Grandpa did it!'

The nobility milled about in their enclosure. As the old man approached, twisted and limping, to receive his prize, Prince John pointedly turned his back.

Guy of Gisborne picked up the golden arrow between finger and thumb and dropped it at the vagrant's feet. 'You shoot quite well, old man,' he said grudgingly, but there was no reply. He saw that the archer's face was turned not towards him but towards the Lady Marian. The mouth was hidden by the bird's nest beard, but the eyes were wrinkled with smiling. And the Lady Marian was smiling back!

'Well done, sir! Oh, well done!' she said.

'You are kind, beautiful maiden, past all my deserving,' said the winner.

Now you ought to know that Sir Guy of Gisborne thought of the Lady Marian as his future bride (even though she did not care for the idea). He was furious to see her smiles wasted on a filthy, decrepit Saxon. He took hold of the shaggy beard to yank the rogue's head round to face him. The beard came away in his hand. The archer sank his teeth in Gisborne's clenched fist, then sprang backwards.

It was as if he had left his old age in Gisborne's grasp and been restored to youth. There stood a handsome youngster, straight-backed, bright-eyed and laughing.

'*Robin Hood!*' breathed Gisborne, and for a moment the two men looked at one another with bitterest hatred.

Then a voice in the crowd shouted, 'Here, Robin! Over here!' A riderless horse, slapped on the rump, galloped towards the pavilion; Robin leapt into the saddle. The flying stirrups struck the faces of the guards who tried to stop him.

Gisborne was first to mount up and give chase, while Marian crammed her long plaits against her mouth and gazed after them. 'Oh ride, Robin, ride!' she whispered under her breath. She alone among the spectators had recognized Robin Hood beneath his disguise – but then she was in love with him, and he with her.

The crowds scattered from in front of the galloping horses, as Gisborne pursued Robin towards the castle drawbridge. The golden arrow shone in Robin's hand. A cry rose spontaneously from the beggars and children by the gate: 'Ride, Robin! Ride!'

But Gisborne was close behind, well mounted, and his sword out, whereas Robin's horse was a poor thing. His disguise allowed for no weapon: a longbow cannot be used in the saddle.

'I've a score to settle with you, you filth, you thief!' panted Gisborne, and the blade of his sword sliced the green feathers from Robin's arrows. 'You've robbed my tax gatherers, stirred up the peasants, and thumbed your nose at me out of the greenwood tree! Well, now I'll show that scum of yours that their magic Robin Hood is nothing but common flesh and blood!' This time his blade shaved the hair from Robin's neck. They thundered over the castle drawbridge side by side.

'And I have a score of scores to settle with you, Gisborne!' panted Robin. 'You robbed me of my father's land. You tread down the poor and make widows and orphans weep! You drove me to live like an animal in the greenwood . . .'

Gisborne swung, and Robin's hot blood flew back in his face, in his eyes.

'. . . *when everyone knows that you are the animal!*' Robin turned in the saddle and struck out, using the only weapon he had.

Watching from the castle yard, the crowds saw the two horses part. One went left, towards the forest, the other right, towards the town. It looked as if Gisborne had unaccountably turned aside and let Robin Hood escape.

A short while later, the bully's horse ambled down the streets of Nottingham town, reins dangling, foamy with sweat, hooves skidding on the cobbles. Shopkeepers and housewives, accustomed to the man's cruelty, drew back fearfully against the walls. Then one by one they stepped out again. They had seen the golden arrow shaft shining in the centre of Gisborne's crested surcoat, its point sunk deep in his heart. And they had seen death staring out of Gisborne's open eyes.

Greater tyrants remained, tyrants who made Gisborne seem like a gentleman. Until the true King of England returned, his subjects would continue to groan and suffer at the hands of Prince John and his robber barons. Only the existence of Robin Hood – out there – dressed like Spring among the greenwood trees – kept poor people from despair. The mere mention of Robin's name kept their hearts beating. The telling of his thousand daring exploits warmed them even when there was no fuel on the hearth. In the depths of a cruel winter, Robin was the green promise that Spring always returns.

Brave Quest

A NATIVE AMERICAN MYTH

H E HAD nothing: no parents, no possessions, no position in the tribe but to be laughed at and scorned. Once, he had been handsome, but being handsome in deeds as well as face, he had tried to return a fallen eagle-chick to its nest and been gouged and gored by the parent birds. Now his face was hideously scarred, and though his name was Man-of-Little, everyone called him Scarface.

'Why don't you ask Marvellous-Girl to marry you?' they jeered. 'You love her, don't you? What a perfect pair you'd make! The dove and the crow!' Their spite rained down on him sharp as arrows.

Of course he loved Marvellous-Girl: everyone did. Braves of every tribe for a hundred miles around came to ask for her in marriage. They all went away disappointed. How could Scarface even tread in the prints of her moccasins or pain her eyes with the sight of his ghastly face? If they had not goaded him, he never would have done so. But their cruelty stirred in him the dregs of an old pride, and he went to the lodge of Marvellous-Girl, and stood by the closed doorway.

'I love you, Marvellous-Girl. If a strong arm and a faithful heart can do you any service, take me for your husband. I stand at your door and sorrow, for what hope of love has a boy like me? But what love can do for you, I will do, for I am filled with love.'

To his amazement, the woman inside did not shriek with laughter. The door flap lifted and her face appeared, as lovely as the new moon. 'I can marry no one, Man-of-

Little, but if I could, there is no one I would sooner have. For you are gentle and good, and your hair would be pleasing under my hand.'

For a moment, Scarface could barely think. The face slipped out of sight, like the moon passing behind a cloud. 'Why can you not marry?' he called, and the pigeons on the corn flew up in surprise.

'Because I am promised to the Sun.'

'No!' He could hear her moving about inside the dark lodge, preparing a meal: the Sun's betrothed, the girl he loved. He bit back his jealousy. 'You are greatly honoured, then.'

Her rustling movements stopped. After a moment she said, 'I would have felt more honoured, Man-of-Little, to be married to you.'

Astonishment, like a fountain, leapt up within Scarface. 'Then I'll shoot the Sun out of the sky!' he cried, and the vultures, picking over bones among the litter, took off in alarm.

'Shssh!' Her face appeared, lovelier than the moon. 'Don't anger him. But you could go to the Sun's Lodge, if you dared, and beg him to release me. He might take pity on us. If he does, ask him to touch your face and heal that scar of yours. Then everyone will know he has renounced his claim and blesses our marriage.'

'I'll go!' cried Scarface, and an eagle flying overhead heard him and dropped its prey.

Though he took food, the journey was so long that it was soon used up, and he lived on roots, berries and wild honey. Though he knew the paths to the east of the village, his journey was so long that he soon reached woodland paths he had never trodden before. Though he asked every person he met, 'Where is the Sun's Lodge?', no one knew, and the journey was so long that he soon met with no more people. Instead he entered wild places inhabited only by animals.

Though he was young and strong, the journey was so long that at last he thought he could go no farther and sat down on a log. Polecat came trotting by, as black and white as snow on coal. 'I am looking for the Sun's Lodge!' said Scarface to the Polecat.

'In all my life I have never seen it. But Bear is wise. Ask the Bear.'

So Scarface searched out the Bear and found him scratching the bark from a tree, licking the insects from his paws. 'I am looking for the Sun's Lodge,' he said, quite fearless (for he had so little to lose that were the Bear to eat him, he would be little worse off).

'In all my days, I have never seen it,' said Bear, 'but Beaver goes where I cannot. Ask the Beaver.'

So Scarface asked Beaver, who was building a lodge in the lake.

'In all my travels I have never seen the Sun's Lodge,' said Beaver. 'But Wolverine is cunning. Ask the Wolverine.'

So Scarface searched out Wolverine, but by the time he found him, he was both famished and exhausted.

'The Sun's Lodge? Of course I know where it is,' said the Wolverine. 'But where is your canoe? You can hardly cross the Great Water without a canoe!'

'If that's where it is, I shall swim across!' declared Scarface. But that was before he saw, for the first time, the Great Salt Waters of the ocean, so vast that a man's life might be swum out amid its valleys and mountains. There on the beach, Scarface sat down and wept tears as salt as the sea. He knelt back on his heels and addressed himself to the sky.

'Rightly was I named Man-of-Little at my birth, for I have neither the face nor the strength, nor the magic, nor the luck to make good of my life. Was it for nothing that I was born? I wish those eagles had eaten me, limb and life, rather than leave me here, on the shores of my short-comings!'

A pair of eagles flying overhead heard him and swooped

down. He raised his arms over his head, but he had no shield or weapon to fend them off.

The eagles' talons closed around his arms, and their beaks gripped his hair. Then, with a deafening clatter of wings, they lifted him – up and out over the ocean.

'There you are, young friend,' they said, setting him down on the farthermost shore. 'We regret that our mistake has spoiled your life so far, but we do what we can in recompense. Follow that yellow path. It leads to the Lodge of the Sun.'

With a whoop of joy, Scarface leapt along the path, his strength renewed, his hunger forgotten. Night had fallen, and he had only the moon to light his way. Presumably the Sun was indoors, sleeping in his lodge.

Just before dawn, he began to see, strewn along the path, various pieces of clothing and weaponry: a quiver of arrows with golden shafts, a headdress of white egret feathers, a gold spear, a tunic sewn with gilt thread, and moccasins of the softest kind. He stepped carefully over them, wondering at what kind of warrior owned such splendid things. Suddenly the leaves of a tree exploded overhead, and a youth plunged down on to his shoulders with a blood-curdling war-cry.

They rolled over and over together on the ground. Scarface easily broke free, but the young man did not seem much put out. 'Why didn't you pick them up?' he asked breathlessly, putting on his tunic again and collecting up his possessions.

'All those beautiful things? Because they weren't mine,' said Scarface.

'Pity. I could have challenged you to a fight for taking them – you must be out-of-the-ordinary honest, that's all I can say!' Scarface sat on the ground, winded and a little bewildered. 'Oh! You don't know me, do you? I'm Morning Star, son of the Sun. He'd like you, my father. I make him angry, because I'm always doing what he tells me not to do. But he'd like you, I should think.'

'I'm not so sure,' said Scarface, with a wry smile. But Morning Star had already run off up the path.

'Let's go killing whooping cranes!' he called over his shoulder. 'The Old Man says I mustn't – so it must be fun. Race you to the lake!'

Scarface got to his feet and ran after Morning Star. 'If your father says you shouldn't, maybe you should respect the wisdom of his age!' His words came back at him, echoing off the shale sides of a valley dry but for a small lake glowing in the dawn. Around it, a flock of cranes sipped the water through long spiky beaks.

As Morning Star rushed at them, brandishing the golden spear, they rose up into the air – a clumsiness of bony wings and horny legs. Then they dropped down again, enveloping Morning Star in a blizzard of feathers. He gave one long, loud scream.

Without time to waste on fear, Scarface ran headlong into the storm of birds. Their long beaks were like tent pegs driven home with mallets. The leading edges of their wings were sharp as blades, and the clawed feet which kicked him were hoof-hard.

But with his fists alone, he bruised their scarlet beaks. With his bare hands he tore tail feathers from them in handfuls until they rose, squawking indignantly, and flapped away down the shale valley. Morning Star lay still along the ground, his body bleeding from a dozen wounds. Scarface lifted him gently and carried him back to the yellow path and up to the door of the Sun's Lodge.

'What have you done?' demanded the fearful orange face which answered his knocking. It was blotched and marked in a hundred places by spots of old age. 'Did you do this to him?'

Scarface could feel the hairs of his fringe frizzle, the lashes of his lids scorch. 'He tried to go hunting whooping cranes by the lake in the valley. The birds mistook him for a foolish boy with too little respect for the advice of his father.'

The heat of the Sun's fury cooled instantly, and he hurried Scarface indoors – into the largest and most magnificent lodge ever raised on a forest of poles. Scarface laid Morning Star on a heap of buffalo hides, fearing he must already be dead. But the merest caress of the old man's hand closed the wounds in Morning Star's body, and restored him to perfect health. So he was able to tell his father about meeting Scarface, about his out-of-the-ordinary honesty, about the whooping cranes blotting out his sky . . .

'You have saved my son's life,' said the Sun solemnly. 'How can I repay you?'

Once, twice Scarface opened his mutilated mouth to speak. But though courage had brought him through woodlands, over the ocean and up to the lodge door, he dared not speak. 'You will destroy me where I stand, if I say the words in my heart.'

'Are you not a guest in my lodge, and my son's best friend? . . . And Man-of-Little, do you think I don't recognize you? Do you think I don't glance down, once in a while, as I cross the sky each day? Do you think I don't listen, too? I was overhead in the sky the day you spoke to Marvellous-Girl at her door.'

'Then touch my face and tell me I may marry her!' Scarface blurted.

The Sun reached out an elderly hand spotted as any leopard, and chucked Scarface under the chin like a little child. 'Let me give you clothes and food for the journey,' he said, 'and water to wash yourself.' As to Scarface's request, he said not a word.

It was not until Scarface looked down into the bowl of water which the Sun brought him, that he saw his face, perfect, restored, healed.

When Marvellous-Girl saw it, she reached out a hand too, through the doorway of her lodge, and touched his cheek. She did not even notice the quiver of golden arrows he was carrying, or the tunic sewn with gilt thread, or the headdress of egret feathers. 'Tell the tribe's women to prepare for a wedding,' she said. 'Tomorrow, I think. At noon. When the Sun will be directly overhead.'

They called their firstborn son Eagle, and the sons which followed after, Polecat, Beaver, Wolverine and Bear. But their daughter, of course, they named Woman-who-loves-Sunshine.

Saving Time

A POLYNESIAN MYTH

THE PACE of life is gentle on the sea-washed islands of Polynesia. Days are long and sunny, and no one hurries to get their work done or rushes a meal when it can be lingered over in the twilight.

It was not always so. Once, the People of the Islands rolled out of their beds at first light and scampered to their boats or to their plantations, dashed to do their work, never stopped to talk or sit – only to snatch a bite of food before the light failed.

'Quick, man, pick those coconuts while you can see which are ripe!'

'Quick, woman, beat that tree bark into cloth while you can see what you are beating!'

'Quick, child, find me bait for my fishing hook while you can still find the worm casts on the sand.'

But many was the time that fishing canoes put out to sea in the morning only to lose sight of land in the failing light and go astray amid the night-dark waves. For the days were very, very short, the Sun speeding across the sky like a thrown ball, the daylight gone in the blinking of an eye.

One day, Maui sat in front of his family hut. The Sun had already set and only firelight illuminated his family's anxious faces as they gathered to eat the evening meal. Some of the food was spilled as the bowls were passed out; there was so little light to see by.

'This food's not cooked,' complained a grandmother.

'I'm sorry. There wasn't time,' said Maui's mother.

'There's nothing for it,' said Maui, jumping up. 'The day

must be lengthened or how can we ever hope to get our work done between waking and sleeping?'

'Tell it to the Sun,' grumbled some of the elders. 'He rushes across the sky like a stone from a catapult and is gone in a twinkling.'

'Then I must make him slow down!' said Maui confidently, and strode off along the beach.

First he fell over a turtle and then he fell over a canoe, for the moon was young and the beach was dark and Maui could barely see his hand in front of his face.

'What are you looking for?' called his sister, Hina.

'For a length of rope,' Maui called back, peering around him without success.

'Don't you think you'd best wait till morning,' suggested his sister, 'when there's more light?'

In the morning, Maui found a length of rope made from coconut fibre and tied it in a noose. Then he walked to the eastern horizon (which took him the rest of the day), where a charred and gaping pit marked the spot at which the Sun leaps into the sky.

He circled the pit with the noose and, holding the other end of the rope, sat well back, through the long night, awaiting sunrise.

With a blinding, blazing bound, the Sun leapt out of his pit, hurtling towards his noonday zenith. The noose snapped shut around his shaggy head of flame – but the old Sun was moving so fast that the rope simply snapped like a spider's thread, and the great ball of fire never even noticed that he had been snared.

Maui returned home and, with the help of all the children, gathered up every coconut husk on every beach of every island. He stripped the hair shells and rolled the fibres into strands of coir. Then he plaited the fibres into a rope so strong he might have towed an island with it. He tied a noose in the rope and took it to the eastern horizon where, once again, he laid a snare to catch the rising Sun.

With one flaring, glaring bound, the Sun leapt into the

sky and pelted towards his noonday zenith. The noose pulled tight around his shaggy head of flame – but no sooner did it touch the great heat of the incandescent Sun than it frizzled into flames, dropping away in a flurry of ash as the Sun hurried onwards.

The day was so short that by the time Maui reached home, it was already night-time again. He crept into the family hut and felt his way to where his sister Hina lay sleeping on her mat. With his sharp fishing knife, he cut off her long hair, purple-black with magic and as glossy as the night sea outside. Plaiting it into a rope, he made one last purple-black noose. By dawn, it was in place around the pit of sunrise.

With a whirling whoop of white fire the Sun leapt into the sky and flew towards his noonday zenith. But he was brought up short by the jerk of a snare. Hina's plaited hair closed tight around his throat, and he choked and struggled and thrashed about, kicking and scrabbling to break free.

'I will let you go on one condition!' shouted Maui, hanging on grimly to the end of the purple-black rope. 'In future you must pass more slowly across the sky, so that the People of the Islands have a longer day, and can get their work done!'

The Sun rolled and spun, tugged and leapt, like a giant tunnyfish caught on a fishing line. But Maui was a great fisherman and he fought the Sun to a standstill. At last he hung panting in the air, great gouts of molten flame dropping like sweat from his golden face.

'I agree. I agree. From now, I shall creep across the sky as slowly as a turtle across a beach. Now let me loose.' Maui loosened the noose of Hina's magic hair, and the Sun walked sedately towards his distant noonday zenith.

The days, after that, lasted from slow lilac dawn through leisurely golden hours and into a sunset as pink and orange as a reef of coral. At such times, when the People of the Islands linger over their meal and watch the beauty of the Sun's descent, they can still see some strands of Hina's hair caught in the Sun's corona, streaking the evening sky.

Of course, what the Sun does when finally he dives into his pit at the western horizon is entirely his own affair. Freed from his promise to Maui, he may soar and swoop, circle and somersault as fast as any turtle beneath the waves.

The Lake that Flew Away

AN ESTONIAN LEGEND

D O YOU suppose a lake has no feelings? No sense of pride? No self-esteem? Do you think that it can lie untended without suffering? Its weeds run riot, like unkempt hair; its fishes choke beneath the autumn leaves; its banks crumble under the feet of drinking cattle.

Lake Eim in Estonia is a vast tract of water a hundred fathoms deep. In the beginning, trees which seeded themselves around it drank its water and flourished, dense and leafy. A forest grew. So did the darkness within it. And soon, within the darkness of trees lurked a darkness of men.

Brigands and bandits made their lairs in the black entanglement of lakeside trees. They fished the lake for their suppers, and they spent long hours sprawled in drifting boats, dangling grappling hooks into the deeps. For it was rumoured the lake held great treasures from an earlier civilization. The men did not dredge the shallows, or clear the weed, or cut back the nettles that mustered at the waterside. That would have been hard work, and they had forsworn hard work.

So why did their pockets jingle with gold, and their gambling last all night? Because each time a traveller passed through the wood – a pilgrim or a merchant – they cut his throat and threw his body in the deep, dark waters. The blood stained Lake Eim. The blood shamed Lake Eim. Red blood stained the bankside flowers and dripped from the bending grasses on to the face of the lake. The blood soured and fouled the still waters of the lake, till it shivered with a hundred cat's-paws, even on a windless day.

In horror and disgust, the lake seethed, and bubbles of marsh gas rose from the rotting weed on its bed. 'I will not be stained with the sin of these wicked men. I shall leave this place!'

The Robber Chief, stirring in his sleep, heard the slap-slap of water on the lake shore. He heard a *suck-shuck* as of mud parting company from a boot or a boat. Drops of water fell on the roof, and he thought. 'Rain,' and turned over to sleep again.

Suddenly, hands were pulling at the covers and voices shouting in his ear: 'Come quick! Come quick! The lake is . . . well, it's . . . the lake, it's . . .'

'The lake is what?' demanded the Robber Chief, grabbing a bandit by the throat. 'What is the lake doing, that you wake me in the middle of the night?'

'Flying away, Chief!'

'Flying away.' The Robber Chief pulled the blankets over his head and cursed his cronies, body and soul.

'It's true, Chief!'

'Like a carpet, Chief!'

'Up and away, Chief, all silver and glittering!'

The Robber Chief rolled out of bed and stumbled to the window. Overhead in the sky hung a billion gallons of water, shining like metal plate, thick as cumulus clouds, spreading out to all points of the compass, a translucent ceiling. If it were to fall . . .

The bandits stood stock still, waiting for a billion steely gallons to fall on their heads like the end of the world. Minute after minute they listened to the gentle hiss of moving water cascading through the sky. Then the moon bobbed into view again, like a fishing float, and the danger was past.

'Well? What are you waiting for?' bellowed the Robber Chief. 'Get out there and make the most of it! There'll be fish by the barrel-load, too, there for the picking up! And treasure! Don't forget the treasure! All there for the taking!'

As they pelted down to the lake, dawn was just rising.

'The boats have gone, Chief!'

'Who needs 'em? We can walk!'

They plunged on, up to their knees in mud. The lake bed was certainly alive with wriggling movement. And treasure chests lay about, smashed open at the hinges and steaming in the early sun.

A bandit thrust his arm into one of the chests, then drew it out with a shriek. The chest was full of frogs! Another was full of water snakes, another lizards. Not a fish, not a single bearded barbel or dappled trout lay stranded by the lake's departure. But every lizard, reptile, newt, salamander, frog and slug that had lived in the mud of the lake was crawling now towards the shore.

The brigands shrank back in revulsion – only to see the nasty slimy livestock of the lake crawl past into their dens, into their beds, into their boots and bags and hats.

They burned everything – their lairs and all they had stolen. They razed the forest to its stumps, then trudged away, their wicked lives in ashes, leaving an empty crater encircled by fire.

Meanwhile, Lake Eim carried its careful burden of fish and treasure through the sky. It flew so high that people below looked up and said, 'What cloud is that hiding the sun?' Hunters looked up and said, 'What flock of birds is that blacking out the sun?'

Then the lake came to a land parched and cracked, brown and destitute for want of water. The poor peasants there held out their hands, hoping the cloud might spare them a few drops of meagre rain. Then suddenly, out of the sky it swooped – a sluicing wealth of water, which seemed to glitter with jewels.

'Make me a bed to lie in, and I shall stay with you,' offered Lake Eim, in a voice like a thundering waterfall.

The peasants snatched up their hoes and spades. The

children dug with their hands; the women wheeled away the dry earth in barrows. Inside a week they made a bed for the lake, and Eim settled into it, with a sound like a weary groan. Fish danced on their tails on the surface, while each circular ripple to spread from the centre to the shore washed up a trinket of gold or a few silver coins. Several little boats bobbed about, too, on the choppy waves.

First the peasants thanked God, with prayers in the church. Then they thanked the lake, with flowers that they floated on its face. They planted willow trees and dug cattle troughs, made osier beds in the shallows, and built jetties out from the shore. They channelled water to their fields, and the fields flourished. They built a town and fed it on fish, and the town flourished. (All the fish fry they returned, so that the fish stocks thrived.) In short, they cared for the lake, and the lake cared for them.

Which is as it should be.

If you don't want your bed full of newts.

Admirable Hare

A LEGEND FROM CEYLON

FOR A few brief years, the ruler of the skies lived on earth as Prince Siddhartha, who was later called Buddha when he became wiser than any other man. But just once, they say, he met an animal whose kindness was an example and a marvel, even to the gods.

One night, the Buddha, who lived as a wandering hermit, got lost in a forest in Ceylon. The dense canopy of leaves overhead obscured the guiding stars. The smooth, blank moon poured its light only into the forest clearings, like milk into cups. In one of these clearings, the Buddha met a hare called Sasa.

'Your face is the face of a good man,' said the hare, 'but your expression is that of a man who has lost his way.'

'True, my velvet-eared friend,' admitted the Buddha. 'I am lost.'

'Then permit me to guide you to the edge of the forest.'

'I'm afraid I have no money to repay such kindness,' said the Buddha, thinking that perhaps the hare earned a living in this way.

'Sir,' replied Sasa, bowing gracefully from his slender hips, 'the debt would be all mine, if you would allow me to help you on your way, and share conversation with me as we go.'

So the Buddha was steered through the wood by this most charming hare, and as they walked, they talked. Sasa was hungry for any wisdom the Buddha could spare him. The Buddha was simply hungry, but did not say so.

At the edge of the wood, Sasa said, 'I know this meagre

forest and how long you have been lost in it. You must be very hungry.'

'You are indeed shrewd in judgement, my velvet-skinned friend,' replied the Buddha. 'I'm famished.'

The hare sat back on his heels. 'That will not do. Indeed, it will not. Please do me the honour of skinning and eating me. I am reasonably plump, as you can see, and too young for my meat to be tough. Here – I'll build you a fire so that you can cook me.'

Leaving the Buddha no chance to protest, Sasa dashed to and fro, gathering firewood into a heap which he lit with the spark from two stones. 'Thank you for teaching me so much of which I was ignorant,' said the hare, bowing once more from his slender hips. 'Enjoy your meal.' And with that, he leapt into the flames.

With the speed of a hawk, the Buddha's hand shot out and caught Sasa by his long velvet ears. Once, twice he swung the creature around, then threw him upwards, upwards. The hare smashed through the spreading canopy of a tree, and leaves and twigs rained down on to the Buddha's upturned face. But Sasa kept on flying, upwards, until he hit the very face of the moon.

'Such a generous creature shall not die – no, never!' the Buddha called after him. 'In future, let the world look up at night and see my friend, Sasa-in-the-Moon, and remember how noble a creature he was, and how kind to a penniless hermit!'

For though he was Buddha-in-the-Wood, with no bite of food to call his own, he was also Buddha, Ruler-of-the-Skies, and had only to reach out a hand to fulfil his every wish.

Sasa lived on in the moon – you can see the happy shape of him dancing. Many a traveller lost at night has looked up and found encouragement in seeing him there.

All Roads Lead to Wales

A WELSH LEGEND

THE countryside of Europe is struck through with roads as straight as if they were drawn on the map with a ruler. Though some have been broken by frosts, and weeds have grown through the cracks, and mud has buried them from sight, still they are there, just below the surface, like the main arteries of the land, bearing blood to its heart. This is a story told by men who found the roads and wondered at their marvellous straightness and excellent construction, wondered at the men who had built them and then disappeared without trace from the ruined villas nearby.

Maximus was Emperor of Rome, and no one was more fit to be so. The known world paid him homage and its merchants met in his market places. When he hunted, it was in the company of great men, and when he hunted that day, thirty-two kings rode in his party.

The heat of the day made the landscape quake. The dogs yelped away into the distance. Sleep rose up from the ground mixed with the dust from his mare's hooves, and cloaked Maximus in weariness. He lay down on a grassy river bank, and his centurions made a shelter of their shields to ward off the sun's heat. Beneath his dark shell, Maximus slept, and while he slept he dreamed – a dream so vivid that the events of the morning grew gauzy and unreal.

He flew along a river in his dream, or leaned so far over the prow of a ship that he saw only the water speeding below him. Upstream he sped, towards the source of the river, higher and higher till he came at last to a mountain – surely the highest in the world. Crossing the peak, he found another river issuing from the far side. He followed it down through the foothills, through fields and forests to its estuary and the sea. At the mouth of the river stood a city, its houses clinging to the skirts of a castle with towers of yellow and green and grey. At the foot of the castle wall, the sea rocked a fleet larger than all the navies of Rome. One ship in particular drew his eye, for its planks were alternately gold and silver and its gangway was a bridge of ivory.

Maximus, in his dream, crossed the ivory bridge just as the silk sail of the gilt and silver ship filled and billowed in his face. The ship carried him over sea lanes and obscure oceans to an island more beautiful than any he had ever seen. Still a strange curiosity carried him onwards, across the island from coast to coast, where he found the far side more lovely yet. Though its mountains were clad in mist, and tressed with rain, its valleys were fleecy with sheep and the river he followed was chased with silver spray. Once again, it was at the river's mouth that his dream brought him to a castle; inside the castle to a hall; inside the hall to a table. There it set him down.

Two princes were playing chess, while an old king sat nearby carving more chess pieces: knights and bishops and pawns. He looked up at Maximus, but a girl seated beside him was quicker in getting to her feet. Her hair, circled with gold, lifted and blew as she beckoned for Maximus to sit beside her in a chair of red gold. Thigh against thigh, arm against arm, hand against hand they sat. Then the Princess rested her cheek against his, turned her face towards him, smiled and offered him her mouth to . . .

A baying of hounds, a blare of horns, a thudding of hooves, and the shell of shields over the Emperor's head fractured and let in the sunlight. 'Your Majesty? Are you well? Such a very long sleep in the middle of the day! Perhaps the heat . . .' The sunlight and noise washed away the dream, the joy, the face of his beloved princess. Maximus awoke with a cry like a man stung by wasps, and clutched his hands to his heart. His hounds tumbled round him, and thirty-two kings stared.

On the way back to the palace, Maximus said not a word, and for a whole week afterwards would neither eat nor sleep, speak nor leave his room. It was as though, with the ending of the dream, he had breathed out a breath and could not draw the next. Physicians whispered outside his door. Rumours spread through the city that melancholy had conquered the invincible Maximus, and the thirty-two kings murmured among themselves.

Suddenly Maximus burst from his room: 'Summon my three finest men and saddle the best horses in Rome!'

He sent the three out into the three divisions of the earth, to search for the pieces of his dream: the country, the river, the castle, the two young Princes, the daughter, the King. He described every detail of his dream and said, 'Look, and do not stop looking until three years of looking have found nothing! For this dream went out of me like blood from a wound, and I fear my life depends on finding that place, that woman, that kiss.'

The three messengers departed into the three divisions of the earth, and each found islands, and each found rivers, each found castles and each found kings within them. But of the beautiful country of Maximus's dream – nothing.

They came home forlorn and fearful, and found the Emperor a shrunken man, like a sail emptied of wind. Rebellion was stirring in thirty-two dark corners of the Empire, because Maximus cared too little to put it down. 'I shall never see her again, and I left my heart in her keeping,' was all he said.

Then one of the messengers said, 'Master, won't you go yourself and look for the pieces of your dream? For the dream was sent to you and not to us!' It was so insolent a thing to say that the messenger trembled with fright.

Maximus lifted his head and parted the fingers which covered his scowling eyes.

'Wise man!' he cried. 'What you say is true!'

Putting on his hunting clothes once more, he took the selfsame mare from the stables, then rode into the green hills, allowing the horse to ramble and amble, on tracks and off. When she grew thirsty, the mare stopped by the banks of a river, and Maximus dismounted too and bent to drink.

'I have been here before,' he said, all of a sudden, as the water raced by beneath his breast. 'This is the river of my dream!'

This time he commissioned thirteen messengers to follow the river upstream to its source. 'Let each man stitch to his cape a sleeve of gold, so that whatever country he comes to, there he shall be recognized as a messenger of Maximus, Emperor of the Romans! I would go myself, but I have rebellions to quell!' The Emperor seemed quite his old self again.

The thirteen messengers followed the river till they reached its source high in the highest mountain they had ever seen. They followed the river which plunged down from the peak and wandered through a dozen countries to the sea. There they found a city and a castle with turrets of yellow, green and grey, a fleet of ships, and a gangplank of walrus ivory. Crossing over it, they took ship on a galleon clinkered with silver and gold.

'. . . Everything was just as you said, master!' they reported back a hundred days later. Their golden sleeves were caked with sea salt and dust, but their eyes shone brighter than gold. 'In a hall, in a castle held in the arms of a river, we saw an old man carving chess pieces, and two boys playing nearby. And there in the centre of the room was a maiden in a chair of red gold!'

'Did you speak? Did you ask her name?' Maximus scarcely dared to hear them out.

'We did as you commanded us, and fell on our knees before her and said, "Hail Empress of Rome," and told her your story from sleeping to waking.'

Maximus was as pale as death. 'What did she say?'

' "Sirs," she said, "I don't doubt what you tell me. But if the Emperor loves me, let him come here and fetch me himself. My name is Elen." '

After that, Rome stirred like a man waking. The army streamed out of their barracks; the shopkeepers swarmed to the palace with supplies; the ladies waved kerchiefs from their windows, and chariots clashed broadside in the gates. The whole might of Rome galloped northwards, northwards and west – across the Alps, across the fields of France. They reached the sea at the castled coast, and took ship for Britain. And every step of the way, Maximus said, 'It is just as I saw in my dream!'

Without pause, Maximus pressed on westward, through the difficult green confusion of Britain's ancient forests until at last he came to Wales. And there, on the farthest shore, amid mountains clad in mist and streams chased with silver spray, he found the castle of King Eudaf.

The Princes Cynan and Adeon sat playing chess, while their father carved new pieces: knights and bishops and pawns. And there, in the centre of the room, in a chair of red gold, sat the Princess Elen.

Into her arms rushed Maximus, and held her close, as though they were lovers who had been kept apart for too long. They married next day.

So dear was Elen to Maximus (and he to her) that he stayed seven years and could not bring himself to leave. His name was reshaped by the minstrels into Maxen, and his nature reshaped into a man of the valleys, where song and poetry are more important than politics of war.

But after seven years, word came from Rome – from a usurper who had filled Maxen's place and wore his imperial crown. '*Since you have been gone seven years,*' he wrote, '*you forfeit the right to call yourself Emperor of the Romans.*'

Then Maxen stirred himself out of his lover's dream, and rode and sailed and climbed and marched back to Rome, to conquer it in the name of Elen. And there he stayed, pruning back the weeds which had overgrown the Empire during seven years of neglect.

Meanwhile, Elen gave orders for straight and sturdy roads to be built across all Italy and Gaul, across Britain and into Wales, so that a man might come and go along them at the speed of a galloping horse, from the centre of the world to the most beautiful corner of the Empire. Felling forests and quarrying hills, fording rivers and draining bogs, her road builders laid down hardcore and clinker, slabs and kerbs, never going round an obstacle but removing it utterly with pick and spade and brute force, letting nothing stand in their way.

These are the roads which the frosts chipped, the weeds invaded, the mud washed out. But they were built so true, so deep-founded, so straight, that they still cross the landscape like ruled lines.

To and fro rode Maxen of Rome, to and fro between the centre of the world and the most beautiful corner of his empire – even in summer's heat, or winter's muddy flood. And all so that he might sleep in the arms of Elen, a dreamless, blissful sleep.

Rainbow Snake

IN DREAMTIME, our ancestors walked the Song Lines of the Earth, and thought about us, though we did not even exist. The Earth they walked was a brown flatness, its only features a few humpy huts built to keep off the sun, the dark, monsters and falling stars. Little tribes of people talked together in their own languages, and sometimes got up and danced their own magic dances. But even magic in those days was brown, drab and unremarkable, for there were no colours to conjure with.

The only colours shone in the sky. Sometimes, after a storm, as rain gave way to sun, a distillation of colours hung in the air, spanning Australia: the Rainbow. And that rainbow, like the people below it, dreamed, thought and had longings in its heart. 'I will go down,' it thought, 'and find a tribe of people who think as I think, and dance as I dance, and we shall enjoy each other's company.'

So the Rainbow drank all its own magic, and writhed into life. Whereas before it had been made only of falling rain and sunlight, each raindrop turned into a scale and each glimmer into a sinew of muscle. In short, it transformed itself into a snake. Twisting and flexing, its body a blaze of colour, it snaked its way down the sky to the edge of the Earth. Its jaws were red, its tail violet, and in between, its overlapping scales passed through every other shade.

But the Rainbow Snake was massively heavy. As it slithered along, it carved a trench through the featureless countryside, and threw aside mounds of mud. Because it was so huge, the trenches were valleys, and the mounds mountains. The next rain which fell was channelled into rivers, and puddling pools, so that already the world was altered by the presence of the Snake.

Rainbow Snake travelled from the Bamaga Point southwards through the bush, and every now and then raised its scarlet head and tasted the air with its flickering tongue. It listened too, with its lobeless ears. Sometimes it heard voices, but did not understand them. Sometimes it heard music, but the music moved it neither to tears nor laughter. 'These are not my kind of people,' it thought, and went on southwards, always south.

Then one day, it found a happy, laughing people whose language it partly understood and whose music made it sway – rear and sway, sway and dance – to the rhythm of the didgeridoo.

The dancing faltered. The dancers froze. The music died away. For towering high above them, jaws agape, the people saw a gigantic snake with scales of every colour in the rainbow. Its eyes closed in rapture, it swayed its sinuous body in time to the music.

When the music fell silent, it opened its gigantic eyes and looked down at them. Mothers drew their children close. Warriors fingered their spears. The Snake opened its mouth . . .

'I am Rainbow Snake, and you are my kin, for you speak the same language I think in, and make the music I have heard in my dreams.'

An elder of the tribe, still balanced on one foot in mid-dance, looked up from under his hand. His bright teeth shone as his face broke into a smile. 'In that case, you're welcome, friend! Lay yourself down and rest, or lift yourself up and dance – but don't let's waste another moment's fun!' The people gave a great shout of welcome, and went back to feasting.

Next day, Rainbow Snake coiled itself round the village, and sheltered it from the wind. Its flanks shaped the land during daylight hours, and in the evening it ate and drank and talked with the villagers. It was a happy time. Even afterwards, it was remembered as a happy time.

After all its travels, the Snake knew more dances than the people did, and from its place in the sky, it had seen more wonders. It taught them all it knew, and in honour of Rainbow Snake, the people decorated their bodies with feathers and patterned their skin, as the snake was patterned (though in plain, stark white).

Then it happened, the terrible mistake.

Dozing one night, mouth wide open, Rainbow Snake felt the pleasant tickle of rain trickling down its back and splashing in its nostrils. The patter of something sweet on its rolled tongue it mistook for rain, and closed its mouth and swallowed. Too late, it realized that the shapes in its mouth were solid.

Two boys, looking for shelter from the rain, had mistaken the Snake's huge mouth for a cave and crept inside. Now they were deep in its coiling stomach, and the Snake could not fetch them back. What to do?

Keep silent and hope the boys were not missed? No. The tribe were certain to notice, and would guess what had become of the lost boys. Admit to eating them, and listen to the mothers weep and reproach it? No. Better to slip away noiselessly, forgoing old friends and seeking out new ones.

Away it went, slithering silently, slowly and sleepily away over the wet ground, colourless in the starlight. It wrapped itself around Bora-bunara Mountain and slept.

Waking to find Rainbow Snake gone and the two boys lost, the tribe did indeed guess what had happened. They did not shrug their shoulders and they did not sit down and weep. Instead, they grabbed their spears and hollered, '*Murder!*' Then they followed the Snake's tracks, plain to see in the wet earth. They sped along the valley carved by its leaving, and had no difficulty in finding its resting place on the peak of Bora-bunara.

The Snake's dreams were pleasant and deep. Its stomach was full, and its contented snores rolled like thunder down every side of the mountain. Boulders tumbled, and shale cascaded, making a climb treacherous. But three brothers clambered nimbly up the rocky escarpments, knives clenched in their teeth. They slit open the side of Rainbow Snake; scales fell in a rain of indigo, green and blue. They opened the wound and shouted inside to the boys . . .

But the great magic of which the Snake was made had part-digested the children. Out past the rescuers fluttered – not boys, but two brightly coloured birds. Their plumage was indigo, green and blue. Soaring high in the sky, they circled the mountain twice, then flew off, singing joyfully in the language of the birds.

The three brothers looked at one another and shrugged. Why grieve for boys who have been turned into birds? Their story has ended happily, after all. Only when they turned to make their descent did they see their friends and neighbours at the bottom of the mountain, jumping, gesticulating and pointing up at the Snake.

The Snake had opened his eyes.

Feeling a pain in its side like a stitch, the Rainbow Snake experienced a sudden draughty coldness in its stomach. It felt, too, a leaking away of its magic, like blood. And worst of all, it felt *betrayed*.

'I knew my little mistake might end our friendship,' it hissed, 'but I never realized it would stir you up to such *insolence*! Attack the Rainbow Spirit? Cut open your benefactor? Shed the scales of a Sky Creature? I'm hungrier now than I was before. And how do you think I shall satisfy that hunger, eh? I know! *I'LL EAT YOU, EVERY ONE!*'

The tongue which darted from its mouth was forked lightning. Its tail drummed up thunder. It crushed the mountain like bread into breadcrumbs, and thrashed the outback inside out and back to front.

In their terror, some people froze, some ran. Some even

escaped. Some wanted so much to get away that they ran on all fours and wore down their legs to the thinness of jumbuck. Some leapt so far and so high that they turned into kangaroos. Some, in hiding under rocks, became tortoises and turtles. Others, who stood stock-still with fright, put down roots and turned into trees; others climbed them and turned into koala with big frightened eyes. Some leapt off Bora-bunara and flew away as birds. And some burrowed deep and became platypuses.

To escape the rampage of venomous Rainbow Snake, they became anything and everything, transforming the landscape almost as much as the angry serpent was doing with its lashing tail.

At last Rainbow Snake exhausted itself and, leaving behind a trail of destruction, hurled itself headlong into the sea. Through the half-circle of the setting sun it slithered, like an eel swallowed down the world's throat.

And next morning, it was back in place again, as though it had never left: the Rainbow, spanning the sky like a breath of peace: a miasma of rain and sunlight, a trick of the light. A reminder of stormy nights.

But when the airy Rainbow Spirit looked down on the Earth below, the landscape it saw was transformed. So too were the lives of our ancestors, for some were animals and some were plants, and those who were still men and women were wiser men and women by far.

Juno's Roman Geese

A ROMAN LEGEND

VEII WAS an Etruscan city, a place of rumour and legend, full of treasure. At the very height of the Roman Empire, Rome set its sights on conquering Veii, but for ten years it stood besieged but unconquered. Camillus, commander of the Roman army, wanted to capture it more than anyone, wanted it more than anything. He fell on his face before the altars of the gods and prayed for success. And he wondered how to enter a city which for ten years had kept out all attackers.

'I shall not enter by force, but by subtlety, silently and in secret,' he thought. Then he summoned his engineers and showed them a plan of the city. 'If we were to dig a tunnel under the walls, here, and bring it out here, by the temple of Juno . . .'

Night and day they dug, passing the loose earth back down the passage. Like moles they tunnelled, silent, and black with Etruscan dirt, working in pitch darkness. Then one evening, the soil gave way to something hard. Camillus wormed his way along the narrow tunnel. He stroked the smooth marble overhead with his fingertips. 'We have come up right *under* the temple of Juno,' he whispered.

So after dark, when no footfall came from overhead, Camillus raised a paving stone and peered about. The dark temple was a vast echoing hollow. He felt like a sailor in the stomach of a whale. He felt, too, as if he were being watched. Camillus looked up, looked higher, and drew a gasp of breath. For looking down at him was the monumental figure of the goddess Juno. Seven metres tall, and clad in slightly ragged, rather grubby cotton robes, her eyes looked directly into his. Scraps of litter blew across the temple floor.

'Phew! Only a statue,' he might have said. But he did not. He took off his helmet, stood to attention, and saluted the Queen of the Gods. His lips moved in silent prayer. 'Oh Juno, prosper me this night, and I shall give you a temple finer than this, filled with the scent of burning herbs, and I shall people it with white geese, so that you never stand lonely in the small hours of the night.'

The white marble face looked down impassively, an artefact carved by human hands, nothing more. And yet the clothing blowing round her lent an impression of movement.

'On, men,' whispered Camillus. 'The city of Veii is ours, if the gods are with us tonight!'

One by one, the Romans crawled through the black tunnel and out into Juno's temple. It stood at the centre of the city, so that when they burst out – like adders hatching from a white egg – the city was stung at its very heart, and fell with barely a cry.

Next day, a queue of wagons stood in the market place. The treasures of Veii were being loaded for transportation to Rome. Statues reclined awkwardly in straw-lined carts – even pillars and mosaics were being loaded: everything beautiful, everything deserving of admiration was carefully stowed and driven away.

But inside the temple of Juno, there was a problem. Camillus went to investigate and found his troops standing stock-still round the statue of Juno. 'What's the matter?'

The troops were tongue-tied, embarrassed. 'We were washing her, right, sir? Bathing her, like you told us, sir, and dressing her in new clothes. Suddenly – now, don't be angry, sir . . .'

'Suddenly what?'

'Suddenly she seemed too . . . too *holy* somehow. We're all afraid to touch her, sir.'

Camillus was not angry. He too had felt the aura of holiness which surrounded the great statue of the Queen of Heaven. Instead of shouting at the men to get on with their work, he took off his plumed helmet, bowed to the statue and called, 'Juno! Great Queen of all the gods! Is it your wish to go to Rome?'

The men stared, transfixed. The horses harnessed to the cart at the temple door trembled in their shafts. Then they saw it – everyone saw it: a serene nod of the marble head, the merest closing of the eyes in affirmation. 'I am content,' said the gesture. 'You may take me now.'

Camillus was as good as his word. He did not rest until Juno was ensconced in the finest temple on Capitoline Hill, her shrine decorated with flowers, and the gardens round about busy with Roman geese. Waddling to and fro, toes turned in and hips wagging, the birds made a comical priesthood. But geese are the sacred birds of Juno, and their honking rang out piercingly, reminding the Romans daily to worship the Queen of Heaven.

Rome gobbled up the treasures of Veii and lauded the heroic victor Camillus, carved his statue, and made speeches of thanks to him in the Senate . . . then they put war behind them, preferring peace.

Once, the Romans had looked towards Veii and thought, 'We wish to have its treasure for our own.' But the conquest of Veii and more such cities made Rome herself a treasure-house. Soon others were looking at Rome with hungry eyes and saying, 'We wish to have its treasure for our own.'

One day, a voice was heard in the streets of Rome. At first the people mistook it for the honking of Juno's geese, but it became more plain – deep and mellifluous, but still, perhaps, a woman's voice . . . It woke them from their sleep. It made the night watch shiver. 'Prepare, Rome, beware! The Gauls are coming!'

The Gauls? It was laughable. The Gauls were uncultured

barbarians who painted their half-naked bodies and wore animal skins. They had no system of government, no great cities, no drama or literature, no education, no empire. Hardly a civilization to be reckoned with, in comparison with the might of Rome! Camillus might have told them to pay more heed to the voice, but Camillus had been banished to the provinces – a man of war put out to grass.

When the Gauls came, they came like beasts, without strategies or cunning, but with brute force. What they fought, they killed. What they captured, they destroyed. Like fire across stubble they came, and all the fine words in the world could not stop them reaching the gates of Rome.

'Where is Camillus to defend us?'

'Gone to the country! Banished to Ardea!'

'Where are the gods to help us?'

'They shouted in the streets, but we wouldn't listen. Too late now! Run! Hide! The Gauls are at the gates!'

Some Romans ran away into the vine-strewn countryside and hid. Those who were fit enough ran with armfuls of belongings for Capitoline Hill. The hill was the city's natural keep – a high, unassailable crag adorned with white temples and glimmering now in the orange light of fires down below. Like surf over a pebble beach, the barbarians, as they pillaged Rome, left no stone where it had lain before. For sheer love of destruction, they pulled the lovely city down round their own ears, for they placed no value on its beauty, found nothing admirable, coveted nothing but blood and terror and death.

Like the sea also, they reached a point beyond which they could not go, for Capitoline Hill could be climbed only by a narrow path, and the besieged Romans could pick off an approaching enemy with ease.

'We have only to wait for you to starve!' bawled the barbarians in their guttural, shapeless language. Then they set about roasting the horses they had slaughtered, and feasting at the foot of the hill. High above them, the Romans watched the fires consume their beloved city, until the heat dried their eyeballs and left them no longer able to cry. Then they wrapped themselves in their cloaks and went to sleep, watched over by the beautiful white statues of their gods.

'Give them time to doze off,' said the barbarian chieftain, gnawing on a hock bone, 'then we'll finish them. Smash their gods and burn their temples.' Beside him, face down on a shattered mosaic floor, a Roman traitor lay amid a pool of bloodstained gold. He had sought to make his fortune by betraying a secret path up Capitoline Hill. The Gauls had taken his information, then cut his throat. Now nothing stood between them and the remnants of Rome.

In the darkest time of night (as when Camillus had burrowed under the walls of Veii), the Gauls crawled and scrambled up the side of Capitoline Hill, daggers in their teeth and rags around their swords to keep metal from clanking against rock. The Romans generally fought their battles by day, after grand speeches, cleansed by prayer, in full sight of the sun. But the Gauls came creeping, sneaking, worming their way up the precipitous path, to slit throats under cover of dark.

At the foot of Juno's statue, the sacred geese fussed and fretted. Their big feet paddled across the chequered floor with a *plash plash plash*.

Hand over hand came the Gauls. Nearly there now. Mouths full of filthy curses, the blood lust rising. An arm over the low wall of a terrace, a knee, a cautious lifting of one eye . . .

'*Haaaaaarkhkh! Haaaaaarkhkh!*'

They were met by orange jabs of pain. Hard white wings beat at their eardrums, and huge black feet, hard as bone, paddled on their upturned faces. Geese!

With pecks and kicks, the geese dislodged the first attackers, then their honking woke the sleeping Romans. '*Haaaarkhkh! Haaaarkhkh!*' It was louder than braying donkeys. One Gaul, in falling, dislodged others: an avalanche of Gauls. Beakfuls of hair sprinkled the marble terraces.

Once awake, the besieged men and women fought with all the valour of true Romans. Morning found the Gauls licking their wounds like kicked dogs, and bemoaning the 'winged monsters' which had beset them in the dark. They would make no more night-time assaults on Capitoline Hill. Besides, the Romans were now on their guard against sneak attacks. And within the week, the cry went up from the roof of Juno's temple. 'Camillus! Camillus is coming!'

Camillus came in behind the Gauls and, scouring them out of the fire-blackened ruins of Rome, drove them into the Tiber. He dealt with them as a man might an infestation of woodlice. And although the destruction left behind was terrible, still forests do grow again after forest fires. In fact, they grow more vigorous and green and beautiful than before.

As for the geese, they were declared heroes and heroines of the battle, crowned with laurel and feted with corn. They fretted and fussed about, like old aunts embarrassed by overmuch attention. But it seemed to Camillus, as he sprinkled corn from a silver pan, that Juno looked on with an expression of pride. Their honking was a note more self-important, too. 'Make way for Juno's geese,' they seemed to say. 'Make way for Juno's *Roman* geese! We saved *her* temple! We saved *her* city!'

John Barleycorn

AN AMERICAN MYTH

NO SOONER did they lay eyes on him than the men of the farms decided to kill John Barleycorn. Though he had never done them harm, Farmer Mick and Farmer Mack, Farmer Mock and Farmer Muck ganged up on him in broad daylight and tumbled him to the ground. They dug a hole and buried his body in a field, and though the rooks flapped out of the treetops and circled overhead, no one else witnessed the dreadful crime.

Fingers and faces numbed by the raw cold, the four assassins trudged silently to the inn and, beside a log fire, tried to warm their hands round tankards of cold water. April rain spattered the windows, and the rookeries in the treetops faded from sight as the afternoon sky grew dark.

The way home took Farmer Mick past the field where John Barleycorn lay buried, but it was too dark to see the place where the clods of earth were piled on his yellow head.

The days grew longer and the sun warmer. Farmer Mick and Farmer Mack, Farmer Mock and Farmer Muck often drank water together at the local inn. They were kept busy milking and lambing, while their wives made butter and skimmed cream off the bowls in the dairy. None of them saw what the rooks saw from high in the trees – a single sharp green finger poking out between the clods, a long, reaching arm . . .

Then one evening, Farmer Mick stumbled into the inn, breathless, pointing back the way he had come. 'Have you seen? Have you seen? John Barleycorn's up again!'

Their arms slung round each others' necks, the farmers

peered out through the low dirty window. 'Ach, he's nought but a green boy. We'd be wasting our time to chase after him!' And they settled to a game of skittles instead.

One particularly sunny day, however, as Farmer Mick walked down to the village, he saw, out of the corner of his eye, John Barleycorn swaying and dancing over his grave, his long yellow beard wagging as he silently sang to the rooks in the trees.

When the others heard the news, Farmer Muck declared, 'Let's get him!' and grabbed up his scythe. Farmer Mock took his sickle, and all four, armed with blades, rampaged out into the field.

Snick-snack, they sliced clean through him at the knees, but John Barleycorn only laughed as he fell.

Whip-snap, they bound him round where he lay, but John Barleycorn only laughed as they tied the knot.

Bump-thump, they manhandled him as far as the barn, and threw him down on the floor, where they beat him with sticks until hairs from his long beard flew amid the sunbeams. So violent and savage were they that sweat poured from their foreheads and dripped in their eyes, and their mouths were circled with a white and dusty thirst. But John Barleycorn only laughed as they pounded him.

They took his blood and bones and hid them in the water butt – and no one knew (except for the rooks in the trees) what they had done.

Then they had a feast, because John Barleycorn was dead. Mrs Mick and Mrs Mack, Mrs Mock and Mrs Muck baked loaves, and the farmers rolled the barrel from the barn all the way to the inn. The innkeeper stabbed a spike through the keg's side, and fitted a tap in the hole. And when the liquor inside glugged out into their tankards, it sounded for all the world like laughter.

'I give you a toast!' cried Farmer Mick. 'John Barleycorn – may he live for ever, God bless him!' and the others took up the toast: *'John Barleycorn!'*

A strange thing to say, you may think, about someone

you have just murdered. But not if you think first of a stalk of barley – how it grows from a seed into a green shoot; how it sways in the wind, ripens to gold in the sun and grows a whiskery beard. Reapers reap it, threshers thrash it, brewers nail it into casks. So next time Farmer Mick and Farmer Mack, Farmer Mock and Farmer Muck stagger home from the inn, their arms round each others' necks, and singing fit to frighten the rooks away, raise three hearty cheers for John Barleycorn and the barley wine that's made from him.

Well? Do you think that's water they've just been drinking?

The Singer Above The River

A GERMAN LEGEND

A HEARTBROKEN girl once wandered the banks of the River Rhine. Her lover had chosen to marry someone else, and her heart was a rock within her, heavy and hard. She searched the fields for somewhere which did not remind her of her lover. She searched the woods for somewhere she could forget him. She searched the riverbank for somewhere she might sleep without dreaming of him. And when she found nowhere, she sought to end all her sorrows by dying. She threw herself from the huge black rock which juts out over the Rhine like an angry fist. Her name was Lorelei.

But even in death, Lorelei found no peace. Her soul was not permitted to rest. She was doomed, for taking her own life, to live on, in the shape of a nymph, perched on the craggy rock from which she had fallen. Her beauty was greater than it had been in life, her voice ten times more lovely. But in place of grief, she nursed a terrible hatred for young men.

As shadows appear with the sunrise, so with sunset Lorelei appeared: a wraith, a twilight shadow. Any sailor, looking up through the dusk as he sailed by, might see a white arm beckoning from the summit of the cliff. A sweet face, barely distinguishable in the half-light, would call to him, sing to him, sing such a song that he felt himself falling towards it. His hand would tug on the tiller as the voice tugged on his heart. Powerless to resist, he would steer for the crag, heel towards the grey crag and the jagged boulders which lay heaped at its feet.

As his boat split, and water closed over his head, each

drowning sailor was still looking upwards, still listening to magic music. Then, as the top rim of the setting sun dipped below the horizon, Lorelei would disappear.

Word spread of the maiden on the rock – the siren who lured men to their deaths. One young man, Ronald, son of the Count Palatine, became obsessed by the thought of her. He boasted that he would lift the curse on the river. He would both remove the hazard to shipping (which was making the Rhine unnavigable) and win himself a bride in the same night. He would climb the rocks, up to the nymph called Lorelei, and snatch her from her dizzy lair. He would close her singing mouth with kisses, and rescue her damned soul by the power of true love.

In short he fell in love with the idea of Lorelei, and believed there was nothing he could not do, because that is what love does to a man.

'Ferryman, ferryman, row me past the Lorelei Rock.'

'No, not for brass money, young sir, I will not.'

'Ferryman, ferryman, I'll pay you silver.'

'Not even silver, young sir, would make me row by the Lorelei.'

'Ferryman, ferryman, then I shall pay you gold.'

The ferryman hesitated. 'How much gold?'

'Enough,' said Ronald.

So, late in the afternoon, the ferryman settled his oars in the rowlocks, and rowed out into the current, with Ronald standing at the bow. The ferryman kept his back always to the rock so that he could not glimpse the nymph and succumb to her magic. But Ronald fixed his eyes on the rock, and his face grew bright in the light of the setting sun.

Suddenly she appeared, the invisible taking shape, like salt settling out of sea water.

'Come,' said her hands, waving. 'Come,' said her arms, beckoning. 'Come,' said her sweet red mouth, 'come and take me home!'

'Row faster, ferryman,' urged Ronald, 'for I must climb the rock before the light fails and she disappears!'

The ferryman did not alter the steady, rhythmic dip of his oars, steering a straight course down the centre of the river.

'Faster, faster, ferryman! Look, she is ready to come with me, if I can just reach her in time!'

The ferryman said nothing, for he had seen it all happen before.

'Faster, faster, you fool!' cried Ronald, as the ferryman eased the boat carefully, carefully down the current. 'You must get closer, or how can I gain a grip on the rock?'

The ferryman shipped his oars. 'This is close enough, young man. You don't want to die so soon. Think what a sweet life lies ahead of you. I'll take you no farther.'

'Cheat! Cheat!' raged Ronald, thinking only of the present. 'I gave you gold to carry me to the rock face!'

'But what good will your gold be to me when I am dead? You have your money back, and I shall row you safe ashore.'

All the while, Lorelei beckoned, whistled, sang like a calling-bird: 'Come to me, love! Come and fetch me down!' In his passion to reach the singing nymph, Ronald snatched one of the oars and began to use it as a paddle. The rowing-boat rocked wildly under him and began to spin. The currents near the cliff face took hold of it and it gathered speed. Ronald gave a whoop of triumph. Too late, he realized that it was speeding towards disaster.

As the boards split between his feet and rocks came through the floor of the boat, Ronald was flung into the cold water. It held him like the arms of a woman. It covered his face with cold, wet kisses, and drew him down to join the company of other sailors wrecked on the Lorelei. The nymph high above smiled, kissed her finger-tips and, leaning over the cliff edge, waved down at the drowning men, laughing.

The Count Palatine broke his chain of office between clenched fists when he was told of his son's death. 'Kill that *thing* on the rock! And if it is dead already, pen its soul and torment it, slowly, for a thousand years!'

Every soldier in his service armed himself with axe or mace, pike or broadsword. The troops set sail for the Lorelei in as huge a ship as had dared to pass through the reach for many years. And when they reached the rock, it was morning and they had all day to make the climb. Studded boots scuffing the rock face, mailed gloves clinging to the fissures, they climbed, with ropes and crampons, pitons and picks. They could not hear the cry of the starlings or the redstart round their heads, for they had wax crammed in their ears to shut out the magic song of Lorelei.

Just as the first man's fingers reached over the brink of the beetling rock, the sun's bottom rim touched land. Lorelei appeared, one moment invisible, the next a woman as lovely as the trees swaying in the distant landscape.

'That's right. Come, my dear fellows. I have kisses enough for all of you! Come here, my handsome soldiers. Come home from the hardships of war to the softness of peace. Come. Come!'

But the soldiers were the cruellest and the bitterest men in all Germany – the Count had made certain of that. They had no daughters, no wives, no sweethearts. As they clambered on to the flat top of the black outcrop, Lorelei could see their ears stuffed with wax, their hands holding maces and pikes and swords.

'Despair, demon, for the Count Palatine himself has called for you to die or, if you are dead, for your soul to be penned and poked like a pig.'

'Then I call on the river!' exclaimed Lorelei, jumping to her feet and raising her voice above theirs. 'You Rhine! Save your daughter Lorelei from these ... these *beasts* disguised as men, who haven't a heart or soul between them!'

Far below, the sound of the river altered, so that the climbing soldiers looked down. They saw a wave heave itself up, as though the river itself were drawing a deep breath. The wave, as it rolled, gathered momentum, sucking water from the shore and piling it, fathom upon fathom, into a tidal wave. The wreckage of thirty ships was stirred up from the riverbed and broken anew, scattering flotsam down the flooding river.

Still the river filled, rising, rising up the sides of the gorge, until it sucked at the boots of the mountaineering soldiers. Just when they thought they had escaped its torrential spray, a second wave broke against the rock, soaking them to the skin. A third plucked men from the rock face and left them swinging on their ropes like spiders on lengths of thread. But those who had reached the top already crawled, relentless as limpets, across the wet black rock, closing in on Lorelei.

With a scream of defiance, she leapt headlong into the mountainous waves . . . and disappeared. She vanished, as surely as salt sprinkled on to water. The setting sun turned the raging river to the colour of blood before the turbulence settled, the waters fell quiet and the Rhine rolled on, black and implacable, into the coming night.

Never again did the nymph beckon from the top of the black rock, luring men to their deaths. But many were the young girls who had their hearts broken by young men, and too many were the young men who went on to become soldiers, steely in body and soul, and deaf to the sweetest singing.

How Music was Fetched
Out of Heaven

A MEXICAN MYTH

ONCE THE world suffered in Silence. Not that it was a quiet place, nor peaceful, for there was always the groan of the wind, the crash of the sea, the grumble of lava in the throats of volcanoes, and the grate of man's ploughshare through the stony ground. Babies could be heard crying at night, and women in the daytime, because of the hardness of life and the great unfriendliness of Silence.

Tezcatlipoca, his body heavy as clay and his heart heavy as lead (for he was the Lord of Matter), spoke to Quetzalcoatl, feathery Lord of Spirit. He spoke from out of the four quarters of the Earth, from the north, south, easterly and westerly depths of the iron-hard ground. 'The world needs music, Quetzalcoatl! In the thorny glades and on the bald seashore, in the square comfortless houses of the poor and in the dreams of the sleeping, there should be music, there ought to be song. Go to Heaven, Quetzalcoatl, and fetch it down!'

'How would I get there? Heaven is higher than wings will carry me.'

'String a bridge out of cables of wind, and nail it with stars: a bridge to the Sun. At the feet of the Sun, sitting on the steps of his throne, you will find four musicians. Fetch them down here. For I am so sad in this Silence, and the People are sad, hearing the sound of Nothingness ringing in their ears.'

'I will do as you say,' said Quetzalcoatl, preening his

green feathers in readiness for the journey. 'But will they come, I ask myself. Will the musicians of the Sun want to come?'

He whistled up the winds like hounds. Like hounds they came bounding over the bending treetops, over the red places where dust rose up in twisting columns, and over the sea, whipping the waters into mountainous waves. Baying and howling, they carried Quetzalcoatl higher and higher – higher than all Creation – so high that he could glimpse the Sun ahead of him. Then the four mightiest winds plaited themselves into a cable, and the cable swung out across the void of Heaven: a bridge planked with cloud and nailed with stars.

'Look out, here comes Quetzalcoatl,' said the Sun, glowering, lowering, his red-rimmed eyes livid. Circling him in a cheerful dance, four musicians played and sang. One, dressed in white and shaking bells, was singing lullabies; one, dressed in red, was singing songs of war and passion as he beat on a drum; one, in sky-blue robes fleecy with cloud, sang the ballads of Heaven, the stories of the gods; one, in yellow, played on a golden flute.

This place was too hot for tears, too bright for shadows. In fact the shadows had all fled downwards and clung fast to men. And yet all this sweet music had not served to make the Sun generous. 'If you don't want to have to leave here and go down where it's dark, dank, dreary and dangerous, keep silent, my dears. Keep silent, keep secret, and don't answer when Quetzalcoatl calls,' he warned his musicians.

Across the bridge rang Quetzalcoatl's voice. 'O singers! O marvellous makers of music. Come to me. The Lord of the World is calling!' The voice of Quetzalcoatl was masterful and inviting, but the Sun had made the musicians afraid. They kept silent, crouching low, pretending not to hear. Again and again Quetzalcoatl called them, but still they did not stir, and the Sun smiled smugly and thrummed his fingers on the sunny spokes of his chairback.

He did not intend to give up his musicians, no matter who needed them.

So Quetzalcoatl withdrew to the rain-fringed horizon and, harnessing his four winds to the black thunder, had them drag the clouds closer, circling the Sun's citadel. When he triggered the lightning and loosed the thunder-claps, the noise was monumental. The Sun thought he was under siege.

Thunder clashed against the Sun with the noise of a great brass cymbal, and the musicians, their hands over their ears, ran this way and that looking for help. 'Come out to me, little makers of miracles,' said Quetzalcoatl in a loud but gentle voice. *BANG* went the thunder, and all Heaven shook.

The crooner of lullabies fluttered down like a sheet blown from a bed. The singer of battle-songs spilled himself like blood along the floor of Heaven and covered his head with his arms. The singer of ballads, in his fright, quite forgot his histories of Heaven, and the flautist dropped his golden flute. Quetzalcoatl caught it.

As the musicians leapt from their fiery nest, he opened his arms and welcomed them into his embrace, stroking their heads in his lap. 'Save us, Lord of Creation! The Sun is under siege!'

'Come, dear friends. Come where you are needed most.'

The Sun shook and trembled with rage like a struck gong, but he knew he had been defeated, had lost his musicians to Quetzalcoatl.

At first the musicians were dismayed by the sadness and silence of the Earth. But no sooner did they begin to play than the babies in their cribs stopped squalling. Pregnant women laid a hand on their big stomachs and sighed with contentment. The man labouring in the field cupped a hand to his ear and shook himself, so that his shadow of sadness fell away in the noonday. Children started to hum. Young men and women got up to dance, and in dancing fell in love. Even the mourner at the graveside, hearing sweet flute music, stopped crying.

Quetzalcoatl himself swayed his snaky hips and lifted his hands in dance at the gate of Tezcatlipoca, and Tezcatlipoca came out of doors. Matter and Spirit whirled together in a dance so fast: had you been there, you would have thought you were seeing only one.

And suddenly every bird in the sky opened its beak and sang, and the stream moved by with a musical ripple. The sleeping child dreamed music and woke up singing. From that day onwards, life was all music – rhythms and refrains, falling cadences and fluting calls. No one saw just where the Sun's musicians settled or made their homes, but their footprints were everywhere and their bright colours were found in corners that had previously been grey and cobwebbed with silence. The flowers turned up bright faces of red and yellow and white and blue, as if they could hear singing. Even the winds ceased to howl and roar and groan, and learned love songs.

Whose Footprints?

A MYTH FROM THE GOLD COAST

D O YOU suppose God made the world all by himself? Of course not. He had help. He had a servant. Every Fon in Abomey knows that. The servant's name was Legba, and he took the blame for whatever went wrong.

Whenever the people saw a wonderful sunset, or made a huge catch of fish, they gave thanks to God and said, 'Great is our Creator, who has made all things wonderfully well!'

Whenever they fell over a rock, or the canoe sank, they said, 'Legba is making mischief again. That villain Legba!'

Now Legba thought this was mortally unfair. 'Why do I get all the blame?' he complained.

'That's what you're there for,' said God. 'It wouldn't do for people to think of God as anything but perfect. It would set them a bad example.'

'But they hate me!' protested Legba. 'They hang up charms at their doors to keep me out, and they frighten their children with my name: "Be good or Legba will come and steal you out of your bed!" How would you feel?' But God had already sauntered away towards the garden where he grew yams. (This was in the days when God lived on Earth, among all that he had made.)

God tended those yams with loving care and attention. If the truth were told, he was kept so busy by his gardening some days, that things could go wrong in the world without him really noticing. It did not matter. Legba got the blame, naturally.

Legba sat down and thought. Then Legba stood up and

spoke. 'Lord, I hear that thieves are planning to steal your yams tonight!'

God was horrified. He sounded a ram's-horn trumpet and summoned together all the people of the world. They came, jostling and bowing, smiling and offering presents. They were rather taken aback to see God so angry.

'If any one of you intends to rob my garden tonight, I'm telling you here and I'm telling you now, and I'm making it plain as day: that thief shall die!'

The people clutched each other and trembled. They nodded feverishly to show they had understood, hurried home to their beds and pulled the covers over their heads until morning. God watched them scatter and brushed together the palms of his great hands. 'That settles that,' he said, and went home to bed himself.

Legba waited. When all sound had ceased but the scuttle of night creatures, the flutter of bats and the drone of snoring humanity; he crept into God's house. God, too, was snoring. Legba wormed his way across the floor, and stole the sandals from beside God's bed.

Putting on the sandals, he crept to the yam garden. Though the shoes were over-large and tripped him more than once, he worked his way from tree to tree, removing every delectable yam. The dew glistened, the ground was wet. The sandals of God left deep prints in the moist soil . . .

'Come quick! Come quick! The thief has struck!'

God tumbled out of bed, fumbled his feet into his sandals and stumbled out of doors into the first light of morning. When he saw the waste that had been laid to his garden, the shout could be heard all the way to Togo.

'Don't worry! Don't worry!' Legba hurried to console him. 'Look how the thief has left his footprints in the ground! You have only to find the shoes that made those footprints, and you will have caught the culprit red-handed . . . -footed, I mean.'

Once more, the ram's-horn sounded, and the people

pelted out of their huts and horded into God's presence, trembling.

'*Someone* has stolen my yams!' bellowed God. '*Someone* is about to *DIE*!'

They all had to fetch out their sandals, and every sandal was laid against the footprints in the garden. But not one fitted. Not one.

'Legba! Try Legba! He's always doing wicked things!' shouted the people, and Legba felt that familiar pang of resentment that God did not correct them. It would have been nice if God could have said, 'Oh not *Legba*. He's entirely trustworthy. He helped me create the world. He's my good and faithful servant.' Not a bit of it.

'*Legba! Have you been stealing from me?!*'

Willingly Legba produced his sandals. Willingly he laid them alongside the footprints in the garden. But not by any stretch of the imagination did Legba's sandals fit the prints beneath the yam trees.

'Perhaps you walked in your sleep, O Lord?' suggested Legba, and the people all said, 'AAAH!'

God tried to look disdainful of such a ridiculous suggestion, but the eyes of all Creation were gazing at him, waiting. He laid his great foot alongside one of the great footprints, and the people gasped and laughed and sighed with relief. It was just God, walking in his sleep, ha ha ha! God was to blame after all!

Then they began to wonder – God could see the question form in their faces – if God had sleepwalked once, perhaps he had sleepwalked before. And if God stole in his sleep, what else might he get up to under the cover of darkness, under the influence of his dreams?

God glowered at Legba. He knew Legba had something to do with his embarrassment, but could not quite see what. Instead, he stamped his sandalled foot irritably and said, 'I'm going! I'm not staying here where no one gives me the respect I deserve! I'm going *higher up*!'

So God moved higher up. And he told Legba to report

to him every night, in the sky, with news of what people were getting up to.

Of course what Legba chooses to tell God is entirely up to Legba. But the Fon of Abomey have been a lot nicer to Legba since God went higher up. A lot nicer.

The Death of El Cid

A SPANISH LEGEND

DON Rodrigo Díaz de Vivar was cursed with pride. It was pride which caused his banishment from the court of King Alfonso of Spain. It was pride which made him swear never to cut his beard until his banishment was repealed. It was pride which made him venture out from Alfonso's tiny corner-kingdom into the part of Spain that had been occupied by Moors from North Africa, where it was certain death for any Christian to go.

Into Moorish Spain he charged, first with a dozen men, then with a hundred, then with a thousand at his back. Before him fell village after fortress, city after port. And from every victory he sent the spoils back to King Alfonso, his King, his lord and master, to whom his obedience never faltered. Still the King did not pardon him, but many more young men left Alfonso's kingdom to join Rodrigo de Vivar and find their fortunes in conquest.

The Moorish occupiers were swept away like rabbits before a heath fire. Families who had lived for generations in Spain, and thought themselves its owners, fled to Africa or had to buy back their lives and freedom from Rodrigo de Vivar. They called him, in their own tongue, El Siddi – the War Lord – and his own men took it up: 'El Cid! Viva El Cid!' He captured Moorish towns like so many pieces in a game of chess.

At last only one black piece was left standing on the board of Spain: Valencia, the treasure-house of the Moors. Not till then did the African might of Islam stir itself. Valencia must not be allowed to fall, or all Spain would be in the hands of Christians.

Before the fleets of Africa could touch Spanish shores, Valencia had fallen, and El Cid, the victor, had made the exquisite city his own. Sending for his wife and family, he celebrated the marriage of his two daughters, and glorified in the King's forgiveness. His joy was complete. He decided to live out his days in Valencia, for there is nowhere lovelier under God's gaze.

On the night of the double wedding, a little, cowardly, creeping man crawled through the flowery grass on his belly, with a heart full of envy. He pushed a knife through the cloth of a tent, and stabbed El Cid in the back, sinking his blade up to the haft.

Within days, the Moorish legions landed in thousands and tens of thousands, and laid siege to the city – pitched their tents among the orange groves and awaited with impatience the day Valencia's citizens would thirst and starve to death.

'But we have El Cid!' cried the people in the streets. 'With El Cid to lead us, we have nothing to fear!' And they jeered over the walls at the besieging army. 'El Cid will crop you like oranges!'

But El Cid lay bleeding on his bed, his life ebbing away. Nothing but a miracle would put him back astride his horse at the head of an army. When word spread of Don Rodrigo's injury, terror and despair poisoned the streets like acrid smoke.

'El Cid is dying!'
        'El Cid is at death's door!'
            'El Cid is dead!'

No word came from the window of his house. No news, either good or bad, came from the lips of El Cid's wife, the lovely Jimena. She sat beside her husband's bed, her long hair spread on the coverlet, and her eyes resting on the distant sea. When at last she opened the door, it was to say, 'Fetch El Cid's horse to the door and you, Alvar Fanez, come and help Don Rodrigo to put on his armour.'

Alvar was El Cid's closest friend, his most trusted

servant. He ran into the room in a fervour of delight. The saints had restored his master's health! El Cid was fit to lead his army into battle!

Alvar Fanez fell back, his mouth open to speak, his heart half broken by what he saw. The craggy features of Don Rodrigo de Vivar lay whiter than the pillow, his eyes were shut, his hands lay crossed on his breast.

'He's dead,' was all he could think of to say.

'Yes,' said Jimena, simply and calmly, 'but his name will live for ever, and it is his name which must save the city today. Help me arm my husband one last time, and tie him on to his horse. I believe that El Cid can still carry the day, if only he shows himself on the battlefield.'

Alvar Fanez did as he was asked. Together – though it was a terrible ordeal for the two alone – they tied Don Rodrigo to his horse for one last ride. Jimena kissed her husband farewell. Alvar Fanez mounted, and led the general's horse to the city gate.

Ahead went the incredulous whispers, the gasps of happy amazement in the half-light of morning.

'El Cid is alive!'

'He's going to head the attack!'

Silently, so as to surprise the sleeping Moors, the army mustered in the streets behind the gate. Division upon division formed rank. As dawn broke, the knights of El Cid struggled to hold their horses in check between the shadowy houses of Valencia.

At the crash of the crossbar unfastening the gate, El Cid's horse Babeica pawed the ground. It leapt past Alvar Fanez in the open gateway and lunged into the lead, as it had in a hundred battles.

The Moors, waking to the sound of galloping horses, looked out of their tent flaps to see the hosts of El Cid riding down on them. The knights of Islam called for their armour. Their squires ran to and fro with weapons and bridles. 'To arms! To arms!'

'Huh!' sneered King Mu'taman of Morocco, walking

with showy disdain to the stirrup of his mount. 'My assassin has cut the heart out of El Cid. My spies have confirmed it. And what is an army without its heart?'

Then he saw a sight which struck such horror into him that his foot missed the stirrup and his shaking legs would not hold him. He fell to his knees, calling on the one true god of Islam for help. 'Can the man not die? Is this why he brought our empires to nothing? Is he immortal? Is it a ghost we have to fight now?' For riding towards him – directly towards him – was the tall, erect, unmistakable figure of El Cid, conqueror of Spain, in full panoply of armour but bareheaded, his long grey hair and beard streaming.

The King's trembling fingers searched for his lance, and he threw it at the chest of El Cid. But though it struck home, the conqueror did not flinch. It was his horse's hooves which trampled the King of Morocco and which tumbled his tasselled tent to the ground. El Cid rode on, so appalling the superstitious enemy that they flung themselves into the sea sooner than face a ghostly enemy who would not, could not die.

Out of the orange groves and along the beaches of Valencia rode Don Rodrigo de Vivar, on his last foray. From the city walls, Dona Jimena watched till he was no longer in sight. But she shed no tears. She knew it was not the ghost of El Cid out there; it was his flesh, his blood. But neither was it El Cid himself. She knew that the soul of El Cid was at rest, and that his spirit was ranging free, untethered and invisible, high above the heads of his victorious army.

The Man Who Almost Lived for Ever

A MESOPOTAMIAN LEGEND

LONG AGO, when the history of Humankind could still be carved on a single pillar, there lived two friends. One, Adapa the Priest, was the wisest of men. The other, Ea, was the friendliest of the gods. But you would have thought they were brothers. Ea taught Adapa many things never before known by mortals – how to speak magic, for instance, and carry it in the fingers of his hand.

Adapa was fishing alone one day, in a stretch of water where the river Euphrates widens into a gleaming lake. A storm sprang up and spilled him out of his boat, wetting his venerable beard and his priestly robes and his dignity. Adapa swam to the shore and pulled himself out, dripping wet. Then he pointed a finger at the South Wind and pronounced a curse, as Ea had taught him to do.

> 'Come down on you the very worst;
> May every power of yours be burst.
> You have a mighty wrath incurred,
> Therefore be broken, like a bird.
> Oh vile South Wind, I call you CURSED!'

Like a great albatross shot from the sky, the South Wind drooped and faltered. One wing was snapped by Adapa's piercing curse, and the wind limped to its nest with an eerie, lamenting cry, and left the banners of seventy kings drooping. The gods in Heaven were shocked.

'Who taught this small worthless man of the Earth the magic words of Heaven? Ea? Why have you shared our secrets with this puny mortal? Summon him before us, to explain himself!'

Ea told Adapa of the summons. 'Don't worry, friend. You have wisdom enough to speak well, and I will commend you to the gods. Tammuz and Gizidu will meet you at the gates, and conduct you before the throne of Mighty Anu. I have asked them, too, to speak well of you in the Courts of Heaven . . . Just one word of advice.' Adapa, who had already begun to rehearse what he would say to the gods, looked round at the change in Ea's voice. 'Be on your guard, Adapa. The gods are cunning, and you have angered them. They may offer you bread and oil to eat. On no account accept it. It may be poisoned.'

Meanwhile, the gods discussed among themselves what was to be done about Adapa and his great knowledge.

'We could strike him dead,' said one.

'We could just tell him never to use magic again,' said another.

'We could always make him immortal, like us,' said a third.

'Or there again . . .'

Shortly, Tammuz and Gizidu led Adapa in front of Anu's throne.

'Adapa, you are accused of cursing the South Wind and of breaking its white wing with the magic words of the gods. Is this true?'

'I admit it,' said Adapa. 'The South Wind wrecked me and endangered my life.' The gods listened. Some nodded, some glared, some leaned their heads together in debate. Adapa began to feel more confident. 'As for the curse I used, I was taught it by my good friend Ea, who has introduced me to many such marvels.'

'Before I give judgement,' said Anu suddenly, 'you must take some refreshment. You've had a long journey. Tammuz! Bring bread and oil!'

It was a gracious offer, courteously made, but Adapa flinched. Tammuz lifted a tray from a table: a flagon of oil and a broken loaf of hot sweet-smelling bread.

Though Adapa was very hungry, he held up a regal hand.

'With your indulgence, I won't eat. I've had enough already. I rarely take more than one meal a day.'

To Adapa's alarm, the Mighty Anu suddenly fell back in his throne and slapped his knees. 'You see? You see!' he bellowed at the other, lesser gods. 'You see how stupid these little Earthmen are? Adapa, you're a fool, for all your wisdom! I said you weren't worthy! I said you wouldn't know what to do with it! But I never thought you'd turn it down! Ha ha ha! Turned it down! No immortal would have been so stupid! Go back to your temples and your prayers. Go back to your *little* life full of *little* achievements. Go back with your talk of visiting Heaven: no one will believe you. Go home now, Adapa, for we offered you the bread and oil of everlasting life, and you turned it down. So die!'

Adapa ran all the way back down to Earth. For the rest of his short life, he went over and over that day in his head – and how he had come to make his worst of all mistakes. Had the gods tricked him? Or had Ea? It was Ea who had told him not to eat. Had Ea given his advice in good faith?

Ea and Adapa no longer fished together in the lakes of the Euphrates, because Adapa could never be sure. Once such doubts have entered a friendship, the friendship has already begun to crumble. Ea and Adapa fished together no more, and one day, when the South Wind had recovered its strength, it spilled Adapa into deeper water, where he drowned.

He was only mortal, after all.

Stealing Heaven's Thunder

A NORSE MYTH

IN THE high halls of Valhalla, across the Rainbow
Bridge in the realm called Asgard, Thor the God of
Thunder woke. He lay for a while between the damp
softnesses of dark cloud, and contemplated the day ahead.

'Today,' he said, 'I shall reshape the mountains with my
hammer, smash the ice cap to the north into glassy
splinters, and make the valleys boom like cannon fire. I'll
strike lightning from the anvil Earth and shoe Odin's horse
with gold from the mines of Middle Earth!' He rolled out
of bed, clutched about him a robe of black fur, and
reached for his blacksmith's hammer.

It was not in its usual place.

He searched under the bed and in every cavernous
cupboard of his chamber. He searched the stairways and
corridors of Valhalla, in every trunk and chest, on every
landing, in the smithy and the treasury, his temper growing
with the increasing daylight.

'WHERE'S MY HAMMER?' he bellowed at last, and
Valhalla shook.

Other gods joined in the search. Queen Freya herself,
wrapped in her flying cloak, soared among the pinnacles of
Heaven, thinking to glimpse the hammer from the air.
Then Odin, King of the Gods, banged a door or two, and
scowled.

'It's plain that Thor's hammer has been stolen. Who
would – who could – steal such a prize, but those grunting
grubs, the Giants?'

'Take my cloak, Loki,' said the Queen, 'and go quickly
to the Realm of Giants. Find out if it is true.'

Loki sped across the Rainbow Bridge, down through the ether, and, tumbling like a pigeon, landed at the gate of the Giants' castle.

'It's true we have Thor's hammer,' bragged the largest of the castle's warriors, Din. 'It's true, too, that you will never find where it's hidden. For I've buried the great hammer called Thunderbolt under clods of clay, one mile underground, and the place is known only to me.' Din scratched his tunic of mangey bear fur, and a cloud of dust enveloped them both. He sneezed, wiped his nose on a mat of greasy hair, and leered at Loki. 'I want a bride, see. And that's my bride-price: Thor's hammer in exchange for a wife!'

Loki was almost relieved. 'I'm certain that somewhere in the world Odin can find you a suitable . . .'

'Oh, I *know* he can,' Din interrupted, cleaning out his ears with a piece of stick, 'and he won't have to look far to find her. I mean to marry Freya. Just for once, what's good enough for the gods might be good enough for me. Now you go and tell Odin: no Freya, no Thunderbolt! And let him send her soon – within three days! I'm weary of being a bachelor.' Loki turned in disgust to go. 'Oh, and say she must bring that flying cloak of hers! And her magic golden necklace!' Din laughed till his nose ran and, blowing his nose between finger and thumb, flapped his hands together with all the grace of an elephant seal.

On the return flight, Loki considered the filthy bargain. Odin would never agree to giving away his wife. He would declare war at the very suggestion. But, in the meantime, what damage would the Giants do to Middle Earth with Thor's hammer? They would flatten its crags, terrorize its occupants. The little humans would blame the gods for their persecution, and the foundations of Valhalla would shake at the consequences. By the time he crossed the Rainbow Bridge of Asgard, Loki had formulated his own solution to the problem.

'Lord Odin, King of Gods and mightiest of us all, I bring

word from the thieves who stole Thor's hammer. They have placed a price on its return . . .'

Three days later, bride and escort set out from Valhalla, canopied beneath Queen Freya's cobalt-blue cloak.

Seeing the two figures descend out of the sunshine, Din clapped his hands once more. 'Prepare a feast! Come, brother Giants, and be my guests! Today is my wedding day!' The worm-eaten table in the Castle of Giants groaned under the weight of food. Barrels of wine were stacked as high as the bat-infested vaults of the roof, and a place of honour was cleared among the litter for the bench of bride and groom.

First Loki entered, then the bride, veiled and shining behind him. 'I bring Freya, formerly Queen of Heaven,' announced Loki grandly, 'to be Queen among Giants and wife to Din!'

Din looked on with a fixed grin of sheepish delight, as the bride seated herself and lifted her veil to eat. Two golden plaits as long as bell ropes coiled themselves on the floor to either side of her. She leaned forward and took a rack of lamb, reducing it to a pile of bones in moments. Next she ate a side of beef and three brace of partridge. Then, impatient of the servingman's slowness in filling her glass, she took the jug from him and emptied it in a single swig.

'You certainly do enjoy your food,' giggled Din admiringly. 'A woman after my own heart. But how do you keep your figure?'

Loki, seated on Din's other side, caught him by the sleeve and whispered confidentially, 'She's been so agitated at the thought of meeting you, my lord Din, that she hasn't eaten for three days. She's making up for lost time, that's all.'

Din scratched his neck with a hambone. 'Agitated, eh? Is that good or bad?' he whispered back.

'Oh, my dear fellow!' Loki had his head almost inside the Giant's gigantic ear, so as not to be overheard. 'I think she must have nursed a passion for you this many a year! You've never seen a woman in such a fever to get to her wedding, I do assure you! That Odin – he may be handsome, clever, noble, brave, powerful . . . but he's not every woman's idea of the ideal lover, you know?'

Din turned crimson with delight, and exhaled a sigh with breath like rotting cabbage leaves. 'She loves me?' Turning to his bride, he said, 'Well, don't be shy, then: kiss me, woman!'

Blue eyes looked back at him, as wild as the sea, then changed to the colour of ice, before darkening to scarlet. They blazed in their sockets, those eyes.

Din gulped and shuffled back along the bench, edging Loki on to the floor without noticing. 'Why's she look at me like that?'

'Passion,' replied Loki succinctly. 'Now, there's just the matter of Thor's hammer . . .'

He had almost reached his feet again when Din clapped him violently on the back and sent him sprawling. 'Of course! I'm a man of my bond! Thor's hammer for a bride, I said, and that's what I meant.' A nod of his great head sent a dozen servants running, spades in hand, to unearth the hammer called Thunderbolt. When they returned with it, Din had just plucked up the courage to tickle the back of Freya's neck with his big fingers.

The servants grunted and staggered under the hammer's great weight, and the table collapsed as they set it down. But nothing could dent Din's pleasure. 'I'd like to see Odin's face when he finds out his beloved Freya's left him for a giant like me!'

For the first time, the bride spoke. 'Then you shall have your wish, Din!'

Pulling off her plaits, the bride snatched up the stolen hammer and whirled it round, before letting it fall on the top of Din's verminous head. Freed of his disguise at last, Odin smashed the tuns of red wine, brought down the vaulted roof. He knocked giants as far as the northern sea and the Baltic Straits. He frightened off their giant cows and stampeded their giant horses, and left their armoury a tangle of twisted metal in the bottom of a fjord.

Only the thin air of Asgard could cool his blazing temper, and he berated Loki continually on the flight back for thinking up such a plan. 'A giant paddling his fingers in my neck, indeed! A giant trying to kiss me!'

Queen Freya saw them rising, like gulls on a warm wind, and greeted her husband's return with pleasure, though she had no idea where he had been.

'Why ever are you wearing that dress, Odin?' she asked. 'It doesn't suit you at all . . . But I'm glad to see you've brought Thor's hammer back. He's been wretched without it.'

Reunited with his Thunderbolt, Thor, God of Thunder, raced around Heaven, striking sparks from the crags of Norway, fires from the peaks of Iceland. He bruised the clouds to a blackness, then split them and loosed a cascade of rain on the fires he had just lit with lightning. Never was there such a storm as the night Thor got back his hammer.

But within the high halls of Valhalla, Freya and Odin slept through the storm undisturbed, while Loki, alone and unthanked, brooded on the idea of making more mischief . . .

Anansi and the Mind of God

A WEST INDIAN MYTH

NANSI was an African. Spider-man Anansi. But he stowed away on a slave ship to the West Indies, so now he turns up in Jamaica and suchlike, as sneaky as a tarantula in a hand of bananas. Spider-man Anansi, Anansi the Trickster. They do say Anansi's the cleverest creature next to God . . . or was it Anansi said that?

Now Spider-man Anansi was a clever man,
But he got to boasting he was God's right hand.
Said God, 'Anansi, if you're really so smart,
You can tell what I'm thinking in my heart of hearts.
There's three things I want, and if you're my peer,
You'll have no trouble in fetching them here.'
Well, Spider-man Anansi, he up and fled,
Swinging down from Heaven on his long black thread.
He ain't one clue what he's s'pose' to fetch back,
But he ain't gonna let God Almighty know that.
He seeks out the birdies, one, two, three;
Says, 'Spare one feather for Mister Anansi!'
Asks every bird for just one feather,
Then Anansi-man, he sews them together.

He sews him a glorious rainbow suit:
Feather pyjamas, feather mask and boots,
Then off he flies high up in the sky,
And he dances about till he takes God's eye.
God says, 'Well Lordy, and upon my word!
Who's gonna tell me 'bout this rainbow bird?
I know I didn't make it, so who else did?'

And he asked the mack'rel and he asked the squid.
He asked the turtle and he asked the dog,
And he asked the monkey and he asked the frog,
And he asked the bird, but it just jumped by,
Giving out a perfume like a rainbow pie.

Now God's advisors racked their brains all day,
But they couldn't find but one thing to say:
'Anansi's the man who could solve this case.'
Says God, 'But I sent him on a wild-goose chase!
I sent him to fetch three things to me:
So I fear that's the end of old Anansi.'
'Why? What did you send him for, Lord?' ask they.
'For the night and the moon and the light of day.
Not that I said so. No, I made him guess,
'Cos he got to boasting he was better than best.
But now he's gone, well, I'm sorry, kinda –
That I told Anansi to be a read-minder.'
All the creatures laughed, but God wasn't luffin',
When away flew the bird like a shaggy puffin.

It was no sooner gone than who comes in,
But Spider Anansi in his own black skin.
In came Anansi with a bulging sack.
Says, 'Sorry I kept you, Lord, but now I'm back.
Anansi-man's back and I think you'll find
I've brought you the three things were on your mind.'
So he reaches in the sack and oh! what a fright,
He plunges Heaven into darkest night.
Out comes the moon next with a silv'ry shine
And God says, 'Mercy me, I thought I'd gone blind!
Touché, Anansi-man, you got me licked.
I don't know how, but I know I been tricked.'
Then Anansi pulls out the great big sun –
All its terrible bright illu-min-a-tion,
And it burns God's eyeball in a place or two,
And it gives him pain, and it spoils his view.

So when God looks down now from his throne on high,
There's a patch he misses with his sun-scorched eye.
You can bet that Spider-man knows where it be –
That patch of ground God Almighty can't see.

Is that where you're hiding, Mister Anansi?

How Men and Women Finally Agreed

A KIKUYU MYTH

HAVING created all the beauties of Africa, the Creator of course chose the most lovely for his home – the Mountain of Bright Mystery. There he lived invisible, like a patch of sunlight travelling over the mountainside, and from there he could see all over the world.

To his three sons, he offered three gifts: a hoe, a spear, a bow and arrow.

Masai, a fierce boy who loved a fight, chose the spear.

'Then you shall be a cowherd and live on the plains where the grazing is sweet,' said the Creator to Masai.

Kamba, who loved to eat meat, chose the bow and arrow.

'You shall be a hunter in the forests where the wild beasts have their lairs,' said the Creator to Kamba.

Kikuyu, a gentle, industrious boy, chose the hoe – which pleased his father greatly. After the others had left, the Creator kept Kikuyu by him and taught him all the secrets of agriculture – where to sow, when to reap, how to graft and propagate, which insects to encourage and which to drive away. He led Kikuyu to the top of the Bright Mountain and pointed far off.

'You see there – in the centre of the world – where those fig trees stand like a crowd of whisperers? Make your home there, my son, and may your life and the lives of your children be happy.'

The figs were large and juicy, the shade deep and dark.

But those were not the best things about the grove of fig trees at the centre of the world. When he got there, Kikuyu found awaiting him a beautiful wife – Moombi – and nine lovely daughters, each as dark and sweet as a fig.

For a long time, Kikuyu lived happily, planting a garden in the shade of the fig trees, as well as fields round about. His daughters helped him, singing while they worked, and the sound of Moombi's laughter rang out from time to time as she pounded maize with her pestle.

But as he watched the bees fumbling the flowers, heard the birds sing in courtship, saw the sheep lambing in the long grass, Kikuyu could not help but wonder how his daughters would ever marry and have children to make them laugh as Moombi laughed. One day, the whole family left the grove of fig trees and trekked back across the plain, past the forests and back to the Bright Mountain, to ask the Creator's advice.

'I would like the sound of men's voices in my fields and, to tell true, my nine daughters would greatly like the sight of men's faces coming home from the fields at night,' Kikuyu confided in his father. 'What should I do to have sons-in-law?'

'Go home, Kikuyu. Go home. And remember – the name of Kikuyu is precious to me, but the name of Moombi is sacred.'

Too gentle to press his request any further, Kikuyu did as he was told, and the family trooped back, past the forest and over the plain, to the fig-tree grove.

There, leaning on their hoes, stood nine fine young men, a little startled to find themselves so suddenly called into being by the Creator. When they saw Kikuyu's nine daughters, their faces broke into the broadest of grins.

'Oh, Papa!' cried the girls, behind him. 'Aren't they *lovely!*'

Kikuyu considered the words of the Creator. 'Is marriage agreeable to you?' he asked the young men.

'Yes, sir!'

'And is marriage agreeable to you, daughters?'

'Oh *yes*, Papa!'

'And is it to your liking, Moombi, that our daughters marry these young men?'

'High time, and none too soon!' declared Moombi, laughing loudly.

'Then I have only this to say,' announced Kikuyu. 'My daughters may marry you, young men . . .'

'Oh, thank you!'

'. . . provided you take the name of Moombi for your family name and obey your wives in all things.'

The young men made no objection, and their marriages were long and happy. When after many years, a couple died, their hut and hoe and inheritance passed to any daughters they might have, not to the sons. The daughters chose whom they wished to marry – taking two or three or ten husbands if they wished, and that is how the family of Kikuyu and Moombi grew into a tribe.

After many generations, the men grew restive. One was jealous of his wife's other husbands. One objected to doing all the washing. One resented bitterly that his wife beat him when the sheep got loose in the garden. One felt sorry for his sons, that they would never inherit a thing. So the men muttered mutinously together, deep in the fig-tree groves, and plotted to end their wives' supremacy. But what could they do? The women fought better, ran faster, cursed louder and thought quicker than their menfolk.

So the men waited their chance. They waited until the women were all expecting babies. They waited till their wives were all half as big as hippopotami and waddling like ducks.

'*We* want to be in charge now,' the men announced one day, and all the women could do was press their hands to the smalls of their backs and groan.

After that, the men took as many wives as they wanted: two or ten or twenty, and some beat their wives when the sheep got loose in the garden, and some put their wives to washing and cooking all day. When they held council, only men were invited, and, of course, they passed laws in favour of men.

'Wives!' they said one day. 'We have decided we no longer want our children to carry your female family names. Our families shall have male names from now on. And no longer will the tribe be called the Moombi Kikuyu, after a woman, but rather the . . .'

'*Enough!*' A sun-wrinkled mother, big as a wildebeest and quite as handsome, stood up. She drew her brightly dyed robes around her big baby-filled belly and settled the scarlet cloths on her head. 'In that case we will bear you no more sons,' she said. 'The name of Kikuyu is precious in the ear of God. but the name of Moombi is sacred. If you do this thing, we who are pregnant shall give birth only to daughters; afterwards we shall bear no children at all! If you want sons, from now on, give birth to them *yourselves*!'

The other women began to laugh and nod. The men looked down at their own thin waists and narrow hips and considered the possibility. Have children? No. That was one privilege the women were welcome to.

'What are we called?' asked the wildebeest woman.

'Moombi! Moombi!' answered the women and began to chant the sacred name of the first wife: '*Moombi! Moombi! Moombi!*'

'What are we called?'

'*Moombi! Moombi! Moombi!*'

The men bowed their heads and shuffled their feet in the dust.

'How are we called?'

'*By the name of our mothers! Moombi! Moombi! Moombi!*'

'Who was our first mother?'

'*Moombi! Moombi! Moombi!*'

'What shall we call our daughters?'

'*Moombi! Moombi! Moombi!*'

'And what shall we call our sons?'

The men drummed their hoes against the ground, joined in the chanting, and consoled themselves that it was a small concession to make. They were still the ones in charge. Really.

'*Moombi! Moombi! Moombi!*'

First Snow

THE WORLD was complete.

'And yet it could be better still,' said First Man, gazing up at the night sky. So he and First Woman and Coyote searched about for something to make midnight still more beautiful: a single golden stone to embed in the northern sky, three glowing red pebbles, and a handful of glittering dust which whirled and whorled in a wild, disordered dance.

'I believe we have finished,' said First Man. 'Life is still hard for the People, with famine and thirst in between the rains, but it is better than before, when we lived below, in the kernel of the world.'

'I have one present more to give them,' said Coyote.

Next morning, the People woke to see a brightness brighter than sunshine in the doors of their hogans.

They ran outside, and saw a strange and beautiful white powder falling from the sky. The first snow ever to fall on the world was whitening the bluffs, pillowing the ground, and settling in glittering swags on the trees. Flakes hung on the warp and weft of the weaving looms, like blossom on a spider's web.

The People stood stock-still, their hands outstretched, catching the snow on their palms. It was not cold. First Woman blinked the snowflakes off her eyelashes and shook them from her hair. She took a spoon and lifted a mouthful of snow to her lips.

It was delicious.

The people licked their snowy fingers.

It was delectable.

Soon everyone was scooping up the fallen snow, cramming it into their mouths. It tasted rather like buffalo dripping. They caught the falling snow in baskets, stuffed it into skin bags and stored it up in jars. They filled their pockets and piled it on the papooses. The women carried the white stuff back to their hogans in their skirts, and kneaded it into wafer bread.

'At last we shan't be hungry any more!' they sang. 'Now everything is perfect!' And they feasted greedily on the magic sky food, until they grew too thirsty to eat any more.

Coyote had filled a cooking pot with white handfuls from a drift of snow. He lit a fire and smoke curled up into the sky, fraying it to grey. He began to cook the snow. The People crowded round to see what delicious stew he was making. But as they watched, they began to shiver.

First the snow in the pot turned grey, then to transparent liquid, seething, bubbling, boiling and steaming, cooling only as the fire burned out. As it did so, the snow on the trees wept and dripped and dropped down in icy tears. The white on the ground changed to a grey slush that soaked the children's moccasins, and the women let fall their skirtfuls of snow, crying, 'Oh! Urgh! So cold! So wet! Urgh! Oh!' The old people drew their shawls about their heads and shook their wet mittens, disconsolate.

'Now look what you've done!' cried First Woman, wrapping herself tight in a dozen shawls. 'Our lovely food has rotted away and there's nothing left but the juices. What a wicked waste! You always were a troublemaker, Coyote! In the time before the world, you were always making mischief, stealing, tricking, complaining. But this is the worst! You've made all our beautiful sky flour melt away!'

The People tried to pelt him with snowballs, but the snow only turned to water in their palms.

Coyote simply drank from the pot of melted snow, then shook his head so hard that his yellow ears rattled.

'You don't understand,' he said gently. 'Snow was not meant for food. It was sent down upon the five mountain-tops for the springtime sun to melt, drip joining drop, dribble joining trickle, stream joining river, filling the lakes and pools and ponds, before it rolls down to the sea. Now, when you are thirsty, you need not wait for the rain, or catch the raindrops in your hands. You can drink whenever you please.

'The snowmelt rivers will water the woods and swell the berries for you to pick. The streams will turn the desert into grass-green grazing, so that your sheep put on wool like fleecy snow. And out there, on the plains, the bison will wade knee-deep in seas of waving grass, and grow into fat and shining herds.

'The dusty hunter can wash the sweat from his face where the young women's long wet hair streams out like weed. The children can leap and swim beside waterfalls where the poet makes verses.

'And at the end of the day, if you are still, and patient and quiet, the deer may come down to drink, and the swallows sip flies off the surface of the stream. The women weavers can wash their wools, and dye them brighter colours of the autumn woods.

'And when the summer dust settles and the ants swarm around the food baskets, and the flies buzz after the dirt, we shall wash our homes clean and sluice the summer sickness out of doors.

'Quick! There will be fish coming down the rivers – gold and silver and speckled like brown eggs. Make fishing rods and nets! Catch and bake the fish over your fires! They will taste better than any snow.

'And when First Snow falls out there in the canyons and winding places, you huntsmen will be able to find the tracks of the woolly bison with barely a glance. The footprints of the secret hare will be as plain to read on the ground, as the stars are in the sky.

'These are the uses of snow.'

'So *that* was the present you had to give us, Coyote!' said First Woman, smiling.

'Oh!' yelped Coyote. 'No! The snow almost made me forget!'

He ran to his hogan and fetched out several bags which he opened and spilled on the ground. There was seed inside – maize and beans and squash – and these were his present to the People. They planted gardens, and the snowmelt watered the soil, so that their gardens grew into magic larders of food far more delicious and nutritious than snow.

So next year, when the First Snow fell, the People held a great feast to celebrate its coming, with sweet, pure water to wash down the food from their gardens. Having drunk snowmelt from the very mountain peaks, it seemed as if they themselves were brothers and sisters of the Five Holy Mountains.

Above them hung the glitter of the stars, below the glisten of snow-flakes and lapping water. And in the lake floated the reflection of Moon and the yellow Dog Star.

Coyote sat back on his haunches and howled his music at the sky.

Ragged Emperor

A CHINESE LEGEND

IF ALL children took after their parents, Yu Shin would have been a wicked, feckless boy. His father was a flint-cold man who thought with his fists, except when he was plotting some new torment for his son. Yu Shin was often lucky to escape with his life.

But Yu Shin was nothing like his father, nor even like his mother, who lifted not a finger to help her poor boy, and let him work like a slave around the farm. 'Fetch the water! Feed the animals! Clean the stables! Weed the ground!'

Yu Shin did it all, and with good grace, too, as though his parents were the dearest in the world, and the work his favourite pastime. Inwardly, though, he was sometimes crushed with weariness and misery at the thought of being so unloved.

In truth, his favourite pastime was to read and study. Whenever he could, he crept away to the schoolmaster's house and sat at his feet, listening to any and everything the wise man said. 'Always remember, Yu Shin,' said the teacher, 'not all men are like your father. Whenever things look black, have courage and pray. Life will not always be this hard.'

Not always be this hard? No. It got harder. Yu Shin's father dimly perceived that his son was becoming more intelligent than he; that bred in him a kind of fear. And when Yu Shin grew tall, strong and handsome, his father grew even more afraid. Soon he would not dare to beat and kick and bully the boy, just in case Yu Shin should hit him back. No, the boy must be got rid of.

'Yu Shin! It is time for you to make your own way in the world. Out of my great generosity, I'm going to give you the Black Field, to live on and grow fat. There! What do you say?'

Now the Black Field was a patch of ground the old man had won playing mah-jong. It was miles away in the shadow of mountains, and having been to look it over, he had come home disgusted, telling his wife, 'It's nothing but wilderness. I was robbed.'

Yu Shin knew all this, and his heart shrank at the idea of banishment to the Black Field. But he remembered the words of his teacher and bowed dutifully to his father. 'I am grateful for your tender care and for this most generous gift, dear Father.' His father gave him one last kick, for old time's sake, and laughed till he split his coat.

Arriving after the long walk, Yu Shin found the Black Field even worse than he had imagined. Thorny weeds and briars choked acres of stony dirt. Here and there lay a dead tree, there and here a boulder big enough to shatter a plough. Not that Yu Shin had a plough – only his bare hands to work the worthless plot. A ramshackle hut no bigger than a tool shed slumped in one corner of the field, empty of furniture and full of draughts.

Yu Shin took a deep breath. 'Oh gods and fairies, you have watched over me till now, watch over me here, too, that I may not die of starvation or despair.' Then he bent his weary back, and began to pick up stones, throwing them aside, trying to expose some little piece of soil to plant.

As he worked, he happened to look up and see a distant dust cloud moving towards him. As it came closer, he could make out large grey shapes. *'Elephants?'*

Not just elephants, but a flock of magpies too, escorting the herd like black-and-white fish over a school of whales.

Yu Shin felt oddly unafraid. Even his malicious father could not have organized a stampede of elephants to trample him. So he stood his ground, and the elephants lumbered straight up to him, streaming past to either side. Flank to flank, trunks waving, they stationed themselves about the Black Field, wrenching up tree stumps, pushing aside boulders. Under their gigantic feet, the smaller stones crumbled to dust. The magpies swooped and darted in between, uprooting weeds and thistles and slugs, fluttering under the very feet of the elephants, perching to rest on their great swaying backs.

'Oh thank you, beasts! Thank you so much!' cried Yu Shin, scrambling to the top of a heap of stones to survey his land afresh. The soil was black and crumbly now, rich with elephant manure and just waiting for a crop. 'Let me fetch you water! Rest now, please! You're working yourselves too hard!'

But until the elephants had finished their work, they neither ate nor rested. Then they formed a line in front of Yu Shin and dropped on to their front knees, in a respectful bow, just as if he were someone who mattered! The magpies circled three times round his head before flying away – a black-and-white banner streaming over an army of marching elephants.

They were no sooner gone than more visitors came into sight. Narrowing his eyes against the low sun, Yu Shin saw nine young men walking ahead of a rider – a girl with a cloak of shining hair reaching almost to her tiny feet. At the gate of the Black Field, the nine bowed low. 'Your field needs planting, sir, and your crops will need tending. Grant us the honour of working for you.'

'Oh but where could you sleep? How would I pay you? How could I feed you until my crop is grown?' Yu Shin cast a desperate glance behind him at the ramshackle hut no bigger than a tool shed. And lo and behold! It was all mended! Big rain clouds were coiling over the mountain-top, and he begged his visitors to hurry inside before the downpour began. But as he opened the door for them, Yu Shin stopped short.

'What do you see, sir?' asked the young men.

'One would think, by your face, sir, that you saw an elephant in your living-room,' whispered the girl.

'No. No elephants,' whispered Yu Shin.

But there *was* room enough for eleven to sit down and dine, and afterwards to lie down and sleep. The inside of the hut had become as huge as a mansion, and along a trestle table lay a feast for eleven, just waiting to be eaten.

Yu Shin did not sit down at the head of the table: he sat the girl there. He did not serve himself until everyone had filled their bowls. He did not bore his guests with talk of elephants and magpies, but asked politely about their journey and what books they had read lately. And, of course, they talked about farming.

But to the girl he barely spoke. His rank was too humble for him ever to speak of love to such an elegant beauty. Even so, when he looked at her, it was the only topic which sprang to mind. 'I would welcome your help,' he told them, 'but as friends not farmhands. For you can't possibly be of lower rank in the world than I am!' and he laughed, so that all his guests laughed too.

Every day, out in the Black Field, Yu Shin worked as hard as anyone. Within the year, the whole province was talking of the Black Field – not just of its record harvests, but of the oddly happy little community which farmed it.

The rumours reached Yu Shin's home. 'Curse the boy,' said his father, grinding his teeth. 'He's done it all to spite me!'

The rumours reached the Emperor, far away in the Imperial City. 'Send for Yu Shin!' said the Emperor, and that is a summons no man can refuse.

Yu Shin had no idea why he had been summoned. His ten friends offered to keep him company, which was heartening, but when, after twelve days of walking, the white spires of the Imperial City came into sight, Yu Shin trembled from head to foot. 'Oh gods and fairies. my dear teacher told me always to have courage. Lend me some now, for mine is almost used up!'

The girl came and put her hand on his sleeve. 'You have done nothing wrong, Yu Shin, therefore you have nothing to fear from the Emperor. Have courage a little while longer.' And it seemed to Yu Shin that she knew something that he did not.

'YU SHIN!' bellowed the court usher. 'BOW LOW BEFORE THE EMPEROR OF CHINA!' Yu Shin's nose was already pressed to the imperial floor. High on the Dragon Throne, clothed in gold, the Emperor clapped his frail, pale hands. 'Listen, Yu Shin! Hear me, people of the Imperial Court! The eyes and ears of the Emperor are everywhere. For many years now my spies have brought strange news from the borders of my empire: of a boy who was meek and obedient to his parents, uncomplaining and brave, who was born wise, but had the greater wisdom to listen to others. I was curious. So I sent my nine sons and my only daughter, to see if the stories were true, to see if this paragon truly existed. They tell me that this same boy is also just, generous and courteous, that all people are equal in his eyes, and all are his friends. I am old now, and my strength is failing. I mean to step down from the Dragon Throne. That is why, Yu Shin, I have sent for you. To take my place.' Yu Shin lifted his nose off the floor, eyes round with wonder. 'My daughter looks on you with love. Marry her. Then if you rule China as you have farmed the Black Field, China will flourish as never before!'

History does not record what Yu Shin's father said when he heard the news. Oh, history says that Yu Shin's rule was a golden blaze of achievement, but rarely mentions that he was a farmer's son, for who would ever dream a peasant boy could become the Emperor of China?

History does not mention, either, what became of Yu Shin's father. But those elephants must have dumped their trunkfuls of tree stumps somewhere, then settled down. Those magpies must have dropped their beakfuls of weeds and thistles somewhere, then roosted.

The Boy Who Lived for a Million Years

A ROMANY LEGEND

THERE was once a boy – the son of the Red King – who had the ambition to live for ever and never to grow old. So he said to his father, 'Give me a horse and my inheritance, and I shall travel the world till I find what I am seeking.'

Now the Red King was rich, and Peter's inheritance came to six sacks of ducats – far too much to carry. So he carved a treasure chest out of rock, and buried it with his treasure inside, under the city wall, marking the place with a cross. 'I shall come back for this when I've found the place where I can live for ever and never grow old.'

Over and under and into and out travelled the Red Prince Peter, for eight years, until he came to a continent called Forest, all covered in trees. In the forest grew an oak tree. And enthroned in the tree sat the Queen of Birds – not an owl or an eagle but a green woodpecker.

'What do you seek in my dappled kingdom, young man?' she asked.

'A place to build my castle where I shall live for ever and never grow old.'

'Then build here,' said the Queen, 'for I and my friends shan't die till I have pecked away the last twig of the last branch of the last tree in this forest.'

'In that case, you will die one day,' said Peter, 'and this is not the place for me.'

He travelled along and throughout, wherever and however the lanes took him, for eight years more. And he came at last to a palace of copper set amid seven mountains, each one a different colour of the rainbow. Inside the gleaming copper palace lived a Princess more beautiful than any in all the undulating world. On her walls were written, a million times, the name 'Peter', and in her picture frames hung nothing but portraits of him.

'In my mind's eye I have seen you, and I have loved you ever so long, Prince Peterkin,' she said.

Now many men would have ended their search for happiness then and there, but Prince Peter was utterly single-minded. 'I shall stay in no place with no woman unless she and I can live for ever and never grow old.'

'Then you were meant for me!' exclaimed the Princess, flinging her arms round his neck. 'For those who live in the Copper Castle shan't grow old or die till the wind and rain have worn the seven mountains flat.'

Red Peter wriggled free and pushed her roughly away. 'Then that day will surely come. I've seen the rain and I've heard the wind, and this place is not for me.'

On and away, farther than far, the Red Prince travelled for eight years more, until he came to a pair of mountains, Gold and Silver, and nearby, the lair of the Wind. To Peter's surprise, the Wind, for all his fame and strength, appeared to be only about ten years old.

'I have searched the world over for a place where I can live for ever and never grow old,' said Peter to the Wind. 'You roam far and wide; tell me where I can find such a place.'

'You have found it,' said the Wind.

'Until?'

The Wind looked puzzled. 'You spoke of "always" and "never",' he said, 'and so did I. Stay if you will, and go if you care to, but here you will never grow old or die.'

Red Prince Peter crowed with delight, and accepted the Wind's invitation. There was fruit enough in the trees and colour enough in the sunsets to satisfy any man. There was water enough in the streams and time enough for everything.

'Only take one piece of advice,' said the Wind. 'Hunt on Golden Mountain; hunt on Silver Mountain. But don't go hunting in the Valley of Regret or you will be sorry you did.'

The mountains of Silver and Gold had game enough to satisfy any hunter. For a hundred years Prince Peter hunted there, and hankered after nothing, not even the beautiful Princess in her palace of copper. Not one hair of his head turned grey, not one joint in his body grew stiff, and it seemed to him that no more than a week had passed. Even his horse remained young.

Then one day in one of the many centuries, found Peter chasing a deer. The deer leapt over branch and log, over river and ditch, off the Mountain of Gold and into more shadowy groves, damper and darker and *deeper down*. Realizing he must have strayed into the Valley of Regret, Peter immediately turned back. But all the way home he had the strangest feeling of being followed – a feeling he could not shake off.

Into his heart crept a small wish: to see his home again. Later it grew to a longing, later still, a burning ambition. After a while, he missed his home so much that he was sorry he had ever left his father's city.

'I'm leaving now,' he told the Wind, who shrugged.

'Tell me something I didn't already know,' said the Wind.

On his way home, Prince Peter passed the place where the seven mountains had stood. Through the teeming rain, all he could see was the copper palace, green with verdigris, overlooking a flat and dismal plain. As he passed by the window of the Princess, the rain washed away the last stony grain of the last mountain, and the palace buckled and fell with a clashing crash. The Princess reached out a withered hand towards the Red Prince, and cursed him as she fell.

Eight years later, Prince Peter passed across the continent called Forest, but all that remained of the forest was a single twig held in the claw of a green woodpecker. The woodpecker, Queen of the Birds, drilled to sawdust that last twig of the last branch of the last tree, then fluttering into the air, fell dead at Peter's feet.

He did not pause to bury her, but galloped on towards home, the city of the Red King, his father. But when he reached the place ... there was no city, hardly one brick on another, and not a living soul he knew. 'Where is the city of the Red King?' he demanded of an old man.

The old man laughed. 'That's only a legend, sir. Never really existed. Or if it did, 'twas in a time before history books were wrote.'

'Nonsense. The Red King is my father, you fool!' said the Prince. 'His city stood here – a city of five thousand souls – not thirty years since! Did it burn? Was it sacked?'

The old man closed one eye and sniffed. 'Were you born mad, sir, or did it come upon you sudden?'

Exasperated, Prince Peter dragged the old man to the spot where his treasure lay buried – six sacks of ducats, under the castle wall. 'I'll prove it to you!' he declared.

Breaking open the ground, he dug out the stone chest and, with his sword, prised it open, breaking the blade as he did so. The lid fell back with a dusty crash. 'There! What did I tell you? Six sacks of ducats!'

'Yes, sir, but you did not speak of the other.'

Peter looked again. To either side of the six sacks sat two old crones, one dark, one fair.

'My name is Old Age,' said the dark-haired one, taking Peter's wrist in a bony hand.

'My name is Death,' said the fair, grasping his other wrist.

And that is where Prince Peter, son of the Red King, met his death after a million years of life.

So I'll wish you happiness and long life – but not so long as a million years, for that, in my opinion, would be a kind of a curse, rather than a blessing.

Sea Chase

A FINNISH MYTH

ILMARINEN the blacksmith knew that only one gift would be good enough to win him the daughter of Lady Louhi of Lapland for his bride. He did not know what it was, but he knew it would be his best work. So he took a swan's feather, a cup of milk, a bowl of barley and a strand of wool, and forged them in his furnace into a single magical gift.

The first time he opened the furnace door he found a golden bowl. But he broke that between his hands and threw the pieces back into the fire, fuelling the furnace even hotter. The next time he opened the door, he found a red copper ship, perfect in every detail. But he crushed that between his hands and threw it back into the flames, fuelling the furnace hotter still. The third time he found a little cow with golden horns; the fourth a plough with silver handles. But none of these things was good enough to win the consent of Lady Louhi. For she ruled the Northland, where the ice growls and night lasts all day and the halls are hung with icicles, like Lady Louhi's heart.

The fifth time Ilmarinen opened the furnace door he found – a something: a sampo. He did not know what it was, but he knew it was the best thing he had ever made. So he sailed with it to the Northland in a boat of copper, and won the daughter of Louhi for his wife. Lady Louhi took the sampo and built for it a hollow copper hill whose door locked with a dozen keys, and inside the hill the sampo worked, its lid whirled and its magic flowed into the icebound ground . . .

Sadly, Ilmarinen's bride was no sooner won than lost

again. She died, melted away in his arms like ice in spring. So he went back to the Lady Louhi and asked for her second daughter.

'No!' said Louhi. 'You have squandered one treasure of mine; shall I see you squander another?'

'Then give me back my sampo,' said Ilmarinen. 'I have not had its worth in wives.'

'Give me back my daughter and I shall give you back your sampo,' said Lady Louhi bitterly. 'Not before.'

Ilmarinen could see why she would not part with the sampo. Since his last visit, Lapland had changed past all recognition. Where there had been snowfields, now barley waved golden and ripe. Where once only reindeer and husky dogs had left their tracks in the snow, fat cows and sleek horses grazed in flowery meadows. And where icicles had hung from the eaves of Louhi's cabin, golden ornaments tinkled in a balmy breeze. Only now did Ilmarinen begin to understand just what a wonder he had made.

Boldly, Ilmarinen seized Louhi's second daughter, flung her over his shoulder and ran for the shore. But though he got clean away, he had sailed only five leagues when the girl, before his very eyes, turned into a seagull and flapped back to land.

By the time Ilmarinen reached his Finnish home, he had abandoned all idea of marrying. All he could think of was getting back the sampo. 'I made it, after all,' he complained to wise old Väinämöinen.

'Then we should share in its magic,' the old man agreed.

Three heroes set sail that summer: and three more different men Finland never forged. There was good old Väinämöinen, sensible and sage; Ilmarinen, dogged and strong; and Lemminkäinen, rash and passionate as a fool in love. With three at the oars, the little boat fairly leapt through the waves.

. . . Too fast for the health of the Giant Pike who lay in wait. Bandit of the sealanes, it plundered the high waves for whale and sturgeon, seizing them in its jaws and eating them, bone and caviar. But when it gaped to swallow the boat of Väinämöinen, the ship's bow rammed it, the proud prow pierced it . . . and the heroes ate pike for five days. Out of the jawbone, Väinämöinen made himself a kantele – a kind of harp with bones for strings; he used the teeth to pluck a tune. And so it was to the sound of music that they came to Pohjola. In place of a beach, huge copper rollers lay at the water's edge for rolling ships in and out of the freezing sea. Beyond the rollers, between the pine trees where day-long dark had once clung, the sun now dazzled on Louhi's cabin and on the copper hill. A gull swooped down and pecked Ilmarinen on the head.

'What brings you here?' asked Lady Louhi, bare armed in the balmy warmth of her cabin's porch.

'The joy of your company and the sampo which has made your frosty land a paradise,' said Väinämöinen. 'Since Finland made it, shan't Finland enjoy its magic too? Let us share!'

But the sun had done nothing to melt the ice in Lady Louhi's heart. 'Can one squirrel live in two trees?' she said. 'Lapland has the sampo now and no one shall take it from us!'

If Väinämöinen was annoyed, he did not show it. He simply took out the kantele – the pike-jaw harp – and began to play. The music was sweeter than mead, the notes softer than snowflakes on the lids of those listening. Louhi made to rise from her chair, but fell back, as all around her the lords and ladies, the soldiers and slaves of the Northland slumped down asleep.

The three heroes tiptoed past them, up to the copper hill. Ilmarinen pushed butter in the keyholes of the dozen locks, while Väinämöinen sang strange and low wordless songs. The door swung open, and the sampo was theirs!

One side was grinding out fair harvests, one peace, one wealth, while the bright lid spun amid a galaxy of sparks.

Past the cabin, over the copper rollers, out into the surf

went the three brave raiders, dipping their oars as softly as wings, stealing away from the Northland. But Lemminkäinen was bursting with pride and pleasure. 'We should celebrate!' he declared. 'We should sing!'

'No. We should not,' said Väinämöinen in a whisper. But Lemminkäinen would not be told.

> 'We came and we stormed the copper hill!
> And now we'll sing till the sun stands still
> How Finland's heroes stole the Mill
> Of Happiness, and took their fill!'

A crane roosting on a sea rock rose lazily in the air and flapped inland. It flew to the cabin of Lady Louhi; it woke the Lapps from their magic sleep. 'The Finns have opened the copper hill! The Finns have stolen the sampo! Arise and give chase!'

Over the copper rollers thundered the Lapp ship – huge as a castle, with a hundred men at the oars and a thousand standing. And Louhi at the stern cursed as she held the tiller:

> 'Come, you Mist-moisty Maiden!
> Come from the seabed, Gaffa's child!
> Stormclouds with thunder laden,
> Come and turn the calm sea wild!'

A hundred miles away, Väinämöinen's boat was suddenly wrapped in mist as thick as sheep's wool. Lemminkäinen's song, first muffled then stifled, fell silent. The three heroes could not see as far as each other's faces; they might as well have been alone on the wide ocean. Without sight of the stars, how could they steer a course for home? Without sight of the sea, how could they avoid the reefs and shoals of shallow water?

Väinämöinen picked up the kantele and began to play. If the mist were magic, so was his music. For the fog began to glow and gleam, to run and steam. It turned to a golden liquor which poured into the sea, a cataract of honey. Lemminkäinen opened his mouth and swallowed the sweetness greedily. Ilmarinen wiped his sticky hands and pulled on his oar. The sea ahead was clear, the water round them a puddle of honey, astonishing the fish.

But Louhi and her men had gained ground.

A mile farther, and the sea around Väinämöinen's boat began to seethe. Out of a geyser of bubbles burst the murderous great head of a sea monster. With scales of slate and teeth of razorshell, the oldest child of Gaffa the Kraken broke surface and gaped its jaws to bite the boat in two.

Väinämöinen threw his cloak, and as the monster chewed it to rags, leaned out over the water and took hold. His fingers pinching both the green frilled ears, he hoisted Gaffa's child high out of the water and hooked it to the mast by its earlobes. The boat sat low in the water and filled up with a terrible smell, but as the monster dried in the sun, its roars subsided to whimpering.

'Tell us, O Gaffa's child, why you have come,' said Väinämöinen (though while he spoke, Louhi was gaining ground).

'The Lady Louhi conjured me to kill you,' sobbed the monster, 'but if you let me down, you may go on your way for all I care.'

What a splash the creature made as it hit the water; for some time it lay rubbing its ragged ears. They were watching it still when the storm came up behind them, and the clouds began to hurl lightning and thunderbolts. The sea rose, the sea rolled, the sea writhed into waves like spires of spume. One after another the pitchy waves beat against the little boat, washing over the low rails, filling the bilges with saltwater and chips of ice. A few more waves, and the boat would founder. Lemminkäinen had no breath left to sing: he was too busy baling.

One wave, bigger than all the rest, crashed down on

their heads and washed the pike-jaw harp out of Väinä-möinen's hands, washing it over the side, sinking it in six thousand fathoms.

Väinämöinen's lips, wet and cold and trembling with sadness at the loss of his harp, would not pucker at first. But he wiped them dry and whistled long and low – a noise so loudly magic that it brought all the way from the cliffs of Finland the great Sea Eagle whose wings span Bear Island and whose beak made the fjords. From its tail Lemminkäinen pulled two feathers the size of castle walls and battened them to the boat's sides; so high that the sea could not break over them, so glossy that the boat slipped all the faster through the vertiginous seas.

But meanwhile, Louhi and her men had gained more ground.

The heroes looked back and thought they saw a cloud. They looked back and thought they saw a flock of birds. They looked back and knew they were seeing a ship as huge as a castle, crammed with warriors. Suddenly Louhi was on them: a hundred men pulling on a hundred oars and a thousand more standing.

Väinämöinen fumbled in his pocket. He pulled out his tinderbox and from it took a sliver of flint. Over his left shoulder he threw it, as you or I throw spilled salt, and as he did so, he sang:

> 'Grow reef, and crack their prow;
> Rocks arise to rack them – now!'

The tiny shard grew to a pebble, the pebble to a stone, the stone to a boulder, the boulder multiplied a millionfold. A reef grew in that instant, so sheer and sharp that it slashed the sea to foam.

Too late Louhi saw it lying across her path. The hull shook and the hundred rowers fell from their benches while the thousand warriors sprawled in the bilges. Seams parted, planks splintered and the sea surged in. As her ship fell apart round her, Louhi clapped the clinker sides under her arms, the rudder under her coat-tails, and telling her men. 'Cling tight to me!', the Lady Louhi took flight.

She became an eagle of wood and bone, with talons forged from swords and a beak from axeheads. With a shriek of hatred, she swooped on Väinämöinen's boat out of the north-western sky, one wingtip sweeping the sea, the other brushing the clouds.

'Oh for a cloak of fire now, to keep off this fearful bird!' muttered the old hero, and he called out, 'One last time I say, let us share the sampo! Let's share its magic!'

'No! I won't share it! I shan't share it!' shrieked the woman-eagle plumed with soldiers, and her metal talons snatched the sampo out of Ilmarinen's lap.

So Väinämöinen pulled his oar out of its rowlock and, whirling it three times round his head, struck out at the swooping eagle of wood and bone. Plank and men and weapons showered down. The wood wings buckled, the tail feathers dropped their burden of men into the sea. But the sampo – oh the sampo! – it fell from her claws into the green, seething sea!

The three heroes leapt to their feet in horror. The Lady Louhi soared into the cloudbanks with a terrible cry. Only the lid of the marvellous sampo dangled from her finger. 'I'll knock down the moon!' she ranted. 'I'll wedge the sun in a cleft of cliff! I'll freeze the marrow in your bones for this, thieving Finns!'

Väinämöinen tossed his long grey hair defiantly. 'You may do much, Louhi! God knows, you have done enough! But the sun and moon are God's, and beyond your reach and mine. Here our battle ends, and here our ways part!'

The enemies turned in opposite directions: Väinämöinen to the south, Louhi to the north. The Lapland she found on her return was very different from the one she had left. Silent, sunless and clogged with snow, groaning under the weight of hard-packed ice, it was once again home to wolves and bears. Only the magic of the sampo's lid brought back the herds of reindeer out of the gloomy forests, brought singing to the lips of the drovers, and pride to the Lapp nation who live at the top of the world.

The three heroes rowed home. No singing now from Lemminkäinen, for the sampo was lost and so was the magical harp. 'The best and the last I shall ever make,' said Väinämöinen mournfully.

But whether by accident of tide, or whether by order of the sea king Ahto (in thanks for the new harp he cradled on his lap), something wonderful greeted them, bright amid the seaweed and shells of the beach. Pieces of the marvellous sampo had washed up on the Finnish shore, and with them better fortune than the Finns had ever known. From then on, the harvests grew taller in the fields, the beasts fatter, the treasury fuller, the people happier than they had ever been before. Poets, most of all, found the air aswarm with words, and dreamed their greatest verses – sagas of sampos, heroes and the sea.

Dragons to Dine

A HITTITE MYTH

Taru took his lightning in one hand and his thunderbolt in the other and went out to fight the dragon Illuyankas. From Aleppo to Kayseri it lay, a mountain range of a monster, armoured with scales as large as oven doors, and green as the mould that grows on graves.

Behind it lay the ruins of cities, fallen forests, plains cracked like dinner plates, lakes drunk dry. One yellow eye surveyed the devastation done, the other looked ahead to lands as yet untouched. That eye came to rest on Taru, god of wind and weather, armed for battle and calling its name.

'Illuyankas! Illuyankas! Stand and fight! You have cracked open this world like an egg and chewed to pieces everything Mankind has made. But you shall not take one step more! All the weather of the world is in my quiver, and the gods have sent me to stop you where you stand!'

Illuyankas yawned gigantically, and licked the moon with a rasping tongue. When Taru mustered the clouds and blew them over the dragon's back, drenching it in rain, the rainwater evaporated in clouds of steam. When blizzards enfolded the beast in driving snow and sleet, the icy droplets simply cascaded off it in torrents of meltwater. Taru tore shreds off the north wind and, shaping them in his hands, pelted the dragon's head. But Illuyankas, though it rocked back on its heels, only snapped its jaws shut around the missiles and cracked them between its bronze teeth.

For a time, Taru drew back his wild weather and let the

sun scorch the dragon's back. But Illuyankas's hide, like a roof of glass, reflected the sunlight, and it rebounded on Taru, dazzling him and wilting the lightning in his hand.

Tara pounded on the dragon with thunder. He whipped it with whirlwinds. But after a day, Illuyankas merely flicked its tremendous tail and flung Taru seven miles into the sky before continuing to graze on the people and villages of the Earth. Lifting its snout and flaring its nostrils, it let out a beacon of fire and a roaring whistle – a summons – and from below the earth, out through the craters of volcanoes everywhere, came smaller, squirming dragons, the children of Illuyankas.

They feared nothing from the paltry people scurrying like ants between their claws. For not even the people's gods could stand in the way of Illuyankas and its kin. Leaping and careering in a boisterous, playful trail of destruction, the great green family came to the palace of the goddess Inaras. That was where, for the first time, they saw a smiling face. It startled them to a standstill.

'Welcome! Welcome, glorious creatures!' cried Inaras, spreading her arms in a gesture of hospitality and gladness. 'Won't you rest and eat? See! I've prepared a meal for you. If you are going to rule the world from now on, you must be honoured as kings are honoured and feasted like emperors.'

Laid out on the ground in front of the palace were white cloths a mile long, strewn with dishes of gold. In the dishes was food of every kind – fish baked and fried, vegetables raw and cooked, meat roasted and rare. There were barrels of wine and casks of beer, sherbets and curds and cheeses. There were cakes and loaves, baskets of nuts and tureens of caramel sugar. Honey-soaked haavala was heaped as high as haystacks.

The dragons browsed at first, taking a lick here, a taste there. But soon they were gorging frenziedly, so delicious were the offerings Inaras laid before them. All day and all night and for three more days and nights the dragons dined, and Inaras never slept, so intent was she on bringing them more food, more drink, more deliciousness.

The dragons began to feel sleepy, and stumbling a little against the pink palace walls, they turned for home. Their bellies were so bloated, their eyes so heavy that it was all they could do to find the individual entrances to their underground lairs. Belching and hiccuping, the baby dragons rolled into their volcanic craters and thrust their heads into the tunnels from which they had emerged. *Oof.* Neck and shoulders passed inside. *Oooff.* Their stomachs did not.

So fat were Illuyankas and the lesser dragons that they could not manage to climb back through their doors. They could not reach their warm nests, their lava troughs, the vats of molten rock at which they drank to recharge their dragonish fire. And when they tried, they could not back out again, either. It was Inaras's turn to light beacons and to whistle. Out from the ruins of their villages, out from the rubble of cities and farms and the fallen forests came all the little people of the Earth, carrying enough new rope to bind the moon to the sun.

They ran to where the dragons stood, heads underground, stomachs and hind-quarters in the sun, writhing and tugging to free themselves. The people bound the dragons and hog-tied them, roped them, knee and ankle, and peeled off their scales, leaving the dragons pink and vulnerable, naked and sunburned.

'Thank you, Taru, for your fierceness and bravery!' they sang. 'But thank you, Inaras, even more, for your cunning and your cooking!'

Inaras inclined her head graciously and invited the people to finish up the crumbs of the dragons' feast. And Taru (when he came back down from the sky) held off bad weather until the people had had time to mend their roofs.

Guitar Solo

A MYTH FROM MALI

IN A place where six rivers join like the strings of a
guitar, lived Zin the Nasty, Zin the mean, Zin-Kibaru
the water spirit. Even above the noise of rushing water
rose the sound of his magic guitar, and whenever he played
it, the creatures of the river fell under his power. He
summoned them to dance for him and to fetch him food
and drink. In the daytime, the countryside rocked to the
sound of Zin's partying.

But come night-time, there was worse in store for Zin's
neighbour, Faran. At night, Zin played his guitar in
Faran's field, hidden by darkness and the tall plants. Faran
was not rich. In all the world he only had a field, a fishing-
rod, a canoe and his mother. So when Zin began to play,
Faran clapped his hands to his head and groaned, 'Oh no!
Not again!'

Out of the rivers came a million mesmerized fish,
slithering up the bank, walking on their tails, glimmering
silver. They trampled his green shoots, gobbled his tall
leaves, picked his ripe crop to carry home to Zin-Kibaru.
Like a flock of crows they stripped his field, and no
amount of shoo-ing would drive them away. Not while
Zin played his spiteful, magic guitar.

'We shall starve!' complained Faran to his mother.

'Well, boy,' she said, 'there's a saying I seem to recall:
when the fish eat your food, it's time to eat the fish.'

So Faran took his rod and his canoe and went fishing.
All day he fished, but Zin's magic simply kept the fish
away, and Faran caught nothing. All night he fished, too,

and never a bite: the fish were too busy eating the maize in his field.

'Nothing, nothing, nothing,' said Faran in disgust, as he arrived home with his rod over his shoulder.

'Nothing?' said his mother seeing the bulging fishing-basket.

'Well, nothing but two hippopotami,' said Faran, 'and we can't eat them, so I'd better let them go.'

The hippopotami got out of Faran's basket and trotted away. And Faran went to Riversmeet and grabbed Zin-Kibaru by the shirt. 'I'll fight you for that guitar of yours!'

Now Zin was an ugly brute, and got most of his fun from tormenting Faran and the animals. But he also loved to wrestle. 'I'll fight you boy,' he said, 'and if you win, you get my guitar. But if *I* win, I get your canoe. Agreed?'

'If I don't stop your magic, I shan't need no canoe,' said Faran. ''cos I'll be starved right down to a skeleton, me and Mama both.'

So, that was one night the magic guitar did not play in Faran's field – because Faran and Zin were wrestling.

All the animals watched. At first they cheered Zin: he had told them to. But soon they fell silent, a circle of glittering eyes.

All night Faran fought, because so much depended on it. 'Can't lose my canoe!' he thought, each time he grew tired. 'Must stop that music!' he thought, each time he hit the ground. 'Must win, for Mama's sake!' he thought, each time Zin bit or kicked or scratched him.

And by morning it really seemed as if Faran might win.

'Come on, Faran!' whispered a monkey and a duck.

'*COME ON, FARAN!*' roared his mother.

Then Zin cheated.

He used a magic word.

'*Zongballyboshbuckericket!*' he said, and Faran fell to the ground like spilled water. He could not move. Zin danced round him, hands clasped above his head – 'I win!

I win! I win!'– then laughed and laughed till he had to sit down.

'Oh Mama!' sobbed Faran. 'I'm sorry! I did my best, but I don't know no magic words to knock this bully down!'

'Oh yes you do!' called his mama. 'Don't you recall? You found them in your fishing basket one day!'

Then Faran remembered. The perfect magic words. And he used them. '*Hippopotami! HELP!*'

Just like magic, the first hippopotamus Faran had caught came and sat down – just where Zin was sitting. I mean *right on the spot* where Zin was sitting. And then his hippopotamus mate came and sat on his lap. And that, it was generally agreed, was when Faran won the fight.

So nowadays Faran floats half-asleep in his canoe, fishing or playing a small guitar. He has changed the strings, of course, so as to have no magic power over the creatures of the six rivers. But he does have plenty of friends to help him tend his maize and mend his roof and dance with his mother. And what more can a boy ask than that?

Sadko and the
Tsar of the Sea

A RUSSIAN LEGEND

THERE was a time when Russia was peopled with heroes, and every day brought adventure. All the deeds were great and worth the doing, and all the cargoes were king's ransoms. Even so, these heroes – the *bogatyri* – were not the greatest powers on Earth, and they were still bound by laws and etiquette and taxes. So when Sadko the Merchant set sail with a cargo of gems, he *ought* to have paid tribute to the Tsar of the Sea.

Suddenly, with a jolt which spilled sackloads of rubies along the deck, the ship stopped moving. The wind tugged at the sail, waves spilled over the stern, but the ship stood as still as if it were rooted to the seabed. The crew looked over the side, but there was no sandbar, no reef. A terrible realization dawned on Sadko.

'The Tsar of the Sea wants his toll!' he exclaimed. 'Fetch it! Pay it! Fetch twice the amount! How could I have been so forgetful, so lacking in respect?' Scooping up a handful of pearls, another of emeralds and two of diamonds, he spread them on a plank of wood and, leaning over the side, set the gems afloat.

'More sail and on!' cried the captain, but the ship stayed stuck fast, like an axehead sunk in a log.

Sadko smote his forehead, tore his coat and leapt on to the ship's rail. 'It's no good! The Tsar is affronted! My offence was too great! He requires a life, and a life he shall have!' So saying, he fell face-first on to the plank, scattering pearls and soaking the fur collar of his coat. 'Take me!' he cried (for this *was* the Age of Heroes).

Nothing happened except that the plank floated away from the ship, the ship from the plank. The captain sailed on without a backward glance, and Sadko lay face-down on the sea, wondering about sharks. The ocean rocked him, the sun shone on his back. Sadko fell asleep.

So he never did know how he came to wake in the palace of the Tsar of the Sea. Its ceiling was silvered with mother-of-pearl, its vaulting the ribs of a hundred whales. Conch-shell fanfares blew from towers of scarlet coral, and where banners might have flown, shoals of brightly coloured fish unfurled in iridescent thousands. Seated on a giant clam shell, among the gilded figureheads of shipwrecks, sat the Tsar of the Sea, half-man, half-fish, a great green tail coiled around the base of his throne.

'Your tribute, my lord . . .' began Sadko, flinging himself on his face and sliding along the smooth-scaled floor.

'Think nothing of it,' said the Tsar graciously. 'I had heard of you. I wanted to meet you. This to-ing and fro-ing over the ocean was your idea, I hear.'

'It shall stop and never be thought of again!' offered Sadko.

'Not a bit. I like it. Good idea,' responded the Tsar, his walrus moustaches flowing luxuriantly about his ears. 'It shall be a thing of the future, believe me. D'you play that?' He pointed a fluke of his tail at the balalaika which had fallen from inside Sadko's coat and was floating slowly upwards and out of reach.

Sadko made a porpoise-like leap to retrieve the musical instrument and began casually to pluck its strings. He claimed modestly to have no skill, no musical talent, nothing worthy of the Tsar's hearing. But he played, all the same, and the Tsar's green face lit up with pleasure. He began to thresh his great tail and then to dance, undulating gently at first like a ray, then tossing aside his turtleshell crown and somersaulting about the palace. The goblets were swept off the tables by the backwash. The hangings billowed, rattling their curtain rings.

Naturally, the courtiers followed suit, plunging and gliding, the narwhal beating time with its twisted horn. But none danced as energetically as the Tsar, hair awash, barbules streaming, as he tumbled over and over, spinning and whistling.

High above, on the surface of the sea, waves as high and white as sail-sheets travelled over the water and fell on ships, shrouding them in spray. Lighthouses tumbled like sandcastles, cliffs were gouged hollow by breaking surf. A storm the like of which the seas had never seen raged from the Tropic of Capricorn to the Tropic of Cancer, because the Tsar of the Sea was dancing to Sadko's balalaika. Sadko's ship and twenty more besides came sailing down, drowned sailors caught in their rigging, spilling cargoes on the tide.

Seeing his mistake, Sadko tried to stop, but the Tsar only roared delightedly, 'More! More music! I'm happy! I feel like dancing!' So Sadko played on and on, in bright, major keys suited to the Tsar's cheerful mood. At last, with a tug that cut his fingers to the bone, Sadko pretended accidentally to break all the strings of his balalaika, and the music twanged to a halt. 'I regret . . . my instrument . . . not another note . . .' he apologized.

'No matter. I was getting tired anyway,' panted the Tsar, throwing himself down on a coral couch. 'My chariot will take you home.' Sadko was conveyed in a shell chariot drawn by salmon, out of the palace caves, in from the ocean and up a saltwater river to its freshwater source.

The experience had so shaken him that, for a long while, he did not set foot on a ship, but made all his journeys overland. Near where the Tsar's chariot had set him down, he built a warehouse where other merchants could store their goods. It was a novel idea no one had ever had before. But the spot was far from his native city of Novgorod, and he did wish to see his home again before (as was the fate of *bogatyri*) he turned to stone, a boulder in the landscape of history.

Apprehensively, he went to the banks of the River Volga with a plate of salted bread and fed it to the river. 'Oh River, will you carry me home to the city of my birth, now that we have dined together?'

The fish ate the bread, but it was the river which thanked him. 'You, Sadko, are a man who knows the worth of water.'

'Of course! No man can live in it, no man can live without it,' said Sadko, and the Volga gurgled with pleasure.

'I must tell my brother that one! "No man can live in it, no man can ..." Very good! On second thoughts, why don't you tell him yourself? Share some of your excellent bread with my brother, Lake Ilmen, and see how he rewards your generosity.'

So Sadko threw salted bread on to the waters of Lake Ilmen, and though the fish ate the bread, it was the lake which thanked him. 'You, Sadko, are a man of the future,' said Lake Ilmen in his whispering, reedy voice. 'May I suggest you cast three fishing nets over me, for I have a present for you from my great grandfather, the Tsar of the Sea.'

Sadko cast the three nets, and to his astonishment and the amazement of everyone who helped him that afternoon, the nets filled with all manner of *salt sea* fish – cod and bass, sturgeon and wrasse – and silver salmon, too, though it was not the season, not the season at all! There were so many fish and it was so late in the day that the catch needed to be stored overnight. Sadko's warehouse was the very place.

But in the course of the night, a subtle change overtook the fish in Sadko's warehouse. By morning, when the doors were opened, there was no smell, no smell at all. And all the fish – stacked high as the rafters of Sadko's warehouse – had turned to ingots of solid silver.

In a way, the end began that day. For afterwards, the *bogatyri* of Russia stopped adventuring and doing great deeds. They took to trade: buying and selling, transport and distribution, marketing and striking deals. They made millions of roubles, and their warehouses reached almost to the sky.

But their wealth fired the envy of foreigners, and Russia was invaded by brutish, bad-mannered barbarians. The *bogatyri* fled – or withdrew, perhaps, to discuss economic sanctions. While they debated, they turned, one by one, to stone – boulders in the landscape of history. Were it not for the rivers babbling about them, the lakes whispering their stories, the sea roaring out their names, we would hardly know they had ever existed.

The Armchair Traveller

AN INDIAN LEGEND

H<small>E WAS</small> no beauty, it's true. In fact compared with his brother Karttikeya, his looks were downright bizarre. There was his colour, to begin with: blue is not to everyone's taste. Nor are four arms and a pot-belly. Nor are trunks and tusks. But then Ganesa's head *was* second-hand, his own having been cut off by Shiva in a moment of temper and replaced with the nearest one to hand, in the hope no one would notice. Even so, elephants are wise animals, and what Ganesa lacked in obvious good looks he made up for in wisdom. His library was huge. He read even more greedily than he ate, and he ate all day long.

Ganesa and his brother wanted to marry. Their sights were set on Siddhi and Buddhi. Although the obvious solution might seem that they should marry one each, fiery and quarrelsome Karttikeya saw things differently. 'I'll race you round the world, Ganesa,' he said. 'Whoever gets back first shall have them both!'

Ganesa munched on a pile of mangoes before answering. 'That seems acceptable,' he said, spitting pips out of the window. Never once did he lift his eyes from the book he was reading.

With no more luggage than his bow and arrows, Karttikeya leapt astride his trusty peacock (laughing aloud at the absurd idea of his fat, squat brother struggling round the globe behind him) and sped into the distance, a streamer of iridescent green and purple feathers and a flash of silver. He would be married and his first child born before Ganesa even got home!

'Well?' squeaked the mouse which lived somewhere between Ganesa's ears. It raced up and down his bony head. It shouted into his flappy ear. 'Hurry! He's faster than you! Get moving!'

'All in good time,' said Ganesa, and went on reading.

'Don't you *want* to marry Siddhi and Buddhi? They're lovely!'

'Intelligent, too,' said Ganesa. 'At least Buddhi is. Siddhi, I would estimate, is more of an achiever.' He chewed slowly on a heap of melons while sucking strawberries up his trunk for later. 'This really is an excellent book.'

'No time for reading!' urged the mouse. 'Aren't you even going to try? Don't you think you can do it? Karttikeya may be fast but you and I can push through jungles better than he. We could make up time in South America and Indonesia! Get on your feet! You won't win just sitting here!'

'Well, that's as maybe,' said Ganesa through a mouthful of onions. 'Let us not pre-judge these matters.' His trunk reached out and took down another gigantic tome from his bookshelves. Then he settled back in his chair and shot peanuts into his open mouth with uncanny accuracy.

Round the fat world raced Karttikeya. He swam rivers, hacked his way through forests, and traipsed over fly-blown deserts. He saw the most wonderful cities in the world, some armour-plated with ice, some half-submerged in flowers and ivy. He met kings and climbed mountains. He watched harvests of wheat and seaweed and olives; he fought wild beasts with fur, with feathers, with scales. There was no time for wondering why the towers of Sumeria lay in ruins, or why the night sky sometimes filled with trickling colours at the top of the world. He was too intent on winning, on beating his elephantine brother, on the stories that would be written of this epic race.

'Summon the musicians! Prepare the wedding feast! I am back! Karttikeya has returned!' His peacock looked bedraggled and tattered. Karttikeya was covered in dust, leaves and barnacles, and his clothes were full of sand. 'Buddhi? Siddhi? . . . *You!*'

There sat Ganesa in his armchair, munching thoughtfully on cumquats and reading a copy of the *Puranas*. 'Where have you been?' he asked his dishevelled brother. 'We couldn't start the wedding without the bridegroom's brother.'

Now Karttikeya, though he did not have the head of an elephant, was not altogether stupid. He suspected that Ganesa had not been *right round* the world, as he had. Indeed, he did not stop short of thinking Ganesa had never even levered his big rump out of that armchair. So he decided to shame him in front of Buddhi and Siddhi, and to show him up for a cheat.

'Tell us, brother. What did you think of China?'

'Which part?' replied Ganesa. 'There's so much. The green pinnacles of the Yangtse, or the man-made marvels of Pekin?'

'Huh! . . . Was Siberia cold enough for you?' Karttikeya persisted.

'I preferred Greenland, myself – all that volcanic activity, those hot geysers – such astonishing shapes they make as the droplets freeze. And the fjords of Scandinavia – ah! – more indentations than the blade of a saw!'

'Since you were ahead of me,' said Karttikeya sarcastically, 'I'm surprised I didn't see the path you beat through the rainforests.'

'Mmm, well, the forests regenerate so quickly,' explained Ganesa. 'That's why they've all but reclaimed those ziggurats. I notice a similarity – don't you? – between the ziggurats and the pyramids of Egypt. Do you suppose there is any truth in that story about Naramo-Sin sailing west with his mathematics?'

On and on Ganesa talked, pausing only to accept a grape from Buddhi, a pomegranate from Siddhi. The women sat at his feet spellbound by the pictures he painted of distant lands, their people, their philosophies, their legends. 'I particularly like the Native American myth – so poetical in form. For instance . . .'

'All right! All right! You win!' said Karttikeya, slumping down, exhausted. 'You win. You may have your brides.'

Siddhi and Buddhi laughed and hugged each other with delight.

'Thank you, brother! How very gratifying!'

'But admit it, brother, just to me, just for the sake of history, *did* you really travel round the world?'

Ganesa tapped his bony skull with one of his four hands. 'In my mind, dear brother. In my mind. You don't always have to visit a place to find out about it. That's why I treasure my books.'

Buddhi and Siddhi gazed round them at the high shelves full of books and scrolls, and smiled as though they had just been given the world for a wedding present. Then they fetched Ganesa another hand of bananas and sat down to hear more stories.

Uphill Struggle

A GREEK LEGEND

YOU CAN defy the gods just so often: they will always have the last word. The Immortals, you see, have time on their side. They only have to wait, and the disrespectful will be brought to their knees by old age and the fear of dying.

Sisyphus, though, feared nothing. He did not give a fig for their trailing clouds of glory, for their thunderbolts or lightning. In fact, as he said more than once, he thought they were a bunch of rogues and that living at the top of a mountain must have affected their brains, for they were all as mad as bats.

When Zeus, King of gods, mightiest of the mighty, stole the wife of River Alopus, Sisyphus went and told Alopus straight out – just like that. 'It was Zeus, the philandering old devil. He's got your wife. I saw him take her.'

That was too much for Zeus, King of gods, mightiest of the mighty. '*Death! Go and tell Sisyphus his time has come!*' he spluttered, as the jealous husband swirled round his ankles, set urns and couches afloat, and rendered heaven awash with mud.

Sisyphus took to his heels and ran. Death lunged at him with a sickle, but Sisyphus ducked. Death tried to fell him with a club, but Sisyphus jumped just in time. Death loosed avalanches and wild animals, but Sisyphus bolted for home and slammed the door, jamming it shut with furniture.

'I can't hold him off for long,' he told his wife. 'So listen. When I'm dead, I want you to throw my body in the rubbish pit and have a party.'

'Oh but dearest . . . !'

The door burst open and, with a gust of wind and a crash of furniture, Sisyphus fell dead, his soul snatched away to the Underworld to an eternity of dark: silenced by the gods.

'He has *what?!*'

'A complaint. He wishes to complain, your lordship.'

Hades leaned forward out of his throne, eyes bulging, and his herald cowered in terror. '*Just who does he think he is?!*'

'A poor benighted soul, shamefully and shoddily treated,' said Sisyphus, entering without permission and stretching himself out face-down before the Ruler of the Dead. 'I complain not of dying, Lord Hades. Far from it! It's a privilege to share the dwelling place of yourself and so many eminent ghosts! But my wife! My wretched wife! Do you know what she has done?'

Hades was intrigued. 'What has she done?'

'*Nothing!*' cried Sisyphus leaping up and clenching his gauzy fists in protest. 'No funeral rites! No pennies on my eyelids. Not a tear shed! She simply dumped my body in the rubbish pit! She's a disgrace to the very word "widow"!'

Hades nodded his infernal head slowly, so that his piles of pitchy hair stirred within his chair. 'The rubbish pit. That's bad. She shall be punished when she too dies.'

'No need, my lord! Don't trouble yourself! Only send me back there, and I shall make an example of her that will teach the Living a lesson in caring for the Dead!'

'SEND YOU BACK?' Hades was stunned by the boldness of the suggestion. 'Would you come straight back afterwards?'

'The moment she's been taught a lesson, I promise,' said Sisyphus. Hades hesitated. 'Do you know, lord? She never even laid a tribute on *your* altar in remembrance of me!'

'*Then go back and teach her the meaning of respect!*'

cried Hades, leaping up in his excitement. '*Appalling woman!*'

'Excelling woman,' said Sisyphus kissing his wife tenderly. 'I did right?'

'You did perfectly. Here I am to prove it – first man ever to escape the Underworld!' He shook vegetable peelings out of his hair, having only just recovered his body from the rubbish pit. He had promised to return to Dis, Land of the Dead, by midnight. But by midnight he would be fishing on the seashore, by morning dozing among the lemon groves, the sun on his back. Sisyphus felt so full of life that he could have palmed Mount Olympus and thrown it out to sea like a discus! 'They haven't the wit they were born with!' he told his wife. 'And I, Sisyphus, have the wit to outwit them from now till the revolution! One day soon, humankind will rise up and rout the gods as they routed the Titans before them. I'm *never* going back!'

When Sisyphus did not return to Dis as promised, Hades loosed his hounds on the scent. Black as tar, they came panting out of the earth, tongues lolling over bared teeth. From their Olympian palaces the gods watched, smirking, as the dogs closed on their prey, submerged him in their pitchy pelts and dragged him down to Dis.

'Such nerve! Such daring!' said Hades towering over his prize. 'I am so impressed, I mean to do a deal with you, my audacious friend. You see that hill, and that boulder? Simply push that boulder to the top of the hill, and you shall go free, leave here, live for ever, *go home.*'

And so Sisyphus pushes his boulder up the hill. He has been doing it now for four thousand years. His hands bleed, his back is twisted and bent. Every time he gets to within one push of the top, the gods on Olympus swell their cheeks and – *pouf* – the boulder rolls thundering down to the bottom. He must begin again.

Nearby, Tantalus, condemned for his crimes to a pool of

fire, never able to taste the sweet cool water placed just out of reach, looks up and takes his only scrap of comfort in an eternity of torment. 'At least I am not Sisyphus,' he tells himself, 'rolling his rock for ever and a day.'

But Sisyphus, as he slides down the rocky slope on his bare feet, and sets his shoulder to the stone for the millionth time, says, 'One day soon Man will rise up against the gods, and then . . . and then!'

Bobbi Bobbi!

AN AUSTRALIAN MYTH

IN THE Dreamtime, when the world was still in the making, the Ancient Sleepers rose from their beds and walked across sea and land, shaping the rocks, the plants, the creatures, arranging the stars to please the eye.

I remember. Or if not I, an ancestor of mine, or if not he, a sister of his ancestor. Our memories are blurred now, but we do remember: how the Ancient Sleeping spirits walked the Earth during Dreamtime, and made things ready for us.

The snake spirit, Bobbi Bobbi, on his walk, heard crying and came upon a group of human beings newly brought to life.

'Does the world not please you for a place to live?' he asked.

'It would please us,' sobbed the people, 'if we were not so *hungry!*'

So Bobbi Bobbi searched his dreams for a kind of food, then gave it shape from a handful of soil. He made one flying bat and then another. Big they were, and meaty, each one a meal to feed a family. By the time Bobbi Bobbi walked on his way, over the brand-new world, the sky behind him was black with bats.

Binbinga lit a fire. Banbangi his sister crept up on a bat where it hung by its toes from a tree.

Crackle-rattle! The bat heard her, for its hearing was sharp and, just as she reached into the tree, it spread its leathery wings and flapped away.

Banbangi tended the fire. Binbinga took a stone and

went to where the bats hung in a row by their toes from a cliff. He leaned back to throw.

Crackle-rattle! The bats heard him, for their hearing was keen, and just as he threw his stone, the bats spread their leathery wings and and flapped away.

Bobbi Bobbi, walking home through the red light of evening, heard crying. Once again, he came across the little new-made people – now looking more gaunt and desperate than before – and asked them what was wrong. But all they could do was point up at the sky at the flittering swarms of bats.

'We can't reach them. We can't catch them. All day we hunt them, but they won't be caught!'

Now Bobbi Bobbi was angry, because when he made a thing, he made it for a good purpose and not to find it fooling about in the red light of sunset. In his anger he beat his chest, till the ringing of his ribs gave him an idea.

With the sharp blade of the sickle moon, he cut a slit in the side of his chest, reached in his hand, and pulled out a rib, a single rib. Taking a squinnying aim on the circling bats, he flung the rib – it flew with a singing whistle – and tumbled a fine fat bat out of the blood-red sky!

The little people jumped and cheered, but not so high nor as loud as they jumped and cheered at what happened next. Bobbi Bobbi's rib-stick came whirling back out of the scarlet sky – right to his hand, right to the very palm of his hand!

Bobbi Bobbi gave his marvellous rib to the hungry newcomers and – wonder of wonders! – even when they threw it, it knocked the bats from the sky then swooped home again to their hands. 'Boomerang', they called it, a treasure entrusted to them by the gods. A very piece of the gods.

No wonder they grew proud.

They knocked down more bats than they could eat, just to prove they could do it. The best throwers even boasted that they could knock down the birds . . .

'. . . the clouds . . . !'

'. . . the moon . . . !'

And as they strove to outdo one another, Binbinga threw the boomerang so hard and so high that he knocked a hole in the sky!

Down fell rubble and blue dust, on to the ground below. Winds escaped through the gap, stars showed at midday, and the handiwork of the Ancient Sleepers was spoiled.

Now Bobbi Bobbi was really angry, because when he made a thing, he made it to good purpose, not to see it played with by fools.

Before the boomerang could arc back through the tear in the sky, Bobbi Bobbi reared up, caught it in his mouth and shook it with rage.

'Quick! Before he swallows it!' cried Binbinga.

'He mustn't take it from us!' cried Banbangi. And they ran at the great snake spirit, scrambled up his scaly body, clambered up his trunk towards the broad, toothless rim of his mouth. They each took hold of one end of the precious boomerang. In their ignorance, they actually tried to pull it out of Bobbi Bobbi's mouth!

But the snake spirit only dislocated his jaw (as snakes can) to widen the gape of his cavernous jaw, and swallowed Binbinga and Banbangi, swallowed them whole.

A great silence fell over the newly made world, broken only by the *rattle-crack* of the last remaining bats.

For a long while, the flying bats cruised the sky above the new-made people. Daily they increased in number, just as the hunger increased in the bellies of those below. When, at last, Bobbi Bobbi relented and gave back the rib-stick, it was only in exchange for their promises to use it as it was meant to be used – for catching food.

The Gingerbread Baby

A MYTH FROM PALESTINE

LEILA put in the bread and closed the oven door. She drew a deep breath and sighed; there was sea-salt in the air. 'While the bread bakes, I just have time to stroll down to the harbour,' she thought. 'I must see the sea today.'

Down at the waterfront, a ship was loading. Leila had no sooner stepped aboard than it set sail, and carried her over three oceans and five high seas till she came to a land rather like her own. Down by the docks, the houses were shabby and the people poor. A home was one room and a meal was one raisin and the reason was poverty.

A young widow stood by her door, big-bellied with yet another baby, and weeping fit to break your heart. 'Another mouth to feed,' she said, 'and where's the food to come from? Even our poor dog is starving to death.'

Leila wished she had brought the loaf of bread with her, for truly this whole family was as thin as a bunch of twigs. The dog, too. As it was, Leila felt in the pockets of her gown and there was not so much as a coin for her to give the widow.

Higher up, the houses were large and beautiful, each room as big as a lesser man's house, each meal a marvel, and the reason was wealth. Even so, a woman stood on her golden balcony and wept fit to break your heart.

'What's the matter?' asked Leila.

'Nothing your kindness can cure, old lady,' sobbed the woman. 'My husband the sultan hates me, because I have given him no children!'

'*He* has given *you* no children, you mean!' said Leila.

'These men! How they complain about the least thing! You dry your tears and let an old lady advise you.' She whispered in the sultana's ear, and the young woman, though she shook her head – 'It will never work!' – did just as she was told.

When the sultan came home, she told him, to his great joy, that she was expecting a baby. Then, every day, Leila padded the sultana's dress a little more, so that she really did look as though she had told him the truth. Meanwhile, each day, Leila also cooked a morsel of gingerbread, and took it down to the garden gate and fed it to a bony little dog who poked his nose through the bars.

After eight months, Leila went to the kitchen and made more dough than usual. She pinched the gingerbread into the size and shape of a baby, and baked it in the palace oven, wondering as she did so, if her own bread at home was baked yet.

Every day, the sultan came asking, 'Is the child born yet?' At last he heard the words he longed for. Leila peeped round the bedroom door and told him, 'Your dear wife has given you a beautiful child, your eminence. As soon as she is strong enough, she will bring the boy to you in the garden.'

There, amid the tinkling fountains and orange trees, the sultan sat singing for sheer joy. Watching from her balcony, the sultana cradled her gingerbread baby . . . and sobbed fit to break your heart. 'Did you really think he would be fooled, Leila?' she wept. 'Do you think my husband is blind and stupid? It is a lovely baby you baked for me, but anyone with two eyes and a nose can tell it's made of gingerbread!'

'Yes, indeed,' said Leila happily. 'Anyone with two eyes a nose and a tail.' She told the sultana to go down to her husband, carrying the child. 'But not too tight, you hear?'

Leila ran downstairs ahead of her, ran to the garden gate where every day she had fed the bony dog. Sure enough, the dog was there again today and, at the smell of

gingerbread wafting over the gardens, began to drool.
Leila unlatched the gate . . .

'I come, O husband, to show you our lovely child,' said
the sultana, her voice full of fright.

The sultan sniffed. 'Well, he *smells* better than most
babies,' he said.

Just then, with a flash of fur, one bark and a rattle of
skinny bones, a dog bounded over the fountain and seized
the 'baby' in its mouth.

'Call the guard! Shut the gates! Stop that dog!' yelled the
sultan desperately. But no one was quick enough to catch
the mongrel with its meal of gingerbread wrapped in
priceless lace. The dog ran straight home – down to the
docks – and shared its good fortune with the widow and
her hungry, fatherless children.

The crumbs were still falling when Leila hurried in,
breathless from the long trot. She went straight to the box
in the corner (which was all the widow had for a cradle)
and lifted out the tiny, half-starved baby boy crying there
with hunger. 'Listen,' said Leila. 'How would you like
your baby to live in a palace, with all the food he can eat,
growing up loved and safe, to be a sultan one day?'

'Better than words can say,' said the widow. 'But how?'

'Trust me,' said Leila. Picking up the beautiful white
shawl from the floor, she wrapped the real baby in it and
carried him out to where the palace guards were searching
the streets.

'All is well!' she said. 'This family rescued the baby
before the dog could hurt him.'

When the sultan heard that, he gave command that the
widow should receive a reward – a reward so huge that the
family need never go hungry again. And hugging the baby
boy to his chest, he carried it home to his wife.

Imagine the sultana's surprise, having lost a gingerbread
baby, when she got back a real live son. She was too happy
to quibble.

Leila sniffed the air and smelled baking bread. 'Time I

was going,' she said, and climbed aboard a ship making ready to sail. Over three oceans and five high seas it carried her, to the harbour below her own little house. As she opened the door, the wonderful smell of baking bread greeted her like a friend. 'Just in time,' she said, and taking her loaf out of the oven, cut herself a slice to eat with a glass of hot, sweet tea.

The Price of Fire

A MYTH FROM GABON

FROM THE leafy canopy of the forest hang the long, looping lianas, leafy ropes of creeper like tangled hair. Within the loop of the longest liana, God used to sleep away the hottest part of the day, swinging in his viny hammock. His mother said the climb was too tiring now, so she dozed on a tree stump down below, remembering.

The dark damp of the forest floor is a chilly place, especially for an old lady. So God invented fire to keep Grandma God warm: a morsel of sun, a kindling of twigs, and there it was one day, crackling merrily and casting an orange glow.

Manwun came shivering down the forest paths, looking for berries. He saw the fire, saw God's mother asleep in its glow, and thought, 'I could use that stuff to keep *me* warm.' So he stole the fire, and ran for home as fast as he could manage with an armful of burning twigs.

Grandma God stirred, shivering, and bleated up into the trees, 'Son! Son! Someone has stolen my fire!'

God leapt from his hammock at once and, using the ropes of creeper, swung from tree to tree with a piercing yell. He quickly caught up with the thief, swooping low over his head and snatching back the stolen fire.

But Manwun went home and told his village about fire. Soon Mantoo came creeping by and, waiting till Grandma God fell asleep, stole the fire from in front of her. She dreamed of ice, and the chattering of her teeth woke her. 'Son! Son! Someone has stolen my fire!'

Swinging hand-over-hand, from tree to tree, God went

after the thief, and though Mantoo had almost reached the edge of the forest, he too felt the red-and-yellow treasure snatched from his grasp as God went swooping by with a whoop of triumph.

'We could just *ask* him for some fire,' suggested Woman, but no one listened to her.

Manthree made careful plans before he left for the forest. He knew that God would be on the look-out for sneak-thieves creeping through the undergrowth. So he sewed together a coat of feathers – one from every kind of bird – and practised hour after hour. First he jumped from logs, then from branches, then from hilltops, until he could fly with all the skill and speed of a bird.

Dozing on his liana swing, all God saw was a flash of colour as Manthree went by. He never suspected a bird-man had swooped on Grandma God's fire and snatched it up, kindling and all.

'Son! Son! Someone has stolen my lovely fire!' she bleated, and God gave a weary sigh, for he had done enough chasing for one day.

Swinging hand-over-hand, whooping from tree to tree, God went after Manthree: he could just make out the glimmer of orange and red among the treetop fruits. Quick as a swallow, Manthree darted between the dense trees. He reached the edge of the forest and burst out into the bright sunlight of the plain, soaring and looping over rivers and valleys. Out in the open, God had to make chase on foot, wading and jumping, running and climbing, till at last, he sprawled exhausted on a sunny hillside to catch his breath. 'All right! All right! You may have fire! The day is too hot and the world too big for me to chase you any more. Have it and be done!'

Manthree (whose feathers were starting to char from carrying the fire) gave a great cheer, and took his prize home. God, on the other hand, dragged his feet all the weary way back to the forest.

'I've given them the fire, Mother!' he called as he approached the tangle of lianas and the dark, damp tree stumps beneath. 'I decided they could have some too. It will set the world twinkling at night, and their cooking will taste better. Was I right, do you think? I'll make you some more, of course. Mother? Mother?'

Grandma God lay curled up beside the circle of ash where her fire had once burned. She was cold as death, and no fire would ever warm her again.

First God wept, then he swore to make Manwun, Mantoo, Manthree and the rest pay for stealing fire from his poor, frail old mother. 'When I made them, I meant them to live for ever. But now, for doing this, let them taste the cold of Death! Let every man, woman and child grow old and cold and die!'

So that is why old folk complain of the cold, and shiver on the warmest days, and why, at last, the flame of life gutters and goes out in their eyes, no matter how close they make their beds to the campfire.

The Hunting of Death

A MYTH FROM RWANDA

AT THE start, God thought the world of his people: their smiles, their dancing, their songs. He did not wish them any harm in the world. So when he looked down and saw something scaly and scuttling darting from nook to cranny, he gave a great shout.

'People of Earth, look out! There goes Death! He will steal your heart-beat if you let him! Drive him out into the open, where my angels can kill him!' And fifty thousand angels flew down, with spears, clubs, drums and nets, to hunt down Death.

All through the world they beat their skin drums, driving Death ahead of them like the last rat in a cornfield. Death tried to hide in a bird's nest at the top of a tree; he tried to burrow in the ground. But the birds said, 'Away! God warned us of you!' And the animals said, 'Shoo! Be off with you!'

Closer and closer came the army of angel hunters. Their beating drums drove Death out of the brambles and tangles, out of the trees and the shadows of the trees, on to the sunny plain. There he came, panicked and panting, to a village.

He scratched at doors, tapped at windows, trying to get out of the glare of the sun, trying to get in and hide. But the people drove him away with brooms. 'Go away, you nasty thing! God warned us about you!'

The angel huntsmen were close to his heels when Death came to a field, where an old lady was digging.

'Oh glorious, lovely creature!' panted Death. 'I have run many miles across this hard world, but never have I seen such a beauty as you! Surely my eyes were made for looking at you. Let me sit here on the ground and gaze at you!'

The old lady giggled. 'Ooooh! What a flatterer you are, little crinkly one!'

'Not at all! I'd talk to your father at once and ask to marry you, but a pack of hunters is hard on my heels!'

'I know, I heard God say,' said the old woman. 'You must be that Death he talked of.'

'But *you* wouldn't like me to be killed, would you – a woman of your sweet nature and gentle heart? A maiden as lovely as you would never wish harm on a poor defenceless creature!' The drum beats came closer and closer.

The old woman simpered. 'Oh well. Best come on in under here,' she said and lifted her skirt, showing a pair of knobbly knee-caps. In out of the sunlight scuttled Death, and twined himself, thin and sinuous, round her legs.

The angel huntsmen came combing the land, the line of them stretching from one horizon to the other. 'Have you seen Death pass this way?'

'Not I,' answered the old lady, and they passed on, searching the corn ricks, burning the long grass, peering down the wells. Of course, they found no trace of Death.

Out he came from under her skirts, and away he ran without a backward glance. The old woman threw a rock after him, and howled, 'Come back! Stop that rascal, God! Don't let him get away! He said he'd marry me!'

But God was angry. 'You sheltered Death from me when I hunted him. Now I shan't shelter you from him when he comes hunting for your heartbeat!' And with that he recalled his angel huntsmen to Heaven.

And since then no angel has ever lifted her skirts to hide one of us, not one, until Death has passed by, hunting heartbeats.

Young Buddha

AN INDIAN LEGEND

SWEET and pure as dewfall on a spring morning, Queen Maya was loved by her husband and people as much as any goddess. One night, she dreamed that an elephant, white as milk, raised its trunk in salute over her. In her dream, its phantom whiteness came closer and closer, trumpeting, moving right through her own transparent body. When she woke, she was expecting a child. With such a beginning, no ordinary boy. His very name meant 'bringer of good'.

From the first moment, Prince Gautama was remarkable. He was no sooner born than he took seven steps, looked around him at the astonished waiting-women and midwives, and said, 'This is the last time I shall come.'

He understood, you see, without anyone teaching him, how life goes round and round, each soul quitting one body only to be born afresh in another: each life a new chance to strive for perfection, to escape the endless treadmill of rebirth. But despite his childish wisdom Gautama was as ignorant as any other newborn baby of the world outside his nursery.

'One day he will give up his kingdom!' cried a woman of such age and wisdom that her milky old eyes could see into the future. 'He will be a mighty teacher, greatest of all the teachers, bringing peace to countless millions!'

'Oh no, he won't!' cried the King, for Gautama was his son and his intended heir. He wanted for Gautama what every father wants – a life of ease, a life of pleasure, a life of plenty. 'My son shall be happy!' said the King.

So, when Prince Gautama went out for a chariot ride,

crowds of people lined the streets: healthy, well-fed, handsome people with smiling faces. Anyone ugly, anyone crippled or pocked by disease, anyone starving or threadbare or weeping was swept off the street, along with the dung and the litter, by squads of royal guardsmen.

The King found his son a beautiful girl to be his wife, and filled the palace with music, fountains and works of art. For all the young Prince knew, the whole world was a paradise of joy and unfailing loveliness. The gods above shook their heads and frowned.

One day, despite the efforts of the royal guards, despite the King's commands . . . and because the gods care only for the truth, Gautama went riding in his chariot. And he saw an old man, wrinkled and bent and weary from a lifetime of work.

'Who is he? *What* is he?' Gautama asked his chariot driver. 'I have never seen the like.'

Then the chariot driver could not help but explain: how everything – people and animals and plants – grow old and feeble and lose their first, youthful bloom. It is the truth; what else could the poor man say? When Gautama got home that day, he did a great deal of thinking.

Next day, despite the efforts of the soldiers, despite the King's commands, and because the gods care only for the truth, Gautama went riding again. And he saw a woman with leprosy lying beside the road, hideous and racked with pain.

'Who is she? *What* is she?' Gautama asked his chariot driver. 'I have never seen the like.'

Then the chariot driver could not help but explain: how sometimes people and animals and plants get sick and suffer pain or are born disabled or meet with terrible injuries which scar and mar their bodies. It is the truth; what else could the poor man say? Before he fell asleep that night, Gautama did a great deal of thinking.

Next day, despite the royal guards, despite the King, and because the gods care only for the truth, Gautama saw a dead body lying unburied at the roadside. 'What is that?' Gautama asked his chariot driver, seized with clammy horror. Then the chariot driver could not help but explain: how everything, everyone dies. It is the truth; what else could he say? Before the moon set that night, Gautama was a changed man.

He no longer took any pleasure in the dancing girls who tapped their tambourines and shook the golden bells at their ankles. He had no appetite for the delicious meals, no patience with the games he had once played. Taking a horse from the stable, he rode like a madman, searching for some solace in the great empty countryside beyond the city wall.

But as he rode, it seemed to him that the very fields were screaming under the sharp ploughshares of the farmers; that the woodsmen were breaking the spines of the trees with their merciless axes; that the insects in the air and worms in the soil were crying, crying, dying . . .

In a lonely glade, under the shade of a rose-apple tree, Gautama found a measure of peace. Like a man balancing a million plates, he reached a perfect stillness and balance. He saw the whole, how the world was, with all its evil, and he perceived that somewhere beyond its noisy hurtling waterfall of misery – if he could just reach through the crashing torrent – there was a place of peace and stillness.

Giving away all his jewels, all his possessions, he left his father, left his wife, left even his young son. It was no easier for him to leave them than it was for them to lose him but as he told them, 'It is the fear and pain of such partings that make life unbearable. That's why I have to go and discover a different kind of life untouched by any such sorrow.'

In his search for understanding, Gautama tried to go without food and drink, to ignore his body so that his mind could fly beyond and away from it. But starving himself only left him sleepy and weak and his thoughts cloudy and muddled. And so he bathed his poor, bony body in the river and the riverside trees reached down their branches in sheer love, to help him from the water. Gautama took food.

Later, as he walked through the forest, a giant snake, king of its breed, reared up before him, its head as high as the tallest tree. 'Today! Today, O wisest of men, you shall have what you desire! Today you will become a Buddha!'

So sitting himself down, cross-legged, under a holy tree, Gautama vowed that he would not move once more until he had grasped the reason for life itself. He practised meditation, freeing his mind like a bird from a cage, to soar through past, present and future, through place and time and all the elements.

At the sound of his whispered chanting, Mara, god of passion, fretted and raged and fumed and quaked. He summoned his sons and daughters, his troops and his weapons. '*Destroy him!*' he commanded. 'If he finds a way to rid the world of Wanting and Longing and Anger and Ambition and Greed and Fright I shall have no empire left, no more power than a blade of dead grass trodden underfoot!' At Mara's command. Thirst and Hunger, Anger and Joy and Pride and Discontent all hurled themselves at the fragile, silent, solitary man seated under the tree.

But they might as well have hurled themselves against rocks, for Gautama was beyond their reach, out of their range, his soul united with the gods, his thoughts as large as the Universe. Gautama had become a Buddha. And now, when the very word 'Buddha' is spoken, *his* is the face which fills a million minds, with its knowing, tender, smiling peace.

The Woman Who Left No Footprints

AN INUIT LEGEND

THEY HAD no children, but they had each other. And so great was the love between Umiat and Alatna that they had happiness to spare for their neighbours. An old lady lived nearby with her granddaughter, and if it had not been for the kindness of Alatna and Umiat, who knows what would have become of them during the harsh winter months? As it was, Umiat caught them meat to eat and Alatna sewed them warm clothes. That little girl spent so much time playing at their house, she might as well have been their own daughter.

Then one day, Alatna disappeared. She did not get lost, for then she would have left footprints. She did not meet with a bear, for then there would have been blood. No. Her footprints went ten paces out of the door and into the snow . . . then disappeared, as if Alatna had melted away.

Umiat was desolated. He beat on the door of every house, asking, 'Have you seen her? Did you see who took her?' But no one had seen a thing, and though the people tried to comfort him, Umiat only roared his despair at them and stamped back home. From that day on, he did not eat, could not sleep, and if anyone spoke to him, he did not answer. Someone had taken his wife away, and he no longer trusted a soul.

Then one evening the little girl came and took him by the hand. Silently she led him to her grandmother's house and the old lady said, 'You and your wife were good to us. Now it is time for us to help you.'

She gave him a magic pole, an enchanted staff of wood. 'Drive this into the snow tonight. Then tomorrow, go where it points. It will take you where your heart desires to be.'

For the first time a flicker of hope returned to the man's sallow face, and he took the stick, stroked the little girl's hair, and went home to sleep. The stick he drove into the snowdrift by his door, and sure enough in the morning it had fallen over towards the north. Umiat's one desire was to be with his wife, so he picked up the stick, put on his snowshoes and tramped north. The old woman and the little girl stood at the village edge to wish him well. 'Remember!' the old woman called. 'The name of the stick is October!'

Each time Umiat rested, he stuck the stick in a snowdrift and, each time, the stick keeled over (as sticks will that are driven into snow). But Umiat trusted the old woman's advice. And after three days' journey through the wildest terrain, the stick sensed the closeness of Alatna. It pulled free of Umiat's hand and set off at a run: it was all Umiat could do to keep up with it! End over end it poled through the snowy landscape, and Umiat sweated in his fur-lined coat with running after it.

The stick led him to a valley well hidden by fir trees and hanging cornices of snow. And in the valley stood the biggest snowhouse he had ever seen, smoke coiling from the smokehole. Outside the door hung something like a huge feathery cloak.

As Umiat watched, a man came out of the hut and lifted down the garment. As he put it on and spread his arms, Umiat could see: it was a gigantic pair of wings.

So *that* was why his wife had left no footprints! This bird-man had swooped down out of the sky and snatched her away. At the thought of it, Umiat's fists closed vengefully round the magic stick. But the bird-man had already soared into the sky and away, the sun glinting on his fishing spear.

Alatna recognized her husband's footfall and ran to the door even before he knocked. 'I knew you'd come! I knew you'd find me! Quick! We don't have long. Eagling will be back as soon as he has caught a walrus for supper. And he has such eyesight, from the air he could spot us for sure!'

'Then we'll wait for him,' said Umiat calmly, 'and buy more time.' Instead of starting back for the village at once, Umiat hid inside the snowhouse.

When, with a walrus dangling from each claw, the villain landed outside the door, Alatna went out to greet him 'Is that all you've brought me? Is that all you care for me? I said I was hungry! A couple of miserable walruses won't make me love you, you know! Now fetch me two whales and we shall see!'

So Eagling put on his wings again, despite his weariness, and flew out of the valley towards the sea. And while he was gone on this marathon journey, Umiat put Alatna on his back and they left the valley. Leaning on the magic stick now for support, Umiat strode out as fast as he could go.

But by the most disastrous stroke of luck, Eagling's return flight brought him swooping directly over their heads! A vast sperm whale dangled from each claw, and at the sight of his prisoner escaping, Eagling gave a great cry of rage and let his catch fall.

The impact half-buried Umiat and Alatna in snow, but they were not crushed. They scrambled over the huge flukes of the whales tails and made for a river gorge where there were caves to hide among. Crawling into one, they lay there holding their breath, hoping Eagling would think them crushed beneath the whales.

Eagling was not so easily fooled. He saw where they had gone, knew where they were hiding, though the narrowness of the gorge prevented him swooping on them. 'You shan't escape me so easily!' he cried in his shrill, squawking voice. And plunging his huge clawed feet into the river, he spread his wings so as to dam the flow completely.

Little by little, water piled up against his broad chest and his massive wingspan, deeper and deeper, flooding the river till it burst its banks, till the gorge began to fill up like a trough.

'Oh my dear Umiat, I'm sorry!' cried Alatna. 'You should never have tried to rescue me! Now look! I've brought death and disaster on both of us!' They held each other tight and tried to remember the happiness of their time together in the village. They thought of the little girl next door and so of the old lady who had lent Umiat the running stick . . .

'*And its name is October!*' cried Umiat, remembering all of a sudden the old woman's last words to him.

Just as the floodwater lapped in at the mouth of the cave, into its menacing, swirling depths, Umiat threw the magic stick with a cry of, 'October!'

In the second that it hit the river, the stick brought to it the month of October – that very day, that very moment in October when the rivers slow and gel throughout the arctic wilderness; when they slow and gel and fleck with silver, thicken and curdle and freeze.

Eagling, submerged up to his chin in the rising river, wings outstretched, was trapped in the freezing water as surely as a fly in amber. Umiat and Alatna stepped out on to the ice and crossed gingerly to the other side, pausing only to pull one feather defiantly from the bird-man's head.

Within the day, they came in sight of the village. And there the old lady and the little girl stood, waiting and waving.

'I'm sorry! I have lost your magic stick, Grandma!' Umiat called as soon as they were close enough to be heard.

'But you have found your heart's desire, I see,' she replied. Then, watching Alatna and the little girl hug and kiss and laugh for joy, she said, 'I think we've all found our heart's desire today!'

Sun's Son

A MYTH FROM TONGA

'Who's your father? Can't you say?
Where's your father? Gone away?'

OVER AND over the other children chanted it, until
Tau burst into tears and ran home to his mother.
'Who is my father? I must have a father! Tell me
who he is!'

His mother dried his tears. 'Take no notice. Your father
loves us both dearly, even though he can't live with us,
here.'

'Why? Why can't he? Is he dead?' His mother only
laughed at that. 'Who *is* he? You must tell me! I have a
right to know!' On and on Tau nagged until at last his
mother gave in and whispered in his ear, 'You are the son
of the Sun, my boy. He saw me on the beach one day,
loved me, shone on me, and you were born.'

She should never have told him. Tau's eyes lit up with an
inner sunlight, and he bared his teeth in a savage grin. 'I
always knew I was better than those other boys. I never
liked them, common little worms. Well, now I've done
with them. Now I'll go and find my father and see what *he*
has in mind for me!'

His mother wept and pleaded with him, but Tau
considered himself too splendid now to listen. Pushing a
canoe into the sea, he paddled towards the horizon and the
Sun's rising place. 'Tell your father I still love him!' his
mother called.

As the Sun came up, Tau shouted into his face, *'Father!'*
'Who calls me that?'

'I! Tau! Your son! I've come to find you and be with you!'

'You can't live with me, child! My travelling has no end. I have always to light the islands and the oceans!'

'Then at least stay and talk to me now!' called Tau.

And the Sun was so moved to see his human son, that he actually drew the clouds round him and paused for a brief time over the drifting canoe. 'I suppose you will become a great chief on Tongatabu when you grow up,' said the Sun proudly.

'Stay on Tongatabu?' sneered Tau. 'Among all those common people? Not me! I want to ride the sky with you each day!'

'I regret, you cannot,' said the Sun. 'But you are lucky. There's nowhere lovelier than Tongatabu and no one sweeter than your mother . . . I must go now. The world expects it of me.'

'Is that all you can say?' retorted Tau resentfully. 'Is that all it's worth, to be the son of the Sun?'

The Sun was rising from the ocean now, shedding his disguise of cloud, shining brighter, and brighter, hurrying to make up time. 'Tonight my sister the Moon will rise in the sky. She will offer you the choice of two presents. One is brotherhood, the other glory. Choose brotherhood, my son! For my sake and for your dear mother: choose brotherhood! It will make you happy!' His booming voice receded to the bronze clashing of a gong, as the Sun reached his zenith in the noon sky.

'Brotherhood, pah! He wants me to be like all those others,' said Tau aloud to himself. 'He wants me to forget who I really am and be mediocre, like the rest. He doesn't want me. He doesn't care one coconut about me.' Full of self-pity, Tau curled up and went to sleep in the bottom of the canoe.

He was woken by a piercing white whistle which made him sit bolt upright. There in the sky, like a mother's face looming over a cradle, the Moon his aunt looked down on

him. 'Have you come to give me my present?' he asked
rudely.

She scowled at him. 'Who do you take after? It isn't
your mother and it certainly isn't your father. But yes, I
have a present for you. Tell me, which do you want?'

Hanging down from her horns, like the pans of a pair of
scales, hung two identical packages. Neither was big and
neither was recognizable for what it was. 'This is glory,
and this is brotherhood,' said the Moon.

'Give me glory!' barked Tau.

'Think, nephew. One of these gifts will do you good,
one will bring you harm. Please choose carefully!'

'I told you already!' said Tau. 'I know what my father
wants: he wants to forget all about me. He wants me to go
back home and forget who I really am – prince of the sky!
He's afraid that if I take glory I'll be greater than him –
burn him out of the sky. That's what. Give me glory! Give
it now!'

She reached out the other package – brotherhood – but
he paddled his canoe directly into her round silver
reflection on the sea's surface, and scratched it, so that in
pain she let drop her other hand. Snatching the parcel
called 'glory', Tau hugged it to his chest.

He ripped off the wrappings and there, as beautiful as
anything he had ever seen, was a seashell round and red
and luminous as a setting sun. 'Now I shall be a god,' said
Tau. 'Now I shall be worshipped instead of doing the
worshipping. Now everyone on Tongabatu will bow down
and worship *me!*'

But first the fish came to worship Tau.

Startled by a sudden rushing noise, he looked up and
saw the surface of the ocean bubbling and churning, as
every fish for miles around came shoaling towards the
magic of the red shell. Dolphins and flying fish leapt clean
over the canoe. Sharks and tunny herded close, rubbing
their sharp scales against the boat in ecstasies of adoration.
The spike of a marlin holed the boat. The fluke of a whale

struck the sea and showered Tau in spray. Shoals of tiny, glimmering fish sped the frail vessel along on a carpet of colour, while ray flapped darkly out of the water to trail their wings over the canoe's nose.

'No! Get away! You'll drag it under! Get off the canoe!'

But the fish were in a frenzy of worship, entranced by the glory Tau held clenched in one hand. The canoe was swamped in seconds and plummeted down from under him. And although Tau was carried along for a time, on the writhing ecstasy of the fish, as soon as the red shell slipped from his hand, they let him go, let him sink. Thanks to the shark, his body was never found: he who would have been elected Chief of Tongabatu, if only he had valued his fellow men. If only he had chosen brotherhood.

Biggest

A JAPANESE LEGEND

WHEN THE people of Kamakura decided to cast a statue of the Buddha, their love for him was so enormous that the finished masterpiece was the biggest in the world. Cast in gleaming bronze, it caught the sun's light like the burnished waves of the evening sea – until, that is, a temple was built to house it, a temple rising almost to the sky. The statue towered over the people who had made it, and they were full of wonder, for they were sure they had never cast the look of calm and kindness on the huge bronze face. News spread through the whole world that the Buddha of Kamakura was the biggest, the loveliest, the most wonderful thing under the heavens.

When word reached the Whale, the Whale said, 'Nonsense!' It shook so hard with scornful laughter that waves slopped against fifteen shores. But on every one of those shores, fishermen mending their nets were busy talking to each other about the wonder at Kamakura: '. . . It's the biggest, the loveliest, the most wonderful thing under the heavens, you know . . .'

'But *I* am the biggest, the loveliest, the most wonderful creature under the heavens,' said the vain creature. 'That's how I know these stories cannot be true!'

Still, the rumours played on his mind, until he could bear it no longer. With a whistle, he summoned his friend the Shark and asked him, 'Can there be any truth in these stories?'

'I'll find out,' said the Shark, and swam to the shore of the ocean at Kamakura. From the water's edge she could see the new temple rising almost to the sky. 'That must house the Buddha,' she thought. 'Big! But how big! And how can I find out? I can't swim up the beach or swing from tree to tree.'

Just as she was about to give up, a small rat came scuttling by with a fishhead in its jaws. 'Sir! Would you do me the very great favour of going up to that temple over there and measuring the statue inside it?'

'The Buddha?' said the rat. 'Certainly! It's always a pleasure to go there. It is the biggest, loveliest, most marvellous thing under the heavens, you know.' Away trotted the rat, up the hill, in under the temple door, and round the base of the statue.

Five thousand paces! The Shark shook and shivered at the sheer sound of the words. Five thousand paces? What would the Whale say?

'*Five thousand paces?* From where to where? From nose to tail? From stem to stern? Whose paces, and how long is their stride? Believe the word of a rat? Never!' That was what the Whale said.

But though he tried to ignore the news, he could not put it out of his mind.

'There's nothing for it,' he said at last. 'I'll just have to go and see this pipsqueak for myself.'

And so he took down from the Continental Shelf his magical boots, and put them on.

The tides rose high that night. Rivers flowed upstream, waves broke with such a surge that seaweed was left hanging in the trees. Moonlit meadows were flooded with saltwater, when the Whale waded ashore that night, in his magic boots. Dripping and glistening, he rolled his blubbery way up the hill and slapped with one fin on the great carved temple doors.

The priests were all sleeping, so no one heard him knock. No one, that is, but the Buddha, dully luminous in the candlelit dark. The candle flames trembled, as a voice like distant thunder said, '*Come in!*'

'I can't come in,' said the Whale. 'I am too vast, too

huge, too magnificent to cram myself into this little kennel!'

'Very well, then, I shall come out,' said the Buddha mildly, and by bending very low, he was just able to squeeze through the temple doors. As he straightened up again, the Whale blinked his tiny eyes with shock. The Buddha, too, stared with wonder at the sight of a Whale in magic boots.

The noise of the temple gongs vibrating woke a priest. Glancing towards the Buddha's bronze pedestal he saw, to his horror, that the statue, the precious wonderful, adored statue, was gone! Had thieves come in the night! Had the Buddha sickened of so many curious visitors? The priest ran shouting out of the temple. 'Help! Quick! The Buddha is . . . is . . .'

There, eclipsing the moon, stood two gigantic figures, deep in conversation amid a strong fishy smell.

'The very person we need!' said the Buddha, spotting the priest. 'Perhaps you would be so kind, sir, as to settle a small query for this excellent cetacean? Could you please measure us both?'

The priest fumbled about him for something, anything he could use for measuring. Untying his belt, he used that. One . . . two . . . three . . . scribbling his measurements in the soft ground with a stick.

When he had finished, the priest fretted and fluttered, he stuttered and stammered: 'I sincerely regret . . . I'm dreadfully sorry . . . I can't lie, you see, I have to tell the truth, your divinity . . . but the Whale is two inches bigger than you.'

'Knew it!' The Whale whirled round in his magic boots, shaking the ground, setting all the temple bells jangling in the breeze he made as he blew out triumphantly through his blow-hole. 'I knew it! I knew I was the biggest, grandest, most marvellous creature beneath the heavens! Never doubted it for a moment!' And away he strode, leaving a smell of fish in the air and large, deep bootprints in the ground.

'Oh master, are you very distressed?' the priest asked of the statue. 'We could fetch more bronze and make your feet thicker, your forehead higher!'

The Buddha smiled a peaceable smile, utterly unconcerned by the night's events. 'It means nothing to me and much to him that he should be the biggest. Think nothing of it. I am very content to be as I am. Please don't lose another moment's sleep over it.'

The priest mopped his brow and crept back inside the temple. A handful of peaceful words followed him, fragrant with the scent of the blossoms outside.

'Besides . . . the Whale has still to take off his boots.'

'I Love You, Prime Minister!'

A FRENCH LEGEND

THE EMPEROR Charlemagne conquered the world . . . then was conquered himself by a woman. He fell in love with Princess Frastrada from the easternmost regions of his vast Empire, and such was his passion for her, his adoration, that Prime Minister Turpin always suspected some magic at the bottom of it.

Frastrada was beautiful, gentle and good, but was she so far above every other woman, that Charlemagne the Mighty gazed at her all day long, could not bear to be apart from her, took her on every campaign, and invited her to every conference of state? Turpin had his doubts.

When Frastrada died, he was certain. Somehow she had cast a spell over Charlemagne, and the magic did not even end with her death. Now the Emperor sat by her body, rocking and groaning, cradling Frastrada in his arms and wetting her cold face with his tears. All government was forgotten, all affairs of state let go. He would not eat or drink, nor leave the room where her body lay; would not permit the Princess to be buried.

The Prime Minister could not let this unhealthy state of affairs go on. So when at last the distracted Emperor fell asleep across the bed, exhausted with crying, Turpin tiptoed in and began to search. He did not know what he was looking for – what charm, what amulet, what magic hieroglyph – but he searched all the same, until just before dawn, he glimpsed something in the dead Princess's mouth.

Poor Frastrada. Her love for Charlemagne had been so desperate, that she had begged her eastern men of magic for a charm: something which would ensure her all-powerful husband never tired of her. They forged her a magic ring. Growing ill, realizing she was about to die, Frastrada looked at the ring on her hand and wondered what would become of it. Would another woman wear it and be loved by Charlemagne as much as Frastrada had been loved? No! The thought was unbearable. So, in the hope of remaining the one true love of Charlemagne's life, she slipped the ring into her mouth just as Death stole her last breath.

'Who's there? Frastrada? What—' Charlemagne was stirring.

Turpin, sooner than be found robbing the dead Empress, slipped the ring on to his own finger just as his master sat up, fuddled with sleep. Charlemagne opened his eyes and saw his . . .

'Dearest Prime Minister!'

'Good morning, my lord.'

'How wonderful to see you! I'd forgotten how very handsome you are. What, hasn't this woman been buried yet? How remiss. Oh, Prime Minister! Oh dear, *dear* Prime Minister, may I just say what a comfort it is, at a time like this, to have a man like you by me I can rely on.' And flinging both arms round Turpin, Charlemagne dragged him away to breakfast.

Inwardly Turpin crowed with delight. He had saved the Emperor from dying of grief, and therefore saved the Empire from crumbling into chaos. Besides, all Turpin's advice would now sound as sweet as poetry in Charlemagne's ears. He got permission for his favourite road-building schemes, he got laws passed, he got posts at the palace for all his friends and relations . . . not to mention the presents – horses, chariots, a few small countries . . . All because he was wearing the magic ring.

Even so, after a time Turpin began to wish that perhaps the ring were not *quite* so powerful. Just when he wanted some peace and quiet, the Emperor always wanted to talk, to hold hands, to listen to music with his dear Prime Minister. On campaign, Turpin had to sleep in the Emperor's tent. And the generals in the army, the princes, the kings of minor provinces gave him very odd looks as Charlemagne stroked his hair and bounced Turpin on his knee. Turpin's wife was put out, as well.

In fact, Turpin began to be extremely sorry he had ever put on the ring. But how could he be rid of it? Give it to someone else? No! That someone would be ruling the Empire before long, whispering new policies in the Emperor's ear and being given all the privileges of a . . . well . . . a prime minister.

Could he bury it? What if Charlemagne became rooted to the spot where the ring was buried, fell passionately in love with a garden bed or half a metre of desert sand? What if Turpin were to drop it in the sea? Would Charlemagne hurl himself into a watery grave?

Turpin examined the ring with utmost care. Around the inside was engraved an inscription: 'From the moon came my magic; in the moon my magic ends.' Had the ring fallen from the moon, then? Oh no! How could a mere prime minister return it there? Night after night, Turpin walked sleepless around palace or camp, turning the problem over in his mind.

One moony night, when the imperial army was camped in a forest, Turpin crept from the Emperor's tent, desperate for a little solitude. He wandered among the trees, a broken man. He simply could not stomach one more poem composed to the beauty of his nose, one more statue of him raised in a public place, one more candlelit supper where Charlemagne gazed at him – 'How I love you, Prime Minister!' – all through the meal. Enough was enough. Turpin resolved to run away.

But just then, he found himself beside a lake. It was large and smooth, with a reflection of the moon floating at its heart. Impetuously Turpin pulled off the ring. A little smudge of gold flew over the water. A small splash at the centre of the moon's reflection set ripples spreading. The ring was gone for ever.

Dawn came up while Turpin walked back to the Emperor's tent. As he lifted the flap, the sunlight fell across Charlemagne's face and roused him.

'Yes, Turpin?' said the great man, raising himself on one elbow. '*Must* you bring me problems of state quite so early in the morning? What is it?'

Turpin bowed low respectfully and backed out, letting the tentflap fall. 'Nothing, my lord. Nothing that cannot wait.'

Outside, Turpin gave a little skip and a hop. The spell was broken. He was a free man, a happy man – apart from the explaining he had to do to his wife.

The army struck camp, the Emperor mounted up, and a thousand banners fluttered on their way through the forest. Within the hour, they came to the lake. 'Stop!' cried Charlemagne. Turpin chewed anxiously on his glove. The Emperor gazed about him, one hand over his heart, smiling open-mouthed with wonder. 'I've never seen anywhere like it! What do you say, Turpin? Isn't this the loveliest spot you ever saw?'

'Magical, my lord.'

His knights and courtiers looked about him, puzzled. Pretty, yes, but a tree is a tree and a lake is a lake. But Charlemagne, not realizing that the drowned ring was still working its magic, found the forest clearing too ravishingly beautiful for words. He could not tear himself away. All day long he strolled its shores, picked flowers from its banks.

'I shall build a palace here, my greatest palace, my home. One day, when the world is all mine, I'll live here, I'll be happy here. If only Frastrada could have seen this place . . .'

True to his word, Charlemagne did build a palace in the forest, beside the lake, and whenever war and politics permitted, he lived there. A little town grew up around the palace – Aix-la-Chapelle it was called – and wherever

Charlemagne travelled, however far afield, he never could quite put Aix from his mind. No more than he could ever quite forget his dear dead wife, Frastrada.

And the Rains Came Tumbling Down

A MYTH FROM PAPUA NEW GUINEA

'WHAT WE need are houses,' said Kikori.

'What's one of those?' said Fly (since houses had not yet been invented).

'Somewhere to shelter from wind and sun and rain – other than this cave, I mean, with its spiders.'

Fly pretended to be unimpressed, but liked the idea. Kikori suggested they build a house together, but Fly had ideas of his own about building the very first house and he was sure they were the best.

Kikori built a wood frame, then wove the leaves of the rei plant into five glossy waterproof mats: one for a roof and four for the walls. It was laborious, painful work. The sharp leaves cut his hands and irritated his skin, but the finished house was so fine that his family broke into spontaneous clapping.

Not Fly. He had long since finished his house and returned to watch, with much shaking of his head and carping. 'How long you took! Look at your hands. Makes me itch just to think. And it's *green*. Do you seriously think people want to live in green houses?'

'How did you make yours, then?' said Kikori patiently.

Kikori examined Fly's house, his head on one side then on the other. Fly's framework of branches had been daubed all over with mud. The mud had dried into clay, and now the hut crouched on the ground like a collapsed beast, bony with protruding sticks.

'What happens when it rains?' said Kikori.

At that moment, a clap of thunder sent them both darting back to their huts, mustering their wives and children. The monsoon broke as if the green sky had split, and the rains came, as they come every year to Papua New Guinea. Every view was lost from sight behind a curtain of rain. Every sound was silenced by the deafening hiss of the downpour.

Inside Kikori's house, he and his family sat listening to the thunderous rattle of water on rei. But the interwoven leaves threw off the rain as surely as a tortoise's shell, and they stayed warm and dry. They sang songs and planned which crops to plant in the sodden earth.

Fly, too, sat with his family inside his new house. The rain ran down its brown sides, and gradually the clay walls turned back to mud around them. The mud oozed and trickled. It slopped down like cow pats on to Fly and his wife and children, smothering them from head to foot in brown slurry.

But not for long. Soon so much icy rain was pouring through the roof that they were washed quite clean again. The children's teeth chattered, his wife moaned gently to herself, ground her teeth and wrung out her hair. When the rain slackened briefly, she went out with a panga and cut a great pile of rei leaves, dropping them down at the door.

'When you've made a house like Kikori's,' she said, 'I and the little ones will come and share it with you. In the meantime, we're going back to the cave.'

Fly, as he sat ankle-deep in mud, contemplated the unfairness of life and whether he ought to invent dry rain.

Four Worlds and a Broken Stone

A NATIVE AMERICAN MYTH

THE PEOPLE of Peace will tell you that three worlds existed before this one, and before that a Nothingness flowing from never to ever.

Taiowa, though invisible himself and without form, pictured a solid universe. So he created a creator – Sotuknang – to be its architect. Sotuknang shaped the First World, called Endless Space, and into it, down a thread as fine as one of his own hairs, dropped Spider Woman, fat with the eggs of magic. Those eggs hatched into the very first people.

If you met them, of course, you would hardly recognize them as kin. There is not much of a family resemblance. For they, those most ancient of our ancestors, never grew old, never spoke, and never hunted the animals with whom they shared Endless Space. Also, they had no tops to their heads. Taiowa was able to drop wisdom into their minds like golden honey off a spoon. No learning by their mistakes, no puzzling or studying, no struggling with the meaning of things. Understanding came to them as sweetly as honey, and in among it were the seeds of language.

After a while, the People of Endless Space were muttering to one another, passing comment on the world around them. The animals, alarmed by this new secret, tried to speak themselves. But beaks and muzzles and snouts are not made for more than calling a mate, warning of danger. Noticing the difference between them, the animals drew away, hid among the trees and down burrows, thinking, 'They are ganging up against us.'

Far from it. The People of Endless Space no sooner had language than they began to quarrel – to lie, to boast, to curse and shout insults. Some drew away from the rest, hoarding their treasure of words like money they begrudged spending.

Sotuknang was disgusted. Like a blacksmith who throws bad work back on to the forge, he lit a fire under that world called Endless Space, and burned it to the ground.

The people saw the flicker of fire, and there was sweet wisdom enough in their heads for them to observe the animals, and learn from them. When they saw the ants run underground, the people followed, sheltering deep under the earth from the inferno. When they emerged, a Second World had been built: a world called Dark Midnight. It was gloomy and a little scary. At either end – at North Pole and South – sat giant brothers, steadying the globular world.

Living underground had forced shut the people's open-topped heads somewhat, so now they found it harder to understand what the gods wanted them to do. Still, one or two things they did invent which Sotuknang had never even thought of. For example, instead of sharing everything, they *sold* what they had for money, or exchanged it for goods. 'What do you mean, you can't afford it?' they would say. 'Nothing comes for free in this life!' They began to haggle, to cheat one another, to steal what they could not afford. Soon the streets of the world were full of people crying their wares.

They sold food to the animals and sold the animals to each other. They sold the land they stood on and the water in the rivers. In the world called Dark Midnight, they sold candles to one another, and complained that times had been better once, in the world of Endless Space.

'Enough!' said Sotuknang. 'Twin of the North! Twin of

the South! Leave your places! The mind of God requires *Change!'*

Twice the earth rolled over, as the Twins let go of its axletree. The round world was as shaken as a pebble in the surf. Oceans slopped over the dry land. Cargo ships far out to sea were picked up and dashed down on market-places miles inland. The deserts drowned, and with them the scaly salamanders and crackling locusts. Freshwater rivers were lost in a saltwater surge, and with them the herons and the turtles.

But the people – some of them at least – had the wit to follow the ants below ground again. And the sea had no sooner withdrawn than out they crawled to inspect the Third World left by the tidal waves: Kuskuara.

Ideal building land. They shaped adobe, they made mud bricks, they cut stone blocks and cut down timber. They built cities in wood and stone and brick and clay, with houses and temples, meeting halls and silos. Before long, someone said:

'Our city is better than your city.'

'Our land stretches to the horizon!'

Banners declared: 'Trespassers will be stoned. Keep out.'

Generals proclaimed: 'We must fight for what we believe in!'

The people answered: 'WAR!'

From the bones of trees and the feathers of birds, they built flying machines, and swooped over rival cities showering them with rocks and pitch. Their enemies built newer flying machines to do combat in mid-air with the bomber flying machines, and when flying machines crashed on to the crowded cities, ran with buckets to put out the fires.

At last there were so many fires that only Sotuknang could put them out. His tears swelled the oceans until the oceans joined hands and bled one into another. Whole cities, whole city-realms drowned – even the ants beneath them. Whole continents softened into mud and slid away, and with them the shape and existence of Kuskuara.

But the people – some of them at least – had had the wit to climb into hollow reeds and float away on the rising water. Bobbing about over acres of ocean, the survivors of Kuskuara kept a lookout for land. But there was no land left. Seagulls perched on the reeds and, riding out the flood alongside them, flew in search of dry land. But they came winging back, beaks outstretched, sagging wearily into the wave troughs, exhausted for want of solid ground to rest on.

'Peace, peace,' said Spider Woman. 'I who saw Endless Space and Dark Midnight, who saw Kuskuara come and Kuskuara go, shall live to see more worlds yet. For if the mind of Taiowa wishes a world to exist, then he won't rest till he has succeeded.'

She was right, of course. One morning they looked out across the oceans and saw land. The Fourth World had come into being: World Complete.

Standing on the shore was a gigantic man – huge, terrifying, his eyes alight with visions he was seeing in his head, and in his hands a hammer and chisel such as sculptors use to carve rock.

'Come ashore!' he told them. 'I am Masaw, Guardian of the World Complete. Come ashore! I have things to tell you.'

Masaw had dreamed dreams. Though the top of his head was closed, the gods had found surer ways of imparting wisdom to this wise giant. He took them inland to a place called Four Corners – a desert landscape planted with towers of dark rock. On one such mesa, Masaw had carved the story of his dreams. The people threw down their bundles of belongings and began to scrape together the dirt for building homesteads.

'No!' said Masaw. 'Not yet! You are not yet fit to settle in the Complete World! You have truths to learn, wonders to see, problems to solve.' Picking up a large flat stone, he broke it, as easily as a biscuit, into four equal parts. Then he parted the people into four groups according to the colour of their skins – red, yellow, white and black – and gave each group one fragment of the stone. To North, South, East and West he sent them, far and wide over the face of the Complete World. 'Come back when you have done journeying and meanwhile remember just one thing.'

'What must we remember?' asked everyone, eager to obey.

'Never to forget,' replied Masaw.

First to come home were the red tribe. Long before the continental plates bumped and groaned into their present positions, the red tribe were back, building their villages around the Black Mesa, calling themselves the Hopi, which means 'Peace'. They read Masaw's carvings now and trembled: his dream carvings spoke of unspeakable terrors to come. But what, and why?

When the white tribe came back, they had forgotten everything – their piece of stone, the words of Masaw, their narrow escape from fire and flood. They did not recognize the red tribe as their brothers – nor the yellow, nor the black. In fact, they came home armed with guns and swords and firebrands, ready to fight or kill or capture anyone who stood in their way. They peered at the Black Mesa with eyes as blind as drunkards, seeing only a jumble of words and pictures, understanding nothing.

'See here?' said the Hopi gently, 'this bowl of ashes falling out of the sky? It will scorch the dry land and set the oceans boiling!'

But the white tribe could only see scribbles and scrawls.

Now, luckily, it is your turn. Look closer. See that blue star drawn on the Black Mesa? One night, when the Fourth World has burned down, wick and wax, and left only a puff of smoke behind, the time will have come for a Fifth World, a final world, just as Taiowa intended, just as

Sokutnang wished, just as Masaw dreamed, just as the People of Peace long for. See that blue star? Watch for it. Everything else has happened just as Masaw said it would. So watch out for the blue star rising.

The Needlework Teacher and the Secret Baby

A EUROPEAN LEGEND

WHEN Anzius was Emperor of Constantinople, a certain Prince Hugh, of the royal house of Ameling, came to manhood. His father was dead; it was time for Hugh to take up his rightful position as king. But he had no sooner grown *up* than he began to grow his hair *down*. He sent for a seamstress and had dresses made. He also took up embroidery. What his family and friends thought, who knows?

Now when Hugh set his mind to a thing, he never gave up. So soon there was no finer 'needlewoman' in all Europe than Prince Hugh of the long-flowing hair and longer frocks.

He had his reasons, of course. Hugh had heard tell of a princess – Princess Hilde – most beautiful, most intelligent, and most wronged of women. For her father had sworn she should never marry, and had shut her away in a tower, out of reach of ambitious men like Hugh. Nothing but rumours about her escaped that tower-palace, like bees escaping a hive.

It was not done out of cruelty. Her father Walgund loved his daughter. Perhaps he loved her too much to share her. Perhaps he thought his brick-built tower and brass locks could keep out Death. For in those days, Death roamed as free and common as the wolves in the great green forests.

Hugh set his heart on having the mysterious princess for his wife. So he travelled to Walgund's realm of Thessaly and, putting on his prettiest dress, presented himself at Walgund's castle with gifts of gold and embroidered linen. He said he was a refugee – a noblewoman orphaned by war, without a friend in the world.

Walgund was a chivalrous man; he could hardly turn the noblewoman away (even if she did make him uneasy, standing three spans taller than he). Besides, his wife had seen the lady's embroidery. 'Oh, such artistry! You simply must teach our daughter Hilde how to sew like this!' she said.

Hugh did.

Princess Hilde took a liking to her needlework teacher which startled even her. Perhaps it was that deep, rich voice, or the strength of those big hands guiding Hilde's fingers over the canvas. Or was it the unusual *smell* of that long coarse yellow hair? Within days, they were the best of friends.

So Hugh taught Hilde his best secret of all. 'I have to admit, I'm not quite what I seem . . .' he whispered, grasping her hand and laying it against the roughness of his unshaven cheek.

The weeks which followed were blissfully happy. Hilde secretly married her needlework teacher, and they spent all day together inside the grim High Tower. Then one day Hugh said, 'I must go home now and tell my ministers that I've found the perfect wife to be my queen. Then I must find some way to persuade your father to bless our marriage. Trust me: I'll be back before you even miss me!' And he cut his long hair and left a hank of it in her trembling fingers. He exchanged his dress for a shirt and trousers he had sewn himself, and slipped away from Thessaly and the High Tower.

But Hugh did not come back in days or even weeks. Though Hilde sighed sighs and wept tears and yearned with all her heart, he did not come. Even nine months later, as she secretly gave birth to a baby in the loneliness of her stone prison, there was no sign of Prince Hugh, though she never lost faith in his promise and her love never wavered.

Naturally she could not keep such a secret all by herself. She told Joan, her most loyal and trusted waiting woman, who came and went with rattles and shawls and washing, and a broad smile on her lips. When the Queen made her daily visit to the High Tower to see her daughter, Joan would smuggle the baby away and hide him, so there was no risk of the Queen hearing him cry. Together Joan and Hilde kept secret the very existence of the baby boy. 'What shall you call him, lady?' asked Joan.

'His father can name him when he returns,' said the Princess, for she never gave up hope that Hugh would come back and claim her for his queen.

So where was Hugh? What business of state could possibly keep him so long from the beautiful Hilde? Nothing but war – a dire and deadly war, which spread like plague sores over the whole body of Europe. Soon even King Walgund was riding out to do battle with the enemy, and in the course of the war, found himself fighting side by side with Prince Hugh.

The war ended. Weary and scarred, but triumphant, a dozen armies turned for home. Peace settled like summer dust over the hills and shores of Thessaly. Hugh travelled home with Walgund. A thousand times he had it in his mind to say, 'I love your daughter. Take me for your son-in-law.' But the time never seemed quite right.

Hilde woke with a start to hear running footsteps on the stairs. 'Joan! Joan, quick! Someone's coming! Take the baby and hide him!'

They passed in the doorway, Joan and the Queen. The Queen never suspected that the bundle of washing in Joan's arms was really her grandchild.

'Hilde! Hilde! get up. Get dressed. Wonderful news! Your father has sent word: he's coming home today! He has friends with him. There'll be banqueting tonight; help me prepare. Think of it, child! The war's over!'

Down the stairs hurried the old nurse, and out at the postern gate. She waded downhill into the deep grass beside the castle moat, and there she laid down the sleeping baby. 'Sleep a while longer, little darling. I'll come back for you in two chimes of the church bell.'

But on the stairs, she met the Queen coming down, and the Queen had things for Joan to do. 'Wash the royal bedlinen and sharpen the King's razor. Mull him some ale, and strew fresh herbs on the floor of the Great Hall. Then go and tell the poultryman to kill some geese for dinner – oh, and gather may branches to decorate the castle.' In fact, she kept the old nurse busy till long after midday.

The very first moment she could, Joan slipped out of the postern gate and down towards the moat. She was worried sick about the baby – big enough to crawl, to cram poisonous berries into his mouth, to grab at wasps. She parted the grass. She parted it again. She stood and listened to the flies hatching on the surface of the moat. But there was neither sight nor sound of the baby, no trail nor trace. It was as if he had never been born. In the distance, the great dark forest seemed to raise its branches in anguish and rend its green hair.

As Walgund rode through the forest, he breathed deep the familiar smells of home. He could just glimpse the tip of the tower he had built to house his beloved Hilde.

'If you ever have a daughter, Prince Hugh, take my advice and lock her in above five storeys of stone and behind seventeen doors of oak. Have her taught needlework and music and solitaire. Then she can't break your heart or her own.'

'She might die of boredom,' said Hugh under his breath, but King Walgund did not hear: he had just glimpsed the fleeting grey streak of a running wolf, and his sword was already half out of its sheath. Walgund dug in his spurs and his horse leapt forwards.

But the horse's hooves all but trampled the she-wolf's den. Five, six, seven wolfcubs, with teeth like needles and eyes as bright as mercury, rolled and wrestled and yelped in a furry heap, and there in the midst of them, a little boy baby sat snatching at their tails and rubbing his face against their fur, laughing with delight.

'By the saints! What a boy!' whispered Walgund, breathless with amazement. 'What I'd give to have a grandson like that!'

Hugh's heart leapt into his throat. 'How?' he wanted to shout out. *'How will you ever have any grandchild at all, unless you let Hilde marry?'*

But just as the words formed on his lips, back came the she-wolf, terrible, murderous, and Hugh did the only thing he could. He leapt out of the saddle and snatched the baby from between the wolf's very jaws.

'Look what we found in the forest, my dear!' called Walgund to his queen as he rode in under the portcullis. 'A wolf child!'

Not only his wife but his daughter came out to see, and yet it was a daughter Walgund scarcely recognized. Her hair was wild and loose, her face white, her eyes swollen from crying.

'She must have missed me a great deal,' thought Walgund.

'She must have thought I was never coming back,' thought Hugh.

Hilde ran towards the men, arms outstretched and shrieking.

'She must have thought I was dead,' thought Walgund.

'She's going to give away our secret!' thought Prince Hugh.

But Hilde ignored both men. She saw only her little boy – the one she had searched for all afternoon, the one she had thought drowned in the moat or eaten by wild beasts.

Pulling him out of Hugh's arms, she covered him with kisses, laughing and crying both at once. The Queen stared. Walgund stared. Hugh stared. But Joan just smiled.

When everything was explained to Walgund, he brooded a long time before he spoke. 'A man may look to his children for obedience,' he said at last, 'but he'll be disappointed. A man may look to his children for surprises: they're guaranteed. A man can ask his daughter to live without love . . . But then how can she give him a splendid grandson like this? Let his name be Wolf! . . . that's if you agree, Prince Hugh.'

'His name shall be Wolf,' said Prince Hugh, 'if mine can be "son-in-law".'

'Then I've gained a son and a grandson, all in one day!' exclaimed Walgund. 'And there aren't two boys in all Christendom I would be more proud to come by!'

Culloch and the Big Pig

A CELTIC LEGEND

CULLOCH was cursed with the curse of Love. His wicked stepmother doomed him, out of magic spite, to love Olwen, daughter of Ysbaddaden. And the curse was no sooner spoken than Culloch fell madly in love – even though he knew neither the colour of Olwen's eyes nor the features of her face. For all he knew, she might take after her giant father and stand head-high to the hills.

'Giant' is not a big enough word to describe Ysbaddaden, for he never sat in one room of his castle but he filled three – one with his head, one with his body and one with his legs. His hair, all unkempt and uncombed, filled a fourth.

As Culloch rode up to the castle, he was greeted by Olwen herself – a comely girl, scarcely two-storeys tall. Cramming her plaits into her mouth in anxiety, she pleaded, 'Turn back! Turn back! No one has ever asked for my hand and lived! For on the day that I marry, it is prophesied my father shall die!'

Pausing only a moment to gaze into Olwen's eyes, Culloch went straight inside. He thought, when he first entered, that Ysbaddaden was asleep. But servants came running with two enormous forked sticks with which they propped open the giant's eyelids.

'What do you want and why are you here?' Ysbaddaden asked in a slurred voice, as if his tongue were similarly heavy.

'Your blessing and the hand of your daughter, sir!'

'Didn't you know?' said Ysbaddaden. 'She weds. I'm dead. It's written in the stars.'

'I'm truly sorry to hear that,' said Culloch. 'But your life seems wearisome to you, anyway, or why do you lie on your face in the straw?'

'I only lie on my face because my hair hangs so heavy. Come back tomorrow, and you shall have my answer.'

Culloch felt he could spare one day, and turned to go. But Ysbaddaden snatched up a sharpened wooden spear, and threw it at Culloch's unprotected back. Cunning Culloch spun round, snatched the spear out of the air and threw it back the way it had come. It struck Ysbaddaden on the knee – 'Ouch!' – but Culloch said nothing, simply walked out into the yard.

When he returned next day, Ysbaddaden had thought up a string of excuses. 'I'm busy. I'm not well. I never see visitors on any day with a T in it. Come back tomorrow.' As Culloch turned to go, the giant threw another spear. This time its point was smeared thick with poison that spattered and scorched the floor as it flew. Culloch caught the spear, spun it round one finger and flung it back the way it had come. It stuck Ysbaddaden in the hand – 'Argh!' – and his groans followed Culloch out of the castle.

Next day, Ysbaddaden, swathed in bandages, began to make more excuses. 'The stars are not favourable. I never liked Wednesdays . . .' but Culloch interrupted him.

'I think we should discuss terms, before you get hurt any more. What must I do to win your daughter? Name it!'

'Very well,' said Ysbaddaden. 'Fetch me the means to cut my hair.'

'That's simple! I'll borrow my cousin Arthur's sword, Excalibur!' said Culloch at once.

But Ysbaddaden shook his fearful head, and set his hair tumbling through all the chambers and anterooms of his castle, lively with lice. 'My hair can only be cut with the magic comb and shears of the Great Pig Troit. Fetch them, and Olwen is yours!' And he smiled at the thought of a task so plainly impossible.

'Now *that* is a quest befitting the Knights of the Round Table!' declared King Arthur, as his young cousin knelt before him in the throne room of Camelot. 'We shall help you, Culloch, and you shall have your bride!'

Arthur and his knights rode with Culloch to the far coast of Wales. When the Great Pig Troit saw the brightness of their armour, saw the boar-spears in their hands, he sharpened his tusks and pawed the ground. 'You may have found me,' said the Boar, 'but now you have to catch me!'

Twrch Troit was no ordinary boar, nor had he always been one. Once he had been a king. But his nature was so evil and his sins so many that they had pushed their way out through his skin – at first like black stubble at his chin, then as thick black bristles all over his body. His dog-teeth had grown into tusks, and his crimes had weighed him down, till he could only move on all fours: a man transmogrified into a boar. It was not hard to find him, for he left a trail behind him of crumpled trees, of houses stove in, of gored hillsides and trampled flour mills.

Now Troit ran down the coastline of Dyfed, past Blaenplwyf and Cei-bach beach, across Ynys-Lochtyn point towards Strumble Head, then inland among the Preseli Hills. Up the watercourses of Taf and Cynin and down the valleys of Tywi, into the Black Mountain crags he ran. Past Castle Cennen they chased that Big Pig, and over the Brecon hills where Troit paused for breath.

'Hold, Troit! We mean to have those shears and comb from between your ears, but you may keep your golden crown and that ugliness you call your face!' bellowed King Arthur.

'The shears and comb are my treasure!' replied Troit in a snarl strung with saliva. 'Before I part with them, I shall carve you into such shapes your own womenfolk will not recognize you!' And he charged, scattering the knights and leaving the prints of his iron hoofs cut in the Beacons for ever. Then he was off again, darting and dodging through the Vale of Ebbw, across Arthur's own estates of Caerleon.

Beating their spears on their shields and loosing blood-curdling yells, the Knights of the Round Table barely paused for breath. Though their caparisons were muddy and their cloaks spiked with thorns, though their faces were masked with dust, and their horses mantled with bracken and ivy, they drove the giant boar over flat water-meadows. Ahead lay the River Severn as big as the sea.

Through the shallows, from sandbar to mudbank, the boar staggered until, on the shoals called Middle Ground, he stood at bay, slashing the water to white rags. Grey waves broke against the bristly flank, and the salt-water washed it white. Arthur's knights threw off their heavy armour for fear of drowning. They whirled their long blades, wiped their spray-wet faces with their hair and sinking up to their knees in the wet sand, circled the Boar Troit as if he were the Round Table itself.

Afterwards, no one man took the credit for snatching the golden comb. A great wave spilled Troit off his feet, and the comb tumbled through the water until Arthur's hand snatched it up.

By then, the Great Pig had gone, swimming and snorting, floating and floundering to the far side of the Severn Estuary, on and into Cornwall. Over river and hills and down steep-hedged lanes, the knights of Arthur hunted the Big Pig Troit. The golden shears clanged against his golden crown. The soft Cornish rocks turned to tin under his hooves as he clattered over them.

The knights on foot climbed up behind those on horseback. Arthur's horse was weary and slowing, but his dog Cabel was as fresh as ever, and ran snapping at the Boar's heels, vexing and harrying him with nips of its sharp teeth. In a frenzy, Troit turned and turned until his tusks were a blur of whirling white.

Spurring on his horse to one last effort, and with a sweep of Excalibur, Arthur sheared through the Boar's topknot of matted bristly hair. The golden crown went spinning one way, the shears another, and Troit bolted baldly over the long peninsula and out into the breaking sea.

He swam on. He may be swimming yet, or rootling and ravening about the seabed, creating havoc among the fishes. But once Arthur had in his hand the comb and shears of the Great Pig Troit, he was content to let him go, out of the Realm of Albion.

Wrapping the strange gifts in white cloth, Culloch bore them back to the castle of Ysbaddaden. Culloch held his breath. Olwen shut her eyes and bit her lip. The servants came running with their forked sticks, and propped open the giant's heavy lids.

'Why have you returned with your quest unfulfilled?' Ysbaddaden demanded, peering at Culloch with bloodshot eyes.

'Our quest is complete. I bring the magic comb and shears from between the ears of the Big Pig Troit. Shall I now cut your hair, Ysbaddaden?'

Locks of the tangled, matted, grimy hair fell, with a noise like autumn. Ysbaddaden lifted his chin off the floor – it was easy now – and sadly smiled. With the merest velvety stubble around his temples and jaw, he looked quite boyish. 'You are to be thanked, Culloch. Your stepmother is to be thanked for bringing you here. For what is life if it must be spent face-down in the dirt? What is a wheel if it does not turn? What is life if it does not end and give way to newness of life?'

Ysbaddaden got up, and the crowd of curious knights gathered by his moat watched him, fingers to his eyelids, leave his castle to tour his lands and estates.

'Culloch. You may consider yourself betrothed to my daughter,' he said as he passed. Then he walked away, head-high with the hills, though his back was bent with age.

'Oh, Olwen!' cried Culloch.

'Oh, Culloch!' cried Olwen, and they kissed there and then on the drawbridge.

The great giant, outlined against the sky, brandished his massive club, in sheer jubilation at the beauty of the spring countryside. Then, leaning his back against a hillside, he melted way, leaving only his white outline in the chalky stone, his shape outlined in sweet green grass.

The Call of the Sea

A LEGEND FROM THE CHANNEL ISLANDS

WHEN THE tide goes out in Bonuit Bay, it leaves rockpools studded with limpets and starry with sea urchins. Joseph Rolande, after a day's fishing, would often stroll along the beach smoking his pipe and watching sunset tinge the sea red. One evening he found more on the beach than peace and tranquillity. A woman lay up to her waist in one of the rockpools – as though taking a bath, but crying bitterly into hanks of her long salt-spangled hair. At the sight of her, Joseph blushed and turned away, for she was wearing not a stitch of clothing. But she called out in panic: 'Please! Don't go! Help me! I stayed too long! The tide went out and left me stranded here. Carry me down to the sea or I shall die!' As she reached out towards him, he glimpsed the ripple of scales and a huge tail fin.

'Oh, no! Oh, no!' said Joseph, backing away. 'You're a mermaid, and I've heard what mermaids do! I've heard how you'll lure a man down into your own world and drown him there!'

The mermaid covered her face with her hair. The water was trickling out of the pool and little by little her shining tail was being laid bare. 'I'll die if I dry!' she sobbed.

Joseph was a good man. Besides, she was far too beautiful a creature for the world to lose. So lifting her in his arms – she smelled of salt and sea-pinks – he carried her past the third wave where she spilled out of his arms like a codling.

'Thank you!' she cried, swimming around his thighs, her hair brushing his hands. 'Come with me and let my father reward you! He's king of the sea people, and his treasures fill the sea caves.'

'Oh, no! Oh, no!' said Joseph stumbling out of the water. 'I've heard how your kind lure a man to his destruction. Be off, you and your salt-sea magic!'

Something sharp pricked his palm. She had slid the amber comb from her hair and was pressing it into his hand – a gift, a thank-you present. 'If you ever need my help, pass this three times through the water and I will come.' With a thrash of her gleaming tail, she was gone.

Those words were like seeds in his brain which sprouted and grew, taking over his every thought. He walked the beach every evening, looking in the rockpools for stranded mermaids. Instead of forgetting her, the features of her face grew clearer in his mind. Those eyes. That mouth. That beauty. Time and again he found himself, without knowing how, down at the water's edge, searching the waves for a glimpse of mermaid. And when he slept, he dreamed mermaid. The amber comb was always in his head when he woke.

'So that's your magic, is it, woman?' thought Joseph. 'That's how you mean to lure me to my death. Well, I'll not give you the satisfaction!' And he left the fishing, left his seashore cottage, and moved inland to farm a field of kale. He put a mountain between him and the sea.

And yet when the sun shone, it drew up seawater to form the rainclouds which gathered over Joseph's field of kale. It was the sea that rained on his roof.

One night, the rain beat on Joseph's roof like a thousand galloping hooves. A storm worse than anyone could remember rived the sea to a frenzy of leaping waves. It drove a ship on to the Bonuit rocks, and the Bonuit maroons sounded.

Every soul who lived in the bay ran to the shore and peered through the downpour. Rain beat so hard on their faces they could barely lift their lids. Waves heaved themselves up to the height of church steeples, and fell in crashing ruins against the shore. All but one of the little boats lying along the shore was overturned and smashed. The screams of the sailors clinging to the wreckage were all but washed away. 'It's hopeless. No one can get to them,' said the Jerseymen.

'Help me to launch my boat!' shouted a voice behind them. Joseph Rolande came running down the beach. There was grass on his boots from his run over the hill, but he was dressed once more in his fisherman's clothes.

He and his boat disappeared beyond the mountainous waves into the hellish maelstrom of Bonuit Bay where rocks chew each wave to shreds and wicked currents knot and plait beneath the surface. Only when the lightning flashed could those on shore glimpse the little rowing boat and the pounded wreck with its sad clutch of crew.

The lightning burst and faded; it scorched eyes, it coloured the sea. But surely they could not *all* have been mistaken? There was someone else besides Joseph out there . . . A gigantic fish? A drowning woman?

'You called me with my comb and I came, Joseph. At last you called me!'

'Help me save these men!' he shouted back to the mermaid, his mouth full of rain.

And she did. With all the tenderness of a human woman, she caught up each sailor washed off the wreck, and swam with them to Joseph's boat. Half dead with drowning, half mad with fear, they hardly remembered afterwards how they had escaped death. But many of the seventeen sailors saved that night spoke of a woman holding them in her arms, of a man pulling them aboard laughing as he did so and crying, 'All this time! All this time! What a fool I was!'

As the last sailor slumped like a wet fish into the bottom of Joseph's boat, and he pulled for shore, the mermaid swam alongside, her hair flowery with sea foam. 'All this while I thought you had forgotten me!' she called.

'All this while I thought your kind was wicked – that I

mustn't give in to your beauty! Thank you for coming. Thank you for helping!' Joseph shouted above the storm's clamour.

He beached the boat, and the locals crowded round, praising his bravery. But as they helped the rescued sailors up the beach to shelter, they looked back, only to see Joseph pushing his boat once more into the dreadful surf. Had he seen another soul to rescue?

'No! You've done enough! Don't go, Joseph!' they called, but their voices were snatched away by the wind.

Joseph put out to sea and never returned. He did not need to. Someone was waiting for him beyond the third wave – 'And all this time you were a true friend!' – someone with an amber comb in her hair and in her hand the keys to the Kingdom of Undersea.

The Crystal Pool

A MELANESIAN MYTH

T HE SEA was not always so big, glazing the globe blue, roaring in the ears of dry land. Believe it or not, the sea was once no more than a single secret saltwater spring where an old woman went to draw water for cooking: it made her vegetables taste good.

Often and often, her two sons, Spy and Pry, saw her go out and come back with a brimming pan. They saw the pan when it was empty, too: rimy with white dust.

'Where do you go to, Mama mine, and where do you fill your cooking pan?' asked Pry, but she would not tell him.

'Let us go with you, Mama mine, and help you carry the pan,' said Spy, but she would not take him: said she knew them both for mischief.

So one day, without asking, they followed her – saw her draw back a cloth, fill her pan and put back the cloth lid.

When she had gone, they crept out. They too pulled back the cloth. There underneath was a small sparkling crystal pool. One stride would have straddled it. Spy cupped his hand, took a taste and pulled a face. Pry tried too: 'Pah!' Nothing but a brackish puddle.

Reflecting the sky, the pool blinked a blue eye. It began to bubble and gurgle, gush and rush. It fountained up between their guilty fingers.

'Oh, Spy, now what have you done?'

'Nothing! It was your idea!'

Water splashed over their feet and went on rising. It swirled round their ankles. Taking fright, they ran in different directions – each still holding a corner of the cloth, so that it tore clean through. They ran, but the water ran faster, curling and coiling into waves, heaping and humping into great glossy swells which swamped the stones, drowned the desert, hid the hills, besieged the mountains. Whole villages were swept away like bird nests. Whole herds and hoards of beasts and birds were rolled off their feet and washed free of their wings and fur.

When the old woman saw the sea coming to submerge the land under sky-high fathoms of salt water, she snapped twigs from a magic tree, hitched her skirt past her knees, and went down to meet it. In a straight line at her feet, she planted the twigs, watering them with magic words.

On came the rolling, smashing, tumbling breakers, crashing into a spray which enveloped the old woman and hid her from sight. But as their foam fringe touched the magic fence, they drew back, sucking the sand, stirring the stones, sinking with a soughing sigh, back, back and back.

The ocean ceased to grow. Though sea now outstretched the land, it never rose beyond those magic twigs. Even now, when the full moon tugs and rucks the seven seas to and fro, to and fro, the twigs do not wash away.

But those two torn strips of sopping cloth dangling from the hands of Spy and Pry can no more cover the ocean now than a butterfly's wings can cover a continent. Nor ever will.

Race to the Top

A MAORI MYTH

IN THE very Highest Heaven, Papa Io prepared three presents for the Human Race. He took three baskets and into one put Peace and Love. Into the second he put Songs and Spells. Into the third he put Help and Understanding. The people of Earth would need all these if they were to get along with one another successfully. And Papa Io knew all about the importance of getting along. He had two sons, Tane and Whiro, who could no more agree than fire and water. He had put Tane in charge of light, Whiro in charge of darkness; the jobs suited their temperaments perfectly, he thought. For Tane was all brightness, kindness and goodness, while Whiro (although Io wept to admit it) was gloomy, evil and dangerous.

Naturally, when the three baskets were ready, it was easy to choose which son should deliver them. Io stuck his head out over Heaven's parapet and called through his speaking trumpet, 'Tane! Come up here! I need you to take these gifts to Humankind!'

Now Whiro knew full well that whoever delivered such fine presents to the people of Earth would win them, heart and mind. They would never stop thanking or praising the messenger. The thought of praise appealed to Whiro. So, while Tane climbed the Great Tower of Overworlds, storey by storey, up the ladders which led from one floor to the next, Whiro set off to climb the *outside* of the Tower. Like ivy, like a fat black spider creeping silently up a wall, he raced his brother skywards, determined to reach the top first. In his pockets were all the tools of his trade, all the tricks which would give him the advantage . . .

It was slow going. But by the time he reached the second storey, Whiro found Tane was already on the third. So, out of his pocket he pulled handfuls of mosquitoes, sandflies and bats. 'Kiss my brother for me, my dearios,' he said, and flung them in the air.

Unsteadily balanced on the ladder between worlds, Tane was suddenly engulfed in a cloud of flying black particles. They flew in his eyes, his ears, his mouth and up his nose. He bent his head down against the swarm, clinging to the ladder with one hand while, with the other, he fumbled in his pocket. At last he tugged out a twist of north wind as big as a towel, and waved it round his head. The insects and bats were swept by a frosty gusting gale miles out to sea.

So, when Whiro, climbing the outside of the Tower, reached the third storey, Tane was already well on his way to the fourth. Whiro put his hand in his other pocket and drew out, like a fisherman's maggots, a handful of ants, centipedes, hornets, spiders and scorpions. 'Say hello to my brother from me, sweetlings,' he said, and threw them in the air.

Half-way up the next tall ladder, Tane heard a crack-ling, and was suddenly, vilely beset by creepy-crawlies. They swarmed through his hair, infested his clothing; they stung his bare arms and cheeks and calves. Feeling in his pocket, he found no rags of wind, nothing at all to swat them away. There was nothing he could do but shut tight his eyes and mouth and go on climbing – higher and higher – from the eighth to the ninth to the tenth storey.

Gradually, the air became thinner, purer. The holiness emanating from the magic realms above filled the upper storeys with a glorious perfume. The disgusting crawling creatures began to fall away, overcome, like mountaineers succumbing to altitude sickness.

Outside, on the wall of the Tower of Overworlds, even Whiro began to flag. His arms and legs ached. His fingers could barely grip. When he looked down, his head swam at the vertiginous drop. He would never make it as far as the eleventh storey before Tane.

Spotting a small window in the side of the Tower, Whiro slipped through it, feet first, and found himself on the ninth floor. Very well. If he could not catch Tane on the way up, he would ambush him on the way down. Hiding himself in the shadows behind the ladder, he settled down to wait . . .

In the uppermost Overworld, welcoming hands helped Tane from the ladder and led him before Papa Io. And there, while pink evening clouds drifted between the white pillars of Highest Heaven, Io entrusted his three precious presents into Tane's keeping. 'Give them to Humankind with my love and blessing,' said Io. 'And tell them to watch out for that infernal brother of yours. He's a tricky one, that Whiro, though I weep to say it about my own son.'

Carefully, carefully, Tane started back down, the baskets balanced neatly on top of one another. The perfumes of Highest Heaven were heady, and he was feeling a little light-headed as he stepped on to the ladder from tenth to ninth Overworld. He had only one hand free to grasp the rungs now, and he could not properly see where to place his feet.

Suddenly a hand grabbed his ankle and wrenched him off the ladder. He fell, the baskets tumbling on top of him, on top of Whiro who was just then sinking his teeth deep into Tane's thigh.

There in the darkness they fought, good and evil, sparks and foulness spilling from the folds of their clothing. Their panting breaths sped the clouds across the evening sky. Against a blood-red sunset, the Tower of Overworlds trembled and rocked, while the birds screamed around its shaken frame: 'Help! Murder! Ambush!'

Whiro was rested. He liked a fight, liked to inflict pain, whereas his brother was naturally a gentle soul. But Tane knew, as his brother's hands closed round his throat to throttle him, that if Whiro once got hold of the baskets, he would either spill them or use them to take control of the Earth and its people. He slapped feebly at his brother's chest, but there was no pushing him away. He reached out a hand across the creaking floor; his fingers brushed a fallen basket; the lid came off and rolled away into the darkness. A wordless song and a single magic spell spilled into Tane's open palm.

Suddenly a sacred, magic warmth crept up his wrist and arm, into his aching muscles, inspiring him to one last effort. Pushing Whiro backwards, Tane toppled him over the edge of the hatchway and – *thud* – down into Overworld Eight; *crash* – down into Overworld Seven; *bang* – down into Six . . . and Five and Four and so, by painful stages, all the way down to the stony Earth.

He was not killed: immortals don't die. And the whole episode did not serve to sweeten his nasty temper. Picking himself up, Whirro snarled, 'Not deliver the baskets? Well then, I shall make Humankind some presents of my own! Sickness for one! Crime for another! DEATH for a third!' And he slouched away to find baskets big enough for all the miseries he had in store.

Small matter. Tane delivered the three baskets safely to the people of Earth. So after that, they were armed against anything Whiro could hurl at them. The only lasting damage was to the Tower. Shaken and rocked by the titanic struggle on the ninth floor, its rickety structure teeters now, condemned, on the world's edge. It would not carry the weight of the smallest child, let alone the great bulk of Papa Io climbing down from the sky. So Humankind are on their own now. They will have to make do as best they can with what the gods gave them.

Lamia

AN INDIAN LEGEND

HE THOUGHT that he came on the place by chance, but that was not quite true. A deer led him to it. Ali Mardan Khan followed the creature deep into the forest, to the shores of a lake, before it eluded him among green shadows. Not two moments later, he heard weeping.

A woman sat with her back to a tree, her hair plaited with wires of gold and silver, her dress bright with mirror sequins, so that she glistened like a fallen star. At the sight of him, she stretched herself at his feet, hands clasped in supplication.

'Don't be afraid,' said Ali Mardan, raising her up. 'You're on my land here, and no harm will come to you. But who are you?'

She said she was a princess from over the mountains – from war-torn China. 'My father was defeated in battle. Of all my family only I escaped. I have wandered for weeks through the mountains.' Not one jet-black hair was out of place, not a fold of her dress creased, but he believed her instantly. For surely the gods had reached out to preserve this unearthly beauty. The flower boats that plied his Kashmiri lakes were no lovelier than Princess Amali, her voice so soft, sibilant and sweet.

'You are welcome to make my home your own,' said Ali Mardan.

'If you were to offer me marriage, I would not refuse,' said the Princess, looking shyly through her lashes. His fate was sealed.

There on the banks of the lake, Ali Mardan built his

bride a palace in keeping with her loveliness. She wanted peace and solitude, she said, and to be alone with him; he was only too glad to agree. Only one thing marred those beautiful early days of marriage: Ali Mardan began to suffer fearful stomach pains.

'Let me nurse you,' said Amali. 'I'm gentler than those brutal physicians of yours with their leeches and scalpels.' And so tenderly did she care for him, night and day, that Ali Mardan every dawn reproached himself for feeling no better.

One day, as his manservant helped him walk about in the garden, breathing the scents of the forest, they came across a wandering holy man, small and bony as a pigeon, asleep under a tree.

'Shall I throw him out of your garden, sir?' asked the servant.

'Certainly not. Holy men are a blessing from heaven. Fetch a bed out here, and have food prepared for him when he wakes. I must lie down now. The pain, it's too . . .'

When the holy man woke, he was delighted to find himself on a soft couch surrounded by trays of food. He sought out his host to thank him. 'I am sorry to find you unwell, sir. Perhaps I can repay your kindness with my own humble knowledge of medicine.'

He examined Ali Mardan, asked questions, and strummed his lower lip, rapt in thought. 'Are you by any chance newly married, sir?'

'Why, yes! I am!'

The man smiled. 'Then the remedy is plain, and I shall supply it! Let me cook dinner tonight.'

He picked all the herbs, ground all the spices. But although he cooked exactly the same meal for Ali Mardan as for the Princess, he sprinkled a handful of salt over Amali's plate. If she noticed, she said nothing and the meal passed without incident.

By midnight Amali had a raging thirst. She got out of bed, and went to the water jug. But the jug was empty. She went to the door. But it was locked. She went to the window. But its grille of wrought iron was designed to keep out thieves: no way out.

With a glance at her sleeping husband, Amali stretched herself, reaching up as though she would touch the ceiling. Her body grew thinner; her bones seemed to melt away. Her skin glistened green in the moonlight, and her hair congealed to her back and legs. A serpent ten feet long reared up from the patch of moonlight where Amali had stood a moment before, its jaws agape for water, forked tongue flickering. Out between the filigree ironwork of the window she slithered, and down to the lake, drinking her fill, dislocating her serpent jaws to scoop up the water. Then she slithered back to the palace.

In the shadow of the wall stood the holy man, a little silver hatchet in his hand. The moment her head was through the bars, he struck. But the snake was too quick for him, the scales too tough.

Next morning Ali Mardan summoned the holy man to his room.

'I'm sorry, sir. I wounded her, but I could not kill her.'

'Wounded whom? Is there an assassin loose in my palace?'

'No, sir. A lamia.'

If for two hundred years a snake lives unseen by human eyes, it becomes a dragon. A hundred years more, and it becomes a lamia – a creature of infinite wickedness, able to change into any shape – a bird, a tiger. Worse, it can become a woman and feed on the lifeblood of a man.

'Your wife, sir,' said the holy man, 'is poisoning you with the venom of her kisses. Your only cure is to kill her.'

'Never! No! You're wrong! Aha, I can prove you're wrong! You may have wounded some snake in my garden last night, but not Amali. I left her asleep in bed. Unhurt! See for yourself: here she comes!'

But as Princess Amali entered the garden, her silken cloak blew back: they saw that one of her arms was in a sling. 'I dropped my mirror. I cut myself,' she said when she saw them staring.

When she had gone, Ali Mardan drew a trembling breath. One hand clutched the pain in his side, one gripped the arm of his chair. 'Tell me what I must do,' he said at last, 'to kill a lamia.'

They built a summer-house of shiny lacquered tree bark, down by the lake. It had just a table, a chair, a bed and a big oven.

'Come with me, Amali,' said Ali Mardan. 'The holy man thinks one of my courtiers may be poisoning me. So I shall eat nothing but what is cooked by your own hand, and have no one near me but you.'

The Princess looked doubtful. 'Cook, my love? But I hardly know how . . . being a princess, you know. Besides, I hate ovens.'

'Only a loaf of bread,' he said. 'You can hardly refuse me that.'

The walls of the summer-house were so thin and fine that the shadows of husband and wife could be seen as they kneaded dough together at the table. The smaller shadow turned to place the bread in the oven. The taller moved painfully across behind – and gave her a push.

Into the oven went the lamia! And Ali Mardan staggered from the hut, his arm across his face. Servants came running with blazing torches, and set light to the summer-house: it burned like a chrysanthemum bursting into crimson bloom.

Next day. Ali Mardan woke feeling stronger. He dimly hoped the pictures in his head were left over from some bad dream. But when he climbed out of bed and found his body free from pain, he realized that the death of the lamia – his bride – had truly taken place.

Outside the door stood the holy man, travelling-staff in hand. 'I can safely leave you now, sir, and return to my monastery. But come with me to the lake, if you will.'

'Must I?'

The summer-house was nothing but a pile of ash around the cast-iron oven. Opening the oven door the holy man swept out a handful of ash and a pretty green pebble. 'Choose: the pebble or the ash?'

'The pebble,' said Ali Mardan without thinking.

'Then I shall keep the ash,' said the holy man.

Ali Mardan sat the pebble down on the oven while he stared out across the lake. The lilies were just coming into bloom. Birds were eating seed from the rushes, dragonflies hovering over their reflections. When he turned back, the oven was solid gold.

He pocketed the stone with a smile. 'And what can the ash do?' he asked. But no one answered. The holy man had disappeared among the trees, and Ali Mardan would never know what the ash of a lamia could do. He was glad it had gone. He used the alchemy of the pebble only rarely, when he most had need. It reminded him of his dead wife and the gleam of gold wire in her plaited hair.

Isis and Osiris

AN EGYPTIAN MYTH

IN THE Ship-of-a-Million-Years, Shu rolled the dice. 'Again!' groaned Troth. 'You win again!' And so the God of Mischief won from the God of Time a whole stash of minutes – enough, in fact, to make a day. And on that new day, Nut, wife of the Sun God himself, gave birth. Her peevish husband had cursed her with childlessness all year round. But on the 366th day of the year, using borrowed time, Nut was at last able to give birth to four babies. She hid them on Earth, as kings and queens: Set and Nephthys, Isis and Osiris.

Set could find no one on Earth fit to be his wife – no one, that is, but his sister Nephthys. So he married her, and they became King and Queen of Nubia. Their love was so great for one another that they had none left for the people of Nubia.

Osiris could find no one on Earth fit to be his wife – no one, that is, but his sister Isis. So he married her, and they became King and Queen of Egypt. Their love for one another was so great that it spilled over on to their Egyptian subjects.

In those days, mortals knew nothing about clothing themselves, growing food, taking shelter from the burning sun. Up until then, they had simply grubbed about like brute beasts. But Osiris taught them how to brew beer and to dance, and Isis taught them how to weave linen, farm crops, make bricks out of the Nile mud. King and Queen were greatly loved for their teaching; greatly repaid for the love they lavished on the people of Egypt.

'What a beautiful statue!' cried Isis, as she took her place

at the banqueting table. Set had invited all his neighbour-
ing kings and queens to a marvellous feast and, naturally,
Isis and Osiris were guests of honour.

'Aha, no statue, this!' laughed Set agreeably, and
showed off his latest work of art. It looked like the figure
of a man, but there were hinges on one side and latches on
the other, and it opened like a trunk. The space inside was
just the size and shape of a man. 'If anyone here fits the
space exactly, he shall have the chest as a present!' Set
announced – astonishing generosity, given that the chest
was inlaid with turquoise faïence, gold, silver and lapis
lazuli.

Up they trooped, those well-fed kings, to try the chest
for size. But either they were too fat to squeeze in, or too
short to fit. Only Osiris, willowy and tall, fitted to
perfection. (But then, of course, it had been tailor-made for
him.)

BANG! Set slammed shut the lid and sprang the latches.

'No, no!' cried Isis. 'He won't be able to breathe!'

'All well and good, then!' sniggered Set. 'All my life I
have had to watch you and him wallowing in the worship
of your loving subjects. Now all that love will come to me
– Set – ruler of Nubia and of Egypt!' His troops picked up
the chest and ran with it, and though Isis tried to follow,
Set held her fast until the coffin-bearers were out of sight.

Alone and bereft, Isis walked north from Nubia back
into Egypt along the muddy gulch which called itself the
Nile. As she walked, she wept – large brilliant tears which,
in falling, startled tufts of dust from the ground. Rivulets
of tears became pools, pools became streams, streams
swelled the trickling Nile to a river, a torrent. It overspilled
its banks, swamping the countryside from the fifth cataract
to the delta plain.

'Stop crying! Don't cry!' said a little voice. Other voices
joined it. 'Please, Queen Isis! Don't cry any more!'

She blinked down and saw seven scorpions gazing up at
her with bulging eyes, imploring her to stop. 'If you cry

any more, the flood will wipe out Egypt!' they said. 'We'll help you look for Osiris. Everyone will help you!'

It was true. Isis and Osiris were so loved that all Egypt was ready to join in the search for Osiris, shut up in his airless coffin, stifling to death with every passing second.

Looking over their shoulders, the troops of Set saw the Nile floods rolling down on top of them and ran for their lives. They flung aside the jewelled sarcophagus, and the floodwaters of Isis' tears caught it and swept it from swamp to reedbed, reedbed to river, from river's reach to cataract, on down the Nile.

With the help of the scorpions, Isis herself found it. Transformed by magic into a sparrowhawk, she was searching, with hawkish eyes, from high in the sunny Egyptian sky. Suddenly she glimpsed the chest floating in mid-river! But her borrowed wings were weary, her bird body on the brink of exhaustion. All she could do was fly down and perch her hawk's weight on the floating coffin, pecking feebly at the lid.

Her feet felt the beat of a heart through the inlaid lid. Not dead yet, then! Half mad with hope, she pecked furiously. Her beak made a hole. The soul of Osiris struggled like a flame through that hole, and singed the feathers of the sparrowhawk!

But, powerless to free him, Isis fell exhausted from the casket and was washed up on the river bank, while the sarcophagus floated on its way into the maze of delta rivulets, and on out to sea. There, waves washed over it, splashed in at the hole her beak had made, filled the trunk with sea brine.

When Isis awoke, bedraggled on the Nile mud, she found she was expecting a baby – Osiris' son. She was forced to call off her futile search until after the baby was born.

Not for a year, not for a handful of sorry years did Isis finish her search for the treacherous casket. It had embedded itself in the trunk of a young tamarisk tree, and the tree had grown up around it, imprisoning the sarcophagus in yet another layer of wood. Only love guided her to it, only absurd, indestructible hope made her hack her way into its sea-filled compartment.

But Osiris was long since dead.

'Dead and never to be buried!' cried a cruel voice behind her. It was Set, as dogged in his hatred as she had been in her love. He too had searched the Red Land and the Black for the lost casket. Bodies could be buried. Graves could become shrines. People could worship at shrines, adoring the memory of the dead; and Set was determined no one but he should be worshipped throughout the length and breadth of Egypt.

So he took an axe and, in front of his sister's horrified eyes, hacked the body of Osiris into fourteen pieces, flinging them into the Nile. '*Now* love him – what you can find of him!' jeered the murderous Set, as the speeding river carried away the parts and pieces of Osiris.

This time Isis did not cry. She tore her hair and rended her fine linen robes, and she screamed like a gull out at sea. '*A boat!*' she shrieked at the people nearby. 'I must gather up the pieces of my husband and give him decent burial! Make me a boat, for the love of pity!'

'But there are no trees to build a boat!' said the people. 'No trees between here and Memphis!'

'Then cut rushes and make a boat from them!' howled Isis, filling her fists with papyrus reeds and shaking them at the sky.

'The crocodiles will tear it apart!' said the people. But they built the boat. And Isis sailed it, too, careless of whether the green Nile crocodiles, large as boats and monstrous with teeth, tore her or her craft in pieces. Blind to their green raft of bodies closing in, she sailed up and down, reaching into the water, reaching into the blood-stained reeds.

'Why do you not fear us?' demanded the largest of the

crocodiles. 'Why do you trespass on our river? Why do you brave our hunger?'

'What do I care about drowning or being eaten?' answered Isis. 'Haven't I pain enough already to fill three worlds? Haven't I lost my darling, body, brain and heart?' And she told the crocodiles (there were several hundred jamming the river now, like logs) the whole story of her husband's murder.

By the time she finished, the log-jam of crocodiles were sobbing and tossing their green jaws from side to side in grief. Some laid water lilies in the bow of the boat, to comfort her. 'Oh, beautiful lady!' wailed the largest, 'we shall cruise the Nile from source to sea and find you every part and piece of Osiris!'

In their baggy green jaws they brought the pieces, as gently as they carried their own eggs. They found every piece but one (which was not important), and Isis took all her husband's remains and carried them ashore.

Far inland she walked, to a place called the Valley of Stones, all boulders and hot rocks cracking in the sun. Only then, in that desolate place, did she really feel her loss. For what good are the parts of a dead man, except for burial in the parched ground? She raised such a clamour of grief that the sky above her quaked. The Ship-of-a-Million-Years, barge of the gods, bucketed about.

'What's that row?' asked Ra, Sun and father of the gods.

'Just a mortal weeping over the body of her mate,' he was told.

'Then for Heaven's sake, someone make her stop!' grumbled the ancient Maker-of-the-World. 'Or how can I sleep?'

Leaning over her parcel of woe, Isis saw the black shadow of a jackal loom over her. 'No! You shan't eat him!' she cried, throwing herself across the body.

'Please,' said Anubis, jackal-headed god, keeper of secrets. 'Don't upset yourself. I have come to help.'

The arts he showed her that day had never been seen

before on Earth: how to bandage and anoint a body, how to clothe it in prayers. 'Now,' Anubis said, stepping back from his work, 'now it is only a question of how much you love Osiris.'

She called his name. She shouted out her love. She called so loudly that even in the World-under-the-World, the great serpent of Chaos heard it and flinched.

Anubis grinned a doggy grin. He reboarded the Ship-of-a-Million-Years, and it sailed on across the heavens towards the Gate of Sunset, leaving Isis and her husband in the Valley of Stones . . . hand-in-hand and talking.

He could not stay long, of course. The Living and the Raised-to-Life cannot live in the same world. Osiris left to become King of the Westerners, guardian of the spirits of the Dead. After that, when Egyptians came to die and make the long journey west out of the living world, they no longer feared the darkness of dissolution. They knew that a familiar face would be waiting to greet them in the Land of the West: Osiris, who would raise them to life with love, just as love had resurrected him.

Nor was Isis left lonely for long on the Earth. Shortly she won herself a place in the Barque of Heaven, alongside Thoth and Shu and Ra, Anubis, Nut and the rest. So now each night, as the ship sails under the Earth, she is able to glimpse the glimmering towers of the Westerners and a lean, willowy figure waving, waving his greeting and his love.

The Flying Dutchman

A SAILORS' LEGEND

His HOLD heavy with precious metals and his decks piled high with spices, Captain Vanderdecken cast off, fore and aft, and gave the order to hoist the mainsail. But the crew at the capstans did not sing as they worked. Even the surf did not whisper under the ship's prow. For the clouds which lay along the horizon were red as fire, and the wind ratched at the sea like a rasp. There was dirty weather ahead; this was no time to be setting sail.

The Dutchman was known for a hard man, but not for a fool. Though he worked his men like dogs, cursing them and keeping their rations short, he was a profiteer, and surely a businessman values his cargo if he cares nothing for his fellow men. Surely the captain prizes his ship, even if he couldn't give a damn for his crew. So, when the storm came, slewing round the bottom of the world, fit to send every ship scurrying for shelter, everyone expected Vanderdecken to turn back and make for shelter.

'We'll all be killed!' the First Mate warned. 'The men are scared silly and there's no priest on board to pray for our souls! Turn back, Captain, turn back, I beg you!'

The Dutchman was sitting in his easy chair on the afterdeck, smoking a pipe, while his cabin boy polished his boots. The chart lay in front of him, a single line marking a route around the Cape of Good Hope. He barely even stirred himself to answer, and then the words crawled from between snarling lips. 'I'll go where I choose, and I'll kill any man who thwarts me,' he said. At his feet, the cabin boy tittered in admiration of his brutal master.

The Mate withdrew, but the frightened crew went on muttering among themselves, scared of their captain, more scared of the sea which rolled down on them like a purple mountain range falling on their heads. The waves were flecked with ice, the wavetops torn ragged by the howling wind.

'If we reason with him, he'll have to see sense,' said one, and led the rest – the entire crew – back down the ship to the afterdeck. 'For the love of God, turn back, sir!' shouted the matelot above the racketing wind. 'It's flying in the face of God to round the Cape in this weather!'

But the only answer he got was the sight of the Dutchman's drawn pistol and the sound of its hammer falling. The seaman fell back over the rail into the boiling sea – fell without a cry. But the wind screamed in the rigging, and the ship groaned from stem to stern. 'I'll go round the Cape whether God wills it or no,' said Vanderdecken, grinning like a fiend, his eyes gleaming. 'Which of you is going to try to stop me now? None? No! Not God nor all His angels shall say me nay!'

The crew stared open-mouthed, each man seeing his own death scrawled in the filthy sky. Then their pallid faces grew whiter still, as that ghostly phosphorescence called St Elmo's fire settled on the ship's mast like a column of cold fire.

A piece broke free and fluttered down to the deck, taking shape, as it fell. Some said wings, some a gown, some a head of snowy hair, some a face of ineffable, unbearable beauty. But only the Dutchman really dared to look into the face of that blazing figure

'Did you never hear tell, Dutchman, that it's a sin to take the Lord's name in vain?'

The Dutchman only swore vilely. 'Get off my ship. I've business in hand.'

'Turn back, Dutchman. Three times now you have been warned.'

But the Dutchman only cursed foully and lifted his pistol a second time, saying, 'Devil take you.'

BANG. The thunder was louder than the shot. And the bullet passed clean through the phantom of flame, melting into a single waterdrop before falling into the vast running seas.

'You have spoken your mind,' said the figure. 'Now I will speak mine. Every trading man looks to profit from his trade. So, from this bitter night's work, you shall earn ten thousand such bitter weeks. In return for your curse, I'll pay you in millions of curses. Sail on, would you? Then sail on for ever, for your blasphemy, never touching port. No sleep, no food, no drink shall comfort you. These men shan't disobey you again, for I shall leave you no men. Hail no ships for company or aid or news; none will ever draw alongside without rack and disaster overtaking it. The world will soon learn to fear the Fleeing Dutchman, to shun him and curse him, as you have shunned and cursed me tonight!'

No tears of remorse sprang to Vanderdecken's eyes. He bit his thumb at the phantom. 'Me, I thrive on terror! It's all I ever looked for in another man's face!'

'Good,' replied the fiery shape. 'For search the world over and you shall never find Love – no, not in one single face. Sail on, Dutchman. You have all Eternity for your voyaging!'

A wall of water as high as a cathedral burst over the ship. The Dutchman was flung against the wheel, and clung there, eyes and mouth tight shut against the swamping salt-water. When he opened his eyes again, the deck of his ship was washed bare – bare of spices, bare of sailors, bare of anchor or chains, ropes and waterbutts. Bare of phantasms, too. But clinging to the Captain's ankle, the little cabin boy spluttered and gasped and gibbered with cold.

'Ah! Not entirely alone, then!' crowed the Dutchman, reaching down to grasp the boy's hand. But the face which turned up towards him was no longer human. It wore the snarl of a dog, and the hand he took hold of was scaly and rasp-rough, like the pelt of a dogfish. Eyes which had once fawned on Vanderdecken now looked at him with unconcealed loathing.

'My waterbutts gone? Then I shall drink beer!' shouted the Dutchmen defiantly into the rainy sky. 'Fetch me beer, boy, and I shall drink myself blind drunk!'

But when the cabin boy brought the beer, it boiled in the tankard, making the metal too hot to hold; the foam scalded as it blew into his face. And the meat on his plate turned to molten lead. The darkness beneath his eyelids was suddenly full of horrors so terrible that Vanderdecken never again dared to close his eyes.

Without his orders, all the flags at the masthead had changed. Now, all that flew there was a ghastly yellow rag with a central black spot: the signal of a ship contaminated by plague. And though he ran that flag down a thousand times, it was always flying there again next time he looked up. So no port would grant him entry. No ship would come near.

Rumours soon spread, in cosy harbour taverns, among old sailing comrades, as they sat drinking together, sharing a supper of cheese and cold collations. The Fleeing Dutchman, the 'Flying' Dutchman was a devil, his ship cursed by God. It was a ship to steer clear of, a ship damned.

Of course pirates and thieves listened in to the gossip, but heard only the words 'treasure' and 'gold' and 'precious cargo'. Far from steering clear, they went looking for the Flying Dutchman. But those that laid grappling hooks on board, and set foot on the bare, silent decks, never disembarked again. For their own ships sank like stones, just from touching rib against rib with the ship of doom. So Vanderdecken's ship did *not* go uncrewed. Indeed, he gathered around him dozens of the scurviest villains ever to escape hanging. But they hated the Captain, because they were powerless to leave him, and they cursed the day they had set eyes on that yellow plague flag, for their souls were everlastingly in thrall to the Flying Dutchman.

Restless, unresting, the ship sails on around and around the watery globe. Though the boards have been chafed through by the salt-sharp sea, and her ribs laid bare, still she does not sink. Though the sails have been blown to the ragged thinness of rotten silk, still she speeds before the remorseless trade winds. The chart on the Captain's desk is blacker now than a spider's web with the courses he has plotted on his never-ending voyage.

Endless hail and wind and sun have beaten down on the Dutchman's head, so that his brown face is scored with creases, his misery etched for anyone to see. Whole centuries have passed since Vanderdecken learned repentance, learned to crave a kind face, a smile, a hand extended in friendship. But he sees only resentment, loathing, hate, contempt, terror.

Now, the sailors in the portside taverns whisper that God's anger is softening – that once every seven years or so, Vanderdecken is seen ashore, walking the streets of some foreign port, lifting his cap to the ladies, in the hope that one will stop and speak to him, listen to his story, pity him – love him.

But looking into those half-crazed eyes, seeing all that horror, hearing his crimes, what woman could ever love the Flying Dutchman? So perhaps God's anger is not lessening. Perhaps God has merely found a new way to torment His damned Dutchman from everlasting to everlasting.

Proud Man

A NATIVE AMERICAN MYTH

WISDOM is power so they say, and that makes Gluskap all-powerful. For Gluskap knew everything, and magic besides. He made the world, he rid it of monsters, he fought the stone giants and sometimes, just sometimes, he granted wishes.

One day, four men came in turn to visit him. Each wanted something, some more than others.

'Please, oh please, mighty Gluskap!' said the first unlucky soul. 'All my crops have died and my well's run dry! Now my wife and children are starving and I haven't a morsel to give them! When I ask my friends for help, they call me a fool and a scrounger. Grant me a bite of bread and a jug of milk, if only for my children's mouths!'

'With friends like that, you really do need help,' said Gluskap, and gave the man a cow and whole basket of seed-corn to replant his field.

'Oh, master of the world, I humbly beg you,' said the second man, bowing low. 'See how sickness has scarred my face and weakened my body? Pity my ugliness. All I long for is to be as I was born, an ordinary man, whole and healthy.'

'Whole and healthy is how I made you,' said Gluskap, 'and so you shall be again!' And he healed the man then and there, and sent him off skipping and dancing.

'Oh, Lord Gluskap, in your great mercy!' shouted a loud and scowling man. 'I am cursed with a wicked temper. I scold my wife and hit my neighbours and make my children cry. Before I do something unforgivable, I beg you, take this demon temper out of me!'

Gluskap smiled. 'I always preferred the farmer to the warrior. Take off your shirt and with it your temper. I grant you your wish.' So the man took off both shirt and temper, and left them in the palm of Gluskap's giant hand. The Great Spirit was still holding them when a fourth man arrived.

'Listen here,' said the man. 'You did a pretty poor job when you made me. But I'm a fair man. I'm going to give you a chance to make up for that. Make me taller, for a start, and more handsome. I want to be admired. I want to be the most admired man in my village! Oh, and make me live longer, too.'

Gluskap smiled, but not in quite the same way as before. His fingers closed around the shirt in his hand, and his skin tasted the temper left in its weave. 'Your wish is granted,' he said between gritted teeth.

But the man did not thank him. In fact he didn't say a word. His feet had burrowed deep into the ground, and his spine had stretched, tall and erect. His hair had lengthened, too, so that now it was spiky and . . . green. There he stood: a fine, tall fir tree, as beautiful as any in the forest.

It is true, he did tower over mere men as they rode by; and those passing travellers did admire him immensely. And though they must have grown old and died since then, the fir tree is still there, thriving, to this day. But whether this height and elegance and admiration and long life were quite what the man had in mind, no one will ever know, because the only noise to come from him is the creak of timber and the singing of birds.

Such were Gluskap's powers. Such was his wisdom.

Perhaps you know someone like him; someone who is always right? Someone perfect who never makes a mistake? Yes. Quite. Such people can be . . . wearing, to say the least.

A day dawned when Gluskap's wife had had too much of her husband's marvellous wisdom and (it has to be said) his almighty conceit.

'Of course, there is *someone* who can resist your great powers,' she said, slipping the comment in between the porridge and bread of breakfast.

'I suppose you mean yourself?' said Gluskap, all set to turn her into a sheep or a bush.

'Heavens, no! I mean him,' and she pointed to the baby wriggling on the mat beside the fire.

'Oh, nonsense!' said Gluskap with a tolerant, condescending chuckle. He whistled to catch the baby's attention, and the boy looked up and smiled. 'You see?'

'Hmmm,' said his wife, unimpressed.

So Gluskap called the child to come. But the little baby just smiled and stayed put.

Gluskap put on his most important and solemn face, and summoned the child in ancient words of antique magic.

. . . But the baby just crawled off and played with a feather.

'COME HERE THIS INSTANT!' bawled Gluskap, and although the child's face crumpled, he only crawled to his mother and hid among her skirts. She did not say, 'I told you so.' She did not even smile behind her hand. No, she was wise enough simply to take the baby in her arms and sing him to sleep.

By that time, Gluskap had swallowed his pride, and come to see that there was indeed someone in the world who knew more than he – at least about babies. He took the lesson to heart.

'Wife,' he said. 'It's a wise man who knows his limitations.'

About the Stories

All these stories have been passed down from generation to generation by word of mouth and changed a little by each successive story-teller, growing and altering to suit the listener. I have retold them – sometimes from the briefest passing reference in dusty old volumes – to please you, the reader.

In doing so, I have made sometimes small, sometimes large changes, but have tried to preserve an inkling of the pleasure each story gave to its original audience.

G McC.

The Golden Wish
In Greek mythology, King Midas of Phrygia represented the height of foolishness. The story of his greedy wish is just one of the follies attributed to him.

Shooting the Sun
This Chinese myth of the Fun Sang tree and the divine family in its branches dates back to the sixth century BC. For his actions here, the archer Yi is banished to earth and mortality, but becomes a hero figure in later myths.

George and the Dragon
When the early Church recorded the life of a young martyr, George of Lydda (possibly d. 313 AD), they embellished it with local legend. But the dragon-slaying story predates Christianity; Theseus, in Greek myth, slew a sea monster and rescued a princess on virtually the same spot.

Skinning Out
The idea of God entrusting animal messengers with crucial information recurs throughout Africa. In Ethiopia, it is the holawaka bird

which takes the blame for human mortality.

ROBIN HOOD AND THE GOLDEN ARROW
Tales concerning the outlaw Robin Hood have set his adventures variously in Nottingham and in Yorkshire, in the 1190s and the 1320s. But all depict him as a champion of the oppressed, who robbed the rich to help the poor.

BRAVE QUEST
This story is adapted from a Sioux myth explaining the origins of the famous Sun Dance – a ritual of cleansing and endurance offered up by a warrior in thanksgiving – not to the Sun, but to Wakan Tanka, the Great Creator.

SAVING TIME
Maui is the trickster hero of Oceanic mythology: a rebel who broke every taboo. He is also said to have created the archipelagos by hauling up each island from beneath the ocean with his fishing line.

THE LAKE THAT FLEW AWAY
Many Estonian myths concern lakes and rivers, for water has a holy, magical quality. God is seen as having filled certain water courses from his own golden bowl, pouring water out on to a riverbed prepared by all the beasts of creation.

ADMIRABLE HARE
We traditionally describe the moon's pitted surfaces as looking like a man with a dog. Many other cultures, including India and Mongolia, make out the shape of a hare. This Sri Lankan myth explains how the hare came to be there.

ALL ROADS LEAD TO WALES
The *Mabinogion* is a collection of eleven ancient Celtic stories. This one can be thought of as an expression of wonder, by post-Roman Britons, at the legacy of straight metalled roads left behind by the Roman occupation.

RAINBOW SNAKE
The Rainbow Snake's writhings through the Australian landscape are held to account for very specific landmarks, rivers and mountain

ranges – a common function of myth.

Juno's Roman Geese
Geese were sacred to the Roman goddess Juno, for they were said to share her attributes of love, guardianship and good housekeeping. Camillus (and perhaps the temple geese) is said to have saved Rome from Gaulish invaders in 365 BC.

John Barleycorn
Wherever barley is grown, the agricultural cycle of sowing, growing, ripening, reaping, threshing and brewing has been celebrated in song. The subject of the song? John Barleycorn himself, indestructible spirit of the crop.

The Singer Above the River
On the banks of the River Rhine, just south of Koblenz in Germany, a rocky bluff disturbs the flow of the river, creating dangerous currents and dismal rumours of evil magic ...

How Music was Fetched Out of Heaven
A sixteenth-century Nahua poem written in Nahuatt, language of the Aztecs, revealed this myth dating from a thousand years earlier. Quetzalcoatl, the feathered serpent, appears in Mesoamerican myth in all manner of guises, from the wind to the planet Venus.

Whose Footprints?
Eshu turns right into wrong, wrong into right. So runs the Yoruba song. The Fon people of Benin call him Legba, that mischievous assistant of God, who causes chaos and strife wherever he goes.

The Death of El Cid
By 1080, most of Spain was occupied by Moorish Africans. Rodrigo Díaz de Vivar entered Moorish Spain and made conquest after conquest. In doing so, he achieved fabulous wealth, glory and a place in Spanish history, his life and character hugely romanticized into an heroic ideal.

The Man Who Almost Lived Forever
The stories discovered in the Sumerian library of Nippur are probably the oldest in the world, already ancient when written

down during the Third Dynasty of Ur (about 2000 BC). The true end of Adapa's story is missing, and can only be guessed at.

STEALING HEAVEN'S THUNDER
Thor, with his mighty hammer, Mjollnir, was the best loved of the Norse gods in Norway and Iceland and the last to be ousted by Christianity, probably as late as 1100 AD. In this story, unusually, Loki's mischief is committed in a good cause.

ANANSI AND THE MIND OF GOD
Anansi is a descendant of the many trickster heroes in African mythology. Travelling over in the slave-ships, spider-man Anansi took up residence in the plantations of the West Indies, resourceful, witty, and with a strong instinct for self-preservation.

HOW MEN AND WOMEN FINALLY AGREED
The Kikuyu people of Kenya believe that God had three sons. From the other two sprang the Masai and Kamba peoples. But God's favourite was Kikuyu, which is why God took him to the top of holy Mount Kenya and showed him all creation.

FIRST SNOW
Coyote is the foremost mythical character in western deserts of America. Without his meddling interference, life would be much easier and pleasanter – and yet he is credited with the introduction of fire, agriculture and snow.

RAGGED EMPEROR
Magic plays a great part in Chinese legend, and though Yu Shin's story is a moral tale of virtue rewarded, it is also just as much of a fairy story as *Snow White*. In longer versions, Yu Shin's guardian fairy repeatedly saves his life in fantastical ways, as his father tries to kill him.

THE BOY WHO LIVED FOR A MILLION YEARS
This gypsy horror story is from Romania, from where the 'travelling people' take their origins and their more correct title of 'Romanies'. It captures something of the restlessness of the roaming soul, though it is a cautionary Christian tale.

SEA CHASE

The *Kalevala* is Finland's epic myth cycle and this story only one episode from the huge enthralling saga. Lapland is an ethnic region straddling the northlands of Finland, Sweden and Russia.

DRAGONS TO DINE

In the land now covered by Syria and Turkey, two thousand years before Christ, the Hittite peoples worshipped the weather god Taru. When Roman invaders took over the country, they also adopted and adapted the myth of Taru and Illuyankas, the chaos-dragon.

GUITAR SOLO

This myth is told on the banks of the upper Niger River by the Songhay people. Though their lives are complicated by countless tricky, malicious spirits, this story shows that evil magic can be overcome by very ordinary individuals.

SADKO AND THE TSAR OF THE SEA

The *byliny*, epic poems of old Russia, tell of a race of demi-gods, ancient champions, *bogatyri*. Massively strong, amazingly brave, capable of magic, they were nevertheless Christian heroes. One, transformed into stone, is still to be seen in Kiev Cathedral which he supposedly built.

THE ARMCHAIR TRAVELLER

Ganesa is the Hindu god most honoured by poets and writers. His likeness – pot-bellied, four-armed, elephant-headed dwarf demon – is found in many houses in India, and offerings of fruit and vegetables are made to him.

UPHILL STRUGGLE

In Greek mythology, Sisyphys is the grandfather of Bellerophon, another thorn in the side of the gods. For Bellerophon, even more ambitious than his grandfather, tried to reach the halls of Olympus, flying upwards on his winged horse.

BOBBI BOBBI!

Most Australian myths are set during the Alchera or 'Dreamtime'. This story, told by aboriginal Australians in the north, is one of them.

THE GINGERBREAD BABY
Many familiar stories begin with a woman unhappy because she cannot have children. In Arab Palestine, it is a particularly common theme, and childlessness is portrayed as the one fault no husband can forgive. Originally, this old lady made seven helpful trips abroad while waiting for her bread to rise.

THE PRICE OF FIRE
Every culture has a myth to explain how fire fell into mortal hands. Mostly the fire is stolen from God at great peril, and someone has to suffer for it, as in this tribal myth from Gabon in West Africa.

THE HUNTING OF DEATH
In some parts of Rwanda, death is blamed on the man who disliked his mother-in-law so much he would not let her come back to life. But this is an alternative explanation.

YOUNG BUDDHA
Two and a half thousand years ago, in the city of Kapilavastu, a prince was born to the King of Shakyas. According to legend, until the age of twenty-nine he lived a life of blissful luxury, then gave it all up to seek perfect wisdom and a solution to suffering and death. It took him six years of trial and error. After his enlightenment he taught the 'Middle Way' which is at the foundation of Buddhist thinking, not just in India but all over the world.

THE WOMAN WHO LEFT NO FOOTPRINTS
The Inuit tribes of Alaska set this story in the village of Na-ki-a-ki-a-mute during the month of Naz-re-rak-sek, or October. This is surely an indication of the myth's significance: a celebration of the coming of the winter freeze, when rivers mystically turn to solid ice.

SUN'S SON
Tonga, loveliest of the Polynesian islands, gave rise to this story of pride. Properly speaking, the boy's choice is between Melaia and Monuia, abstract magical words not easily translated.

BIGGEST
Japanese merchants measure soft goods, such as material, with one yardstick, and solid goods, such as metal, with another. The soft 'whale yard' is five centimetres longer than the other – surely the

origin of this legend ... unless the legend is the origin of the difference. Castastrophic storms have destroyed much of Kamakura, including the temple, but the huge Buddha still stands.

'I LOVE YOU, PRIME MINISTER!'
The epic French *Chansons de geste* or 'songs of deeds' written by troubadours in the eleventh and twelfth centuries, mostly concerned the Emperor Charlemagne, his champions and enemies. Robert Southey, the English poet, translated the one from which this story is taken.

AND THE RAINS CAME TUMBLING DOWN
This myth from Papua New Guinea claims to recount the origin of traditional building techniques used universally in this wild, wet territory.

FOUR WORLDS AND A BROKEN STONE
The Black Mesa stands at Four Corners, Arizona and is crucial to the religion of the ancient indigenous Hopi tribe. The word 'Hopi' itself means 'Peace'. The Hopi currently consider that the time of the Great Purification has begun, which will result in the destruction of the Fourth World and establishment of the Fifth.

THE NEEDLEWORK TEACHER AND THE SECRET BABY
The Langobardic cycle of legends are just as complex as the more famous tales of King Arthur. Set down in the fifteenth-century Book of Heroes, these stories – of Constantine and the Amelings, of Ice Queens, bear-witches and more – date back six centuries earlier than that. All trace is lost of whatever true-life events and people gave rise to them, but they originated in a region known then as Pannonia (now Hungary and its surrounding territories). The action roams, though, as far afield as Sweden and Greece, Heligoland, Constantinople and Germany, depicting a war-torn Europe rich in chivalry.

CULLOCH AND THE BIG PIG
The oldest Culloch legend is actually older than King Arthur. It gave rise to (or arose out of) various piggy place-names and landmarks in Wales and Cornwall. The name Culloch itself means 'pig-boy'. Long ago, haircutting once had ritual significance, too. Culloch, for

instance, promised his mother on her deathbed that only King arthur would cut his hair for the first time

THE CALL OF THE SEA

Generally, the mythical mermaid is brought ashore as an unwilling wife an d ultimately returns to the sea. This legend from the Island of Jersey in the English Channel is different. It also involves historical events

THE CRYSTAL POOL

The people of Melanesia, like so many other places, widely recall a Great Flood turned back by a serpent during the dawn of time. This particular story, however, from the Bainang peoples of New Britain, accounts for the origins of the oceans.

The creation myths of the Maori people of New Zealand are epic and complex. Tane, both the god of forests and of light, is often found in conflict with his scheming brother. This battle is the third and last war to involve the seventy immortal offspring of Rangi and Papa (Earth and Sky). The original story in fact accounts for many very specific rituals of worship among priests and worshippers.

LAMIA

Legends of lamias are amazingly widespread. From Greece to China people have believed in snake-women deadly to their human mates, unmasked only by goodness or wisdom. John Keats wrote a poem about one. This legend, though, comes from Kashmir.

ISIS AND OSIRIS

Even after the wondrous Old, Middle and New Kingdoms had declined, and the Romans subjugated Egypt, Isis and Osiris were still being worshipped far and wide. Her tears swelling the Nile was the mythological explanation of a yearly event, when the river, swollen by rains upriver, overspilled its banks. Though dangerous and unpredictable, it spread the banks with fertile black silt: a greater blessing to Egypt than all its gold and silver.

THE FLYING DUTCHMAN

For at least two centuries, sailors have been telling tales of a ghost ship regularly sighted off the coast of the Cape of Good Hope. Given the distances sailors travel, and their liking for a good yarn, the story quickly circled the world on the trade winds. It was Sir Walter Scott's theory that the legend originated in a plague-ship forbidden permission to dock anywhere, its crew forced to live out their short, doomed lives at sea. It took more detailed shape in the nineteenth century, in a short story written by Auguste Jal and entitled *The Flying Dutchman*. In the opera of the same name, Wagner allows the Captain finally to find the salvation of true love.

PROUD MAN
The Algonquin tribe who inhabit the northern forests of the United States have a richly complex culture. They tell a great, widely renowned poetic cycle of stories about Gluskap (or Glooskap), their creator god, and his brother Malsum the Wolf, the evil antithesis of Gluskap's goodness. When Malsum has been defeated, the world perfected, and Gluskap's many adventures are complete, he sails towards sunrise in his canoe, watched by the animals who love him, perhaps to return one day.